ROGUE MOM

ROGUE MOM

CASE FILES OF AN URBAN WITCH™ BOOK FOUR

MARTHA CARR

MICHAEL ANDERLE

DISRUPTIVE IMAGINATION®

LMBPN Publishing
PMB 196, 2540 South Maryland Pkwy
Las Vegas, NV 89109

First Edition, May, 2021
ebook ISBN: 978-1-64971-742-9
Print ISBN: 978-1-64971-743-6

THE ROGUE MOM TEAM

Thanks to the JIT Readers

Dave Hicks
Misty
Wendy L Bonell
Diane L. Smith
Angel LaVey

If we've missed anyone, please let us know!

Editor
Skyhunter Editing Team

From Martha

To everyone who still believes in magic and all the possibilities that holds.

To all the readers who make this entire ride so much fun.

To Louie, Jackie, and so many wonderful friends who remind me all the time of what really matters and how wonderful life can be in any given moment.

From Michael

To Family, Friends and
Those Who Love
To Read.
May We All Enjoy Grace
To Live The Life We Are
Called.

CHAPTER ONE

Lucy Heron walked down the deserted streets of Echo Park. She had never seen the place so quiet. No one walked the sidewalks, stood in their gardens, or looked out through their windows. No cars or bikes roared back and forth. Not even a single bird in the trees. The only exception was Buddy, the family dog, who walked along beside her, wearing a pair of sunglasses and a pork pie hat.

"Nice outfit," Lucy said. "Are you planning on becoming a jazz musician?"

"I would, but I don't have the paws for it." Buddy waved his tail in time to an unheard beat, then started dancing, a fancy routine from an old-fashioned movie, but for four paws instead of two.

"Since when do you dance?" Lucy asked, taken by surprise.

"Since always." Buddy did a side shuffle, and a chorus of backing dancers appeared behind him, all of them cats in sequined outfits with ostrich feather fans spread around their tails. "Remember that night in Paris? I was the talk of the Moulin Rouge."

"No, that was Nicole Kidman." Lucy frowned. "Since when do you talk?"

Buddy shrugged, an impressive gesture for a dachshund, whose body wasn't built for such things. "I've been practicing."

"I'm sure I would've seen that."

"I've been practicing in the caves, with the kids and Batman."

"Well in that case…" Tingling in the palm of her hand made Lucy look down. Her wand had appeared, where previously there was nothing. Something about its dark, unevenly shaped handle cut through the fuzz that had been clouding her thoughts. "Oh, this is a dream."

"You're one smart cookie." Buddy did a spin around a lamppost and moonwalked through a puddle that hadn't been there ten seconds before. "Not many people would have realized."

"I don't normally, not until I wake up."

"So, what's different today?"

"I don't know, but I want to find out."

"In that case, pick up the rhythm and follow me."

Lucy could hear the music behind Buddy's routine now, a trad jazz tune with a trumpet solo rippling over piano and bass. A snare drum kicked in, and she picked up her feet, dancing after the dog.

Now that she wasn't walking, the world moved by faster. One moment they were in Echo Park, the next they were in La Brea, standing by the tar pit. A mammoth with the voice of her manager, Roger Applegate, was hauling itself out of the lake.

"My trunk!" Applegate exclaimed. "Some blighter has stolen my trunk!"

He was right. The mammoth's long, flexible nose was gone, leaving a truncated face with mournful eyes.

A large figure stood nearby, tar oozing from his orange skin—the murderous loan shark named Zero.

"Give him his trunk back!" Lucy demanded, pointing her wand at Zero.

"It wasn't me," Zero said. "I'm dead, remember?"

Then he split in half and collapsed on the ground. Behind him, a shadow shifted, a slender figure of deep black carrying the mammoth's trunk.

"Silver Griffins," Lucy said. "You're under arrest."

However, the figure was gone.

She raced after him, still dancing to the rhythm of the music, Buddy twirling and spinning beside her. Within moments, they stood on the roof of an abandoned office block, looking out across the city. Lucy's husband Charlie stood in the middle of the roof, staring at the screen of a computer.

"Thank goodness you're here," he said. "There's been a crime." He held out his arms. Where his hands should have been, there were smooth stumps. "Someone's taken my programming hands."

A woman's laugh sawed through the air. Lucy spun to see the witch and would-be crime boss Meredith Womack poised at the top of a fire escape.

"Give him his hands back!" Lucy shouted while pointing her wand at Womack.

"It wasn't me," Womack said. "I'm still in jail."

The fire escape twisted, turned into chains, and wrapped itself around Womack, then dragged her cackling out of view. Beyond her, a shadow shifted on the rooftop opposite, that same dark and slender figure, a featureless form dropping Charlie's hands into a sack alongside the mammoth's trunk.

"Stop!" Lucy shouted. "Silver Griffins!"

The figure ducked out of view and was gone.

Lucy danced to the edge of the roof and leapt, soaring into the air, Buddy gliding along beside her.

"This is fun," he said.

"No, it isn't." Those stumps at the ends of Charlie's wrists had made Lucy feel sick to the pit of her stomach.

They landed in Lincoln Park in a swirling mass of smog. Sarah Smith, one of Lucy's best friends, stood in the middle of the dark clouds, wearing her hospital scrubs and a stethoscope around her neck. Lucy strode toward her, hand outstretched. As she lost her dancing rhythm, the music died, and Buddy fell still.

"Watch out," Lucy said. "Something's coming."

"Too late," Sarah said. "He's already here."

Sarah's head vanished. With no neck to hold it in place, the stethoscope slid from her shoulders and fell to the ground, but her body stayed upright.

Lucy screamed.

The clouds of smog swirled in and became a single dark pillar standing behind Sarah: Blight, the pollution monster that had tried to drown LA in smog.

"Give her head back!" Lucy shouted at the monster.

"Blight did not take it," the cloud replied. "You destroyed Blight."

"I know," Lucy snapped. "I have to go through this, don't I? I have to follow the dream to find out where it leads."

She didn't know where that idea came from. It popped into her head fully formed, as sure and real as the fact that the sun would rise in the morning.

The cloud exploded, flying off in every direction, leaving the air clear where it had stood. Through that space, Lucy saw the black figure, stick-thin and sliced from darkness as deep as the midnight sky, drop Sarah's head into his sack.

"Enough." Lucy raised her wand and summoned her magical power. "I'll get you this time."

"No," the figure said in a voice like the sharpening of a knife blade.

It raised its hand, and the whole world went black.

Lucy woke with a start and sat bolt upright in bed, sweat running down her skin. She pulled the sheets tight around her and stared into the pre-dawn gloom, looking for any sign of a stick-thin figure of darkness, but there was nothing to be seen.

"Wussgoanon?" Charlie mumbled, half-asleep.

Lucy drew a deep breath and pulled back the sheet, revealing one of his arms. The hand was still there. She sighed in relief. It was a nightmare, that was all. A weird, unsettling dream, but no more than that.

It was only then that she realized she was clutching her wand and had been since she woke up.

She set the wand down, lay back, and tried to get to sleep, but the dread she had woken with left her heart beating too fast, and her mind was awash with strange and unsettling images. Dawn was creeping in, and though she wouldn't normally get up this early, there was no point trying to get back to sleep.

She got out of bed, pulled on yoga pants and a Black Canary t-shirt, grabbed her phone and wand, and tiptoed out of the bedroom, closing the door behind her to avoid waking Charlie. She crept past the kids' rooms and into the kitchen, then put on the kettle and put a teabag in the biggest mug she could find. If anything could soothe her, it was a good cuppa.

Once the kettle had boiled, she brewed her tea, added milk, and made her way to the living room, where she settled down on the couch. Buddy was surprised to see a human moving around already. He got up out of his basket and came to sit with her, laying his head in her lap.

"I don't suppose you've been learning to talk, have you?" Lucy asked.

Buddy flopped one ear over and dribbled sleepily onto her leg, but if he'd learned words, he was keeping them to himself.

Lucy unlocked her phone and checked her emails. There was nothing urgent although a yoga class she'd booked had canceled due to lack of interest. More encouragingly, there was a nice long message from her parents back in England, talking about their holiday and including a couple of pictures of the Dorset coastline. She'd have to make time to write back later. One of her messaging apps had some late-night activity on the group chat with Sarah and Jackie. Apparently, Jackie's date had stood her up, saying that he "couldn't be bothered."

"Wow," Lucy typed back. "Even by men's standards, that's a terrible excuse. Hope his boss can't be bothered to pay him at the end of the month."

Next, she opened a web browser and skimmed through the news from the mundane and magical worlds. A big celebration of Gnomish culture planned for next month had been canceled, with the organizers announcing that it had "proved to be too much work for the benefits involved." An art exhibition Lucy had been looking forward to was also canceled, as the two main contributors hadn't produced the pieces for display. Meanwhile, three leading players in the Dodgers' lineup for next week's game weren't going to appear, and the news site's sports commentator hinted that some strange arguments were going on behind the scenes at the club.

"What's with everyone this week?" Lucy scratched Buddy behind the ears. "Maybe I'm tired and grumpy, but it seems like a lot of things are falling apart."

Buddy made a happy noise and shifted his head to get a better scratch. Lucy smiled. It was hard to stay in a bad mood when you had a dachshund in your lap.

Dawn light crept in between the blinds, casting a series of long thin shadows across the wall. Lucy remembered the figure in her dream with a shudder. She pulled her wand close, just in case.

CHAPTER TWO

Gruffbar rode into the parking lot of the motel, the roar of his black Harley-Davidson Deluxe chasing off the few birds that had gathered on the lot in the first light of dawn. As far as Gruffbar was concerned, it was good riddance to feathered pests. When nature got into the spaces occupied by humans and magicals, it only added chaos and mess.

He pulled up in front of his motel room and parked the bike. For a dwarf, there was a special art to dismounting a Harley, even one that he'd modified to suit his frame. He hopped down, checked that the bike was secure, and grabbed the bag off the back that hid his custom shotgun with the ax-blade head. He hadn't gone anywhere without the weapon since leaving LA. Things were too uncertain. You never knew when past trouble might turn and bite you in the ass or when a new business arrangement might turn out to be less than it seemed.

Florida was fine so far. It lacked the dynamism he liked about LA, as well as the mass of contacts he'd built up there, but it also lacked the smog monster he'd been dealing with and the set of Silver Griffins who had brought Blight down. The magical authorities out here seemed less diligent, which was how he liked it, and there were still magicals who needed the services of a criminal lawyer because there always were.

His key card *clicked* in the lock, the door swung open, and he trudged into his room, then slammed the door behind him. Dealing with creatures of the night was all very well, practically a necessity for a dwarf of his talents, but establishing those contacts was trashing his sleep schedule. He flung his bag and bike helmet down, dropped the latest set of contracts on the table, took off his jacket, and removed his hefty boots. At last, he lay back on the mattress, which was only slightly lumpy and a little infested. So, this was his Florida life—bed bugs and a broken schedule. It could have been a whole lot worse.

He figured that he should probably sort himself out before he fell asleep. His beard needed trimming, an idea that would have appalled his ancestors but that was a necessity when passing for human, and his leather trousers would get disgusting if he kept sleeping in them. Still, it wouldn't do any harm to close his eyes for a moment, to take a brief rest before anything else. It wasn't like he was going to doze off. He was a lawyer. He knew all the tricks to…

Mount Steelstrike towered over Gruffbar, twenty-five thousand feet of barren gray stone, capped with ice and snow on the upper reaches. Down the sides, black and brown streaks marked where mining refuse had been tipped out of the tunnels for centuries, staining the earth itself in deep and comfortingly familiar hues. Smoke trickled from the openings at the tops of some peaks as the foundries turned broken rocks into pure and malleable metal.

Gruffbar walked up a path that ran beside the wagon rails. His grandfather stood by the path, his beard as white as snow and dangling past his knees, a measuring stick in his hand.

"We're going to build new rails this spring," Grandfather said. "More reliable, with wagons powered by both steam and magic. It'll take an effort, but we'll save a fortune in the long term shipping down to the big cities."

"You say that every year," Gruffbar said. "It doesn't happen until after I've gone."

"This spring," his grandfather repeated, tapping the measuring stick against the rails. Then he sat down, laid his arms across his knees, and promptly fell asleep.

Gruffbar walked toward the entrance of Number Seven Shaft. How long was it since he'd been here? He ought to know. He counted everything so precisely. He could remember, down to the minute, how long was left on a contract with a client. He could count dollar bills by their weight in his hand. He had been tracking the days and years since the moment he walked away from the mountain. So why—now, when he was back here at last—couldn't he remember?

The doors of Number Seven Shaft were ancient slabs of bronze, embossed with runes that warded off the dangers of the mine shafts: bad air, rockfalls, stone elementals, and giant rats. However, there was a blank space that Gruffbar didn't remember being there before. Something he'd forgotten. What was it?

Dark spots appeared on that blank space and crept out, tarnishing the doors. When they swung open, it was on rusted creaking hinges, not the well-maintained ones he was used to.

A familiar voice emerged from the deep, echoing up the shaft. Gruffbar followed it. He walked past a cart loaded with ore, with a mule tethered to the front. Two dwarves sat beside it, staring down at their hands.

"Shouldn't you be taking that to the smelter?" Gruffbar pointed at the ore.

"Not worth it," one of the dwarves said.

"Why bother?" the other added.

Other dwarves lined the shaft as he went deeper. Most had picks and shovels, but none of them were digging. They stood idle, eating pies, talking to each other in slow whispers, or just staring at the ground. The dynamism and energy that had driven his community for millennia were gone. The people had no sense of purpose, no desire to delve or to build. It was unsettling but also familiar.

"I remember this day," Gruffbar said, his voice echoing back from the stone walls.

"Of course you do." A dwarf looked up at him. "It was your last day."

A lump filled Gruffbar's throat. The dwarf was right. This was his last day, the final few hours before he had turned his back on everything he had ever known. After this, he would stop being Gruffbar of Clan Steelstrike. He would become a dwarf untethered from his life, out there alone. This was the day when he made that terrible decision.

Deeper he went. The lanterns on the walls grew dimmer until he couldn't see where he was treading. It didn't matter. He knew every rise and dip of Number Seven Shaft, every nuance of its length. He could walk it with his eyes closed.

A light appeared ahead. The tunnel turned into a workshop in a way that tunnels didn't. Between the workbenches, the anvil, and the blazing forge, two figures stood by a table. One of them was tall, slender, clad in black, with a pale face and narrow features, like a warped and mocking exaggeration of everything Elvish, his head completely bald. The other was a dwarf dressed in a crafter's heavy apron, goggles hanging around his neck, his tar-black beard hanging almost to his knees. He held up a sketch for a drilling machine, and his eyes shone with enthusiasm.

Gruffbar looked at his younger self, appalled and envious at what he had been.

"This is going to be the greatest mining machine anyone's ever made," the younger Gruffbar said. "We'll reopen Number Five Shaft, start Fifty-two and Fifty-Three. We'll delve deeper into the mountain than ever before, dig out unmapped veins, find ores that no one has even heard of. When grandfather opens his new rails, we'll fill the wagons every day. The whole world of Oriceran is going to hear about Mount Steelstrike."

"Such grand dreams." The black-clad figure licked his lips and stretched out thin fingers, holding them an inch away from young Gruffbar's head. His voice grated like a blade against a whetstone. "I can taste your ambition, boy, rich and powerful and complex. A sophisticated ambition, not like the idle dreams of the other dwarves here. Their aspirations were barely morsels to tempt my appetite."

"Then why did you take them?" young Gruffbar asked, setting the diagram down. There was sadness in his eyes, and he let go of those plans with painful slowness. "Why make me your enemy, Mr. No?"

The black-clad figure drew a step back, and a chain rattled. There was a scraping noise, and his foot came into view, pinned in a complex version of a bear trap, magical runes glowing on every component.

"Perhaps I was too ambitious," Mr. No said. "Or perhaps I underestimated you. Who else could create a trap that would reach into the dream realm?"

Gruffbar went to the wall and took an ax off the hook.

"No one else," he said. "No one thinks like me."

"Yet here you are, waving an ax around like any old dwarf."

"I'm an engineer, not a warrior, but I can still see what I need to do."

He drew the ax back, ready to strike Mr. No.

"Wait," No said. "If you kill me, the dreams of these other dwarves, your whole community, will be gone forever. They will aspire to nothing. They will sit around, idle, until they wither away and die. The grandeur of Clan Steelstrike will crumble to dust. I can return their dreams and with them the future of your clan."

"In return for your life?"

"My life, and something more. Your greatest hope. Your most delicious aspiration. Your dream of engineering glory. Feed me your future, your driving force, the thing that pushes you to greatness as an engineer, and I will return the smaller goals of your clansmen. Their flickering candles of ambition in return for your raging blaze."

Young Gruffbar stood for a moment, frozen in the second before swinging his ax. Then he set it down.

"Damn you, but I accept, for their sakes." He picked up parchment and a quill pen. "Still, we're doing this properly, setting limits, making sure I don't give you more than I mean to. I'm an engineer, not a lawyer, but we'll make a contract and bind it in magic. When that's finished..." He ran a hand sadly across his design for the mining machine. "When that's finished, you can take what makes me unique."

"Good boy." No ran his long fingers down the back of young Gruffbar's head, and older Gruffbar shuddered. As if hearing the movement, No looked over at him. "So good to see that you remember me. Look at the fresh drive you found for yourself. I'd hoped to feast on you again, but it seems you're out of town. Still, LA has so much potential. All those starlets, those tech bros, those witches, and wizards. I'll have myself quite a feast while you enjoy your motel. What's that saying... If you're tired of life, you're ready for Florida?"

Mr. No laughed, a sound like fingers scraping across a blackboard, and the workshop faded away.

Gruffbar woke with a start. It was the middle of the morning, and the cleaner's trolley was rattling past outside.

"By my beard," he muttered to himself, "the bastard's back."

He stared at the ceiling. If he stayed here, he would probably be safe. Backwater Florida was no place for a psychic predator like Mr. No. Whatever happened in LA, Gruffbar would survive, and wasn't that why he had come here in the first place?

Then he thought of Mr. No repeating what he'd done at Mount Steelstrike. He thought of people he knew, like Gunther the mechanic, left listless and lifeless, empty shells of who they had been.

He pulled his boots on, shoved his few belongings into a bag, and headed out to his bike.

CHAPTER THREE

"Come and get it," Charlie Heron shouted as he set the lasagna dish down on the dining table.

Lucy walked in from the back yard, where she had been trimming the roses.

"Smells delicious." She kissed him on the cheek. "I love a lad who knows his way around the kitchen."

"I'd hope so, after all these years." Charlie grinned and poured dressing over the salad, then mixed it around.

Dylan, their eldest, was the first of the kids to arrive at the table. He was tall for a twelve-year-old, with dark hair that refused to accept the control of a comb, and his wand stuck out from the back pocket of his jeans. Close behind came eight-year-old Ashley, her hair tied neatly back, carrying the parts of a half-assembled robot cat.

"I know that we're not allowed magic at the dinner table," she said, "but…"

"No inventing either," Lucy said firmly. "If your brothers are going to spend some time behaving like ordinary children, you can too."

"I'm not ordinary."

"None of us are," Dylan pointed out. "We have to be able to blend in. Besides, do you want to get cheese sauce on your latest tech breakthrough?"

With a piercing cry, an eagle swept into the room, circled above their heads, and landed on the remaining seat. The air around it shimmered, and the bird disappeared, turning into three-year-old Eddie, the youngest member of the Heron clan.

"Eddie, you know the rules." Lucy pointed at a jar on the counter. "No changing into animals at the table."

"I didn't," he said.

"Birds count as animals."

"Didn't change into a bird at the table. I changed into a boy."

Lucy looked at Charlie and raised a questioning eyebrow. Technically, Eddie was correct, and they wanted him in his human shape for dinner, but this felt like pushing the edges of what was allowed.

"No magic full stop," Charlie said. "You should have changed before you got here. Now go put a note in the magic jar."

Eddie sighed dramatically, jumped down from his seat, and stomped over to the jar with such exaggerated indignation that Lucy struggled not to burst out laughing. The little boy took a square of colored paper from next to the jar, wrote a wobbly "E" on it in felt-tip marker, and thrust it into the jar.

"The jar's getting crowded," Lucy observed. "Looks like you kids owe us a lot of chores. Maybe we should have a day soon where we clear out the jar and get some house-work done."

"And get some candy too." Dylan pointed at the money down one side of the jar, donated by Charlie and Lucy as their punishment for magic at the table.

"Candy too," Charlie agreed. "For now, dinner."

He dished up platefuls of lasagna then passed the salad bowl around.

"What's tonight's quiz?" Lucy asked.

"Science." Ashley sat up straight. "My turn as question master."

It was Dylan's and Eddie's turn to exchange a look. Ashley had a habit of setting tough questions based on things she was passionate about. Her brothers could guess, more successfully in Dylan's case, but they stood little chance of knowing the right answers.

"Could you make things a little easier today, sweet-heart?" Lucy asked. "Your dad and I really struggled with your last few quizzes."

"It's a test," Ashley said. "It's not meant to be easy."

"A quiz, not a test, and it's not supposed to be impossible."

Ashley stuck her fingertip in her mouth and sucked on it for a moment while she thought about the questions she'd come up with. They were ones she could answer, of course, but other people often didn't know about things that seemed obvious to her. Even grownups were strangely ignorant about basic science like the periodic table, cova-lent bonds, or the anatomy of common animals and birds.

"I might need to make a different quiz," she said at last. "Can we start dinner again in, like, twenty minutes?"

"Eat now!" Eddie shoved a large forkful of lasagna into his mouth, just in case someone tried to stop him.

"How about if you run your quiz another day?" Lucy said. "We can talk about something else over dinner instead."

"Like what?" Ashley's mind brimmed over with possibilities. She had read a fascinating paper on offshore wind turbine design, or there were the latest satellite launches, perhaps the recent breakthroughs in DNA editing coming out of China…

"Well, where would we like to go on holiday next year?"

"You mean vacation?" Dylan said.

"I don't think that…" Lucy sighed. "Yes, vacation, that's what I mean."

"Oh." It wasn't the stimulating scientific debate that Ashley had hoped for, but at least she had an opinion on this. "Science camp?"

"Absolutely, you can go to science camp, but that's not much of a family holiday, is it?"

In Ashley's opinion, there was no better choice for a family holiday. How else were her brothers going to learn anything about physics or engineering? Still, she understood enough about people to understand when they weren't going to see the world the same way she did.

"In that case, could we go somewhere with interesting scenery?" she asked. "I'd love to look at the geology of the Alps."

"Alps are an option." Lucy smiled. "What about you, Dylan? Where would you like to go?"

"Somewhere old, with lots of cool history to see, like Paris or Rome or London."

"If we went to England, we could see your grandparents while we're over there."

"Sure, that too. I mean, that would be great, but we can see them when they visit us. I want to go around the British Museum, see the Rosetta Stone and the Elgin Marbles, and visit the Tower of London. Did you know they used to put people's heads on spikes there?"

"We should probably avoid spiking any heads ourselves, but London has a science museum for Ashley, and there's a zoo for Eddie." Lucy turned her attention to the youngest Heron. "I mean, assuming that's what you want out of a holiday?"

"Penguins!" The air around Eddie started to shimmer.

"No magic at the—"

It was already too late. The over-excited boy had become an over-excited penguin, flippers waving up and down as he wobbled in his seat.

"Magic jar," Charlie said, hiding his amusement beneath a forced frown.

The penguin jumped down from its seat and went to write a note using its flippers.

"What do you think?" Lucy asked Charlie. "Fancy a trip back to your old stomping grounds?"

Charlie laughed. "I don't think I'd be doing the same things I did as a student, but sure, I could give London another go. It's been a while."

Dylan raised an eyebrow. "What did you do as a student that you won't do now?"

"Um..." Charlie froze. He didn't think that "spent all day in the pub" was the sort of example he should be setting his son, especially not with the teenage years around the corner.

"Science fairs and tech shows," Lucy said. "Your dad went to anything with a gadget, right Charlie?"

"Absolutely. Tech shows. Lots of tech shows."

"You still go to those. You took Ashley to one last weekend with your friend Ringo."

"I went to way more as a student. I wanted to be the next Steve Jobs, so I was learning everything I could about technology."

"What do you want to be now?"

"Being part of this family is good enough for me."

"Aw, honey, that was adorable." Lucy leaned over to kiss Charlie on the cheek. "You can want to be Steve Jobs too. Just don't turn into Elon Musk. We can't afford to shoot your car into space."

"What about you kids?" Charlie asked. "What do you want to be when you grow up?"

"I'm going to be an archaeologist," Dylan said. "I'll go dig up forgotten civilizations, find the pieces of history everyone has forgotten about. Because I know about magic and Oriceran, I'll understand things that the other archaeologists don't. I'll write books about mundane history, but I'll write secret ones too, about magical history, for magicals to read. Maybe I'll even find ancient artifacts and keep them safe for the Silver Griffins."

"Very *Indiana Jones*," Lucy said. "Be careful you don't get your face melted off." She turned to Eddie, who was back in human form and back in his seat, pushing pieces of lasagna around his plate with a fork, then picking out the pasta to eat with his fingers. "What about you, sweetheart? What do you want to be when you grow up?"

She assumed that the answer would be an animal of some sort, but the fear of silly answers was no reason to keep a three-year-old out of the conversation. He was often at his most entertaining when his expectations were most at odds with the world.

"Zookeeper," he said. "I'm-a feed all the animals, and teach them tricks, and pat them on the head, like this."

He patted himself on the head with one sticky hand, leaving his hair smeared with cheese and tomato sauces.

"Which animals do you most want to look after?" Lucy asked.

"Dinosaurs."

There it was, the answer that took them safely away from reality.

"You should be careful with that," Charlie said. "It didn't go well for *Jurassic Park*."

Eddie grinned and raised his hands like claws. The air started to shimmer again.

"No!" Lucy and Charlie cried in unison.

The shimmering stopped, Eddie lowered his hands, and he went back to eating his pasta.

"What about you, Ashley?" Charlie asked. "Are you going to be the next Steve Jobs instead of me?"

"I'm going to be the next Ada Lovelace."

Lucy looked at her in confusion. "Is that someone from *Game of Thrones*?"

"She was the first computer programmer," Dylan said. "She invented algorithms before there were even computers to run them on." He beamed at his sister. "Great choice."

"Thank you." Ashley looked at her parents. "This is why I should be allowed devices at the dinner table because it will help me to develop my skills and become the world's greatest tech entrepreneur. You want that, don't you?"

"Nice try, sunshine." Lucy laughed. "You can storm Silicon Valley after you've finished eating. For now, would you like a bit more lasagna?"

CHAPTER FOUR

Ellis Ellis walked into his latest hotel room and set his suit-case down next to the bed. There was no point unpacking. He had suitcase management down to a fine art and could find whatever he needed without searching around. Besides, no amount of hanging would get the creases out of his suits as well as a quick blast of magic. He probably wouldn't be in LA for long, so there was no point getting comfortable.

That said, there was one thing he wanted to make sure he did while he was in town, regardless of how little time he had. He scrolled through his contacts until he found the special one he'd been thinking about all through his flight, then hesitated a moment, gathering his thoughts and his courage. At last, he hit the call button. Its recipient answered straight away.

"Hi, Ellis!" Sarah said from the other end of the line. "Does this call mean you're in town?"

"I certainly am, ma'am. I wondered if you'd do me the honor of sharing dinner this evening?"

"I'd love to, but I have a shift at the hospital tonight. How long are you around for?"

"Not sure yet. I have a critter I need to track down. Then I'm on to the next job."

"I guess that means you'll be quite busy while you're here too, huh? Having to chase after leads at a moment's notice."

"You sure know your Silver Griffins."

Sarah laughed. "Years of trying to arrange nights out with Lucy and Jackie. My schedule might shift from week to week, but it's still easier for me to plan than it is for them. How about if I send you my work schedule? Then whenever you're free in a gap in that schedule, you can call me and we'll meet up."

"Don't you have other plans?"

"I can reschedule other plans, but who knows when you'll be in town again."

"All right then, send that timetable over, and I'll see what I can do."

"Great. See you soon."

After hanging up, Ellis stood for a minute grinning at his phone. He didn't have a date for tonight as he'd hoped, but this still sounded awfully promising.

Meanwhile, he had a monster to catch, and if he could, he wanted to do it during the day. The Wilderghast didn't only give people nightmares. It fed off the energy that bad dreams created. That meant that it would be easier to defeat while most folks were awake.

One of the apps on Ellis's phone had an icon consisting of a wand in a box. He opened the app and switched it to receive.

"Deprendo Wilderghast." He waved his wand. That wasn't the whole of the spell to detect the Wilderghast, which was a complex collection of different enchantments cast over several days and bound together using rare ingredients. However, it was the trigger, the final piece he had set for the puzzle, ready for when he reached LA.

As the spell settled, the air in front of him sparkled. An image appeared: a homeless woman sleeping under a tree in a park, with a gray-robed creature lurking by her head. The image showed Ellis the Wilderghast as it was, or at least as it had been recently. A single point of light hanging in the air showed him which direction he'd find the creature.

"Well, looky here," Ellis said. "We got ourselves a target."

He lifted his phone into the spell's aura. The magic disappeared from the air and instead appeared on the screen. With the image reduced to something far more portable and far less conspicuous, Ellis headed out the door.

The bright dot on the screen led him out of the hotel and down the street, his chunky red sneakers slapping against the sidewalk. A couple of times recently, his boss suggested that he dress less conspicuously so his targets were less likely to notice him coming. In Ellis's experience, there was nothing inconspicuous about a magical pursuit. Most of his targets didn't even notice what was or wasn't normal dress for a human, so if they noticed him, it would be because of his magical aura, not his suit and sneakers.

The big downside of his complex mass of spells was that while he got a direction, he didn't get a distance, so he had no idea how far it was to the Wilderghast. He walked for over an hour before the directional dot shifted, drawing his attention to a park that included a kids' play area, a bunch of picnic tables, and a posse of seniors taking an outdoor exercise class.

Ellis made his way past a chapel, across the street, and into the park, to all appearances engrossed in his phone. It was a look that had gotten him a few snippy comments down the years from those who thought that young folks should look up from their phones and pay more attention to the world. Never mind that Ellis was into his thirties and feeling that age. Still, it was better to get judgmental looks as a smartphone addict than to draw attention to what magic looked like.

As he crossed the park, he caught sight of a tree like the one in the image the spell had conjured. That image hadn't changed much in the past hour, which meant either the signal had slowed, a real possibility in such a high magic environment, or the Wilderghast had taken its time playing with the sleeping woman's head. As Ellis slid his phone into his pocket and looked ahead, he immediately saw that it was option two.

The Wilderghast, knowing that it was normally invisible to mundane humans, lurked over the woman, its frayed gray robes hanging limply while skeletal fingers pressed against the side of her head. The woman's foot twitched, and she moaned in her sleep, clearly in some distress. Strands of blue light ran from her head into the Wilderghast, the emotional power that it was drawing off from her nightmare.

As Ellis got closer, approaching at an angle so that the creature wouldn't realize he was heading for it, the

Wilderghast didn't look up. It felt safe and satisfied. It had its best daytime feed in months.

Ellis glanced around. No one else was in sight. It was time.

He flicked his hand and his pine wand shot from the quick-draw holster up his sleeve. The moment he felt the wand in his hand, he started to chant.

The Wilderghast looked up. It lurched back from the woman and flung up a hand. As Ellis's magical net descended, a protective field appeared around the monster, glowing with ghostly blue energy. The air crackled as the spells met, strands of raw magic tangling, canceling each other out, spent power blackening the grass as it grounded itself.

The Wilderghast pointed its other hand at Ellis, and the air billowed between its fingertips, like drops of black ink spreading through clear water. A nameless fear gripped Ellis, making his muscles tense and a cold sweat break across his brow. Images from the worst moments in his life appeared at the corners of his vision.

He'd been ready for this. He reached behind his tie and took a grip on his Silver Griffin amulet, a small silver thing of two interconnected circles on a chain but a sign of authority and a ward of protection. The extra protective spells he had cast into it that morning emerged, chasing back the nightmarish visions and forming a protective barrier around his mind.

"I ain't going down that easy." He advanced on the Wilderghast.

Magic still flowed from both of them, Ellis pushing the bars of the ethereal cage forward, the Wilderghast straining to hold them back. Slowly, moment by moment, its defenses weakened. Another push, a little more strength, and Ellis would have it trapped.

The Wilderghast flicked its arm down and pointed its bony fingers at the sleeping woman. Moments before, power had flowed from her head into the Wilderghast. Now it went the other way around, a thread of blackness piercing her forehead. The woman leapt to her feet with a shriek and flung herself at Ellis.

Ellis fell, and the woman landed on top of him. She battered at him with her hands, which were dirty and ragged-nailed. He held his arms up to fend her off, not wanting to hurt her but not willing to let her beat him senseless.

"You bastard!" she shrieked. "You're on their side. You were with…with…with…"

Her words trailed to a halt, as did her blows. She looked down at Ellis in confusion, a gray-haired woman who had taken too many knocks from life and now found herself in one more bewildering situation.

"I'm sorry, sonny." She climbed off him. "I don't know what happened. I just… I thought…"

"It's okay, ma'am." As Ellis stood, he slid the wand into his pocket before she could notice it. "Reckon you were having a nightmare and I happened past at the exact wrong moment."

"It was so real," the woman whispered, looking down at her hands. "I haven't seen Bert in years, but he was there, with his belt, and the police, and…"

Ellis looked around. The Wilderghast was gone, and there was no point in pursuit now that it had a head start.

He would have to reassemble his web of spells to find it again, so there was no rushing that either.

He looked back at the homeless woman, bewildered and dirty and looking like she hadn't been eating properly. He didn't know anything about LA's provision for folks in her position, but he had a phone and probably enough charm to keep her with him while he got hold of someone who could help.

"Reckon I saw a hot dog cart down by the park gates. You want one?"

The woman looked at him through narrowed eyes, hunger and suspicion warring for dominance.

"It's okay, I ain't gonna do anything bad," Ellis reassured her. "I'm hungry, I could do with some conversation, and if you don't like me, you can walk away. How about it?"

"All right," the woman nodded. "You lead the way."

It wasn't the dinner he'd planned or the woman he'd hoped to share it with, but that hot dog in the sunshine gave Ellis a friendly, satisfying start to his latest LA stay.

CHAPTER FIVE

Night fell across Los Angeles.

In a dimension that all humans entered but whose existence few knew about, Mr. No stalked like an angular shadow through a landscape as varied and miraculous as the human mind. There was everything to see here, from the tallest mountain peaks to the depths of the ocean trenches, ancient monuments to shining tower blocks of glass and chrome. In this realm, people walked on the moon, and lovers separated by half a world spent their nights in each other's arms.

This was where the two forms of dreams collided. There were the ones that Mr. No traveled through, those lands of surreal images and wild fantasies of the unconscious, of broken pieces of memory reshuffled to make something new. Then there were the types of dreams that Mr. No stole and hoarded to himself, dreams in the sense of ambition, of aspiration, of the grand things that people hoped to do with their lives. Those other types of dreams brought these to the surface, where Mr. No could see them, smell them, cup them in his hands like precious jewels, and like the robber he was, whip them away.

In a Disneyland hotel room, a girl named Ines dreamed of the holiday that was beginning. Her part of the dreamscape was a wild whirl of bright colors and ceaseless movement. A princess palace towered over her, with a roller coaster racing around its walls. She took a giant candy floss from a cartoon duck in a top hat, ate it all in one go, and climbed up the palace stairs. A roller coaster car stopped in front of her, and she stepped in.

The roller coaster rushed into movement, racing around the towers and high above the park. From the ground below, Ines's parents waved at her, and she waved back. She had never been more excited in her whole life.

As the roller coaster emerged from a tunnel, she noticed the tall man sitting next to her, with his pale face and black suit.

"This is exciting," he said. "Is it everything you dreamed of?"

"Yes," Ines said. "This and more. I'm going on Splash Mountain, and the pirate boat, and the Finding Nemo submarine. I'm going to meet Mickey and Minnie and Donald and all the others. I'm going to eat candy floss every day. It's going to be amazing."

"Have you dreamed of this for long?"

"Ever since I was tiny and saw it on TV for the first time. My parents have been saving up all these years, but it was never this year, never yet. Always something else had to be paid for. Now we're here! I'm going to go on every ride in the park. It's everything I've ever wanted."

"How inspiring. That's quite a dream." The man tapped the side of Ines's head. His finger was cold. "To think you kept it all in here, building up such excitement, propelling yourself toward this moment for so long. Honestly, there's no enthusiasm like that of a child."

"Thank you, I guess." Ines looked at him in confusion. "Are you from one of the films? I feel like I've seen you somewhere."

"Oh, that wasn't me. That was only a pale reflection." The man let out a satisfied sigh as if he'd just eaten a really big burger. "Now, which ride would you like to go on next?"

"I...I don't know." Ines stared vacantly around the park. "It's only a place, with some machines and some people in silly costumes."

"You don't want candy floss?"

"No. It doesn't taste of much."

The man took a step back, a cartoon dog walked between them, and the man was gone.

When Ines's parents woke her in the morning and asked her eagerly which ride she wanted to start with, they were startled to see their daughter shrug and say that she didn't care about theme parks.

In Farhad's dream, he was still a rideshare driver. Instead of the little car he'd bought with all his savings when he arrived in LA, he drove a limousine. Rather than ferrying passengers back and forth between LAX and their hotels, he drifted down Sunset Boulevard or across the hills, looking out over the city. Buildings towered like monuments over the streets, and every one was a celebration of him. When he stopped at traffic lights, a Bollywood dance troupe appeared and sang a song about his financial success, while his mother told him what a good son he had been and how proud she was of him.

He didn't even notice that he had a fare in his car until he was driving through Chinatown, basking in the glowing of a thousand paper lanterns.

"It's a glorious city, isn't it?" said the passenger, a pale man in a dark suit, his long legs stretched out across the back seat. Farhad was pleasantly surprised to hear the man speaking in Urdu.

"Yes." Farhad smiled widely. "It's a wonderful place."

"You came here alone?"

"Yes, but I am saving up to bring my family over. I work all day, every day, gathering the money we will need for visas, plane tickets, and a home. Soon, this will be ours."

Farhad pulled the car up in front of a suburban rancher. The sprawling house was pastel blue and perfectly maintained, with a lush lawn and trees in the yard. Across the road, his mother waved from her own, distinctly separate, house.

"The American dream." Farhad beamed at the sight. "It's everyone's dream now, isn't it?"

"Not everyone's," the pale man replied. "Still, those who dream of it do so deeply, passionately, deliciously."

He tapped the back of Farhad's head with one icy cold finger, and a shudder passed briefly through Farhad. In front of him, the house shrank, then faded away, until he sat in heavy traffic in his car, one more day stalled on the streets of LA.

The back door opened. His passenger stepped out onto the sidewalk and vanished into the crowd.

When Farhad woke up, there were already requests for rides popping up on his phone, but he couldn't be bothered getting out of bed. He switched the TV on and lay there, watching nothing that mattered.

The hall in Selma's dream was grander than any she had been to in real life. Bigger than any lecture hall she'd sat in at MIT, any concert hall she'd been to as she improved herself culturally, any hotel function hall she'd been in for the Silicon Valley tech events and weekend presentations by motivational speakers. It was the sort of lecture hall that gods would have delivered speeches in, and it was packed full of people, all there to listen to her.

She walked out to the podium in the center of the stage to a wave of polite but enthusiastic applause. She was the woman who had given the world its great next technological leap forward, and they were all here to hear what she had to say. There were Einstein, Newton, Hawking, Gates, her parents, her ex-husband, the fifth-grade teacher who had told her that she would never amount to anything and the sixth-grade one who had inspired her to take up technology. Everyone who had ever made a difference in her life, from the biggest relationships to the smallest conversations to the figures of history and fiction which inspired her, they were here for her presentation.

She took a black cube out of her pocket and put it on the podium. Even she didn't know what it did yet, but she knew that they would be amazed.

A tall, pale man in a black suit, presumably technical staff, walked over to her while the crowd kept applauding.

"It's everything you dreamed of, isn't it?" he asked. "The exalted master of technology, scientific genius, celebrity CEO, and entrepreneur."

Lights flashed as the press took her pictures and the television cameras moved in closer to get the best view of her. All over the world, people were watching.

"Yes," she said. "It's all I've ever aspired to."

"Good."

The man raised a finger. She thought that he would tap the microphone to test that it was working, but instead, he tapped the center of her forehead. That touch was unnaturally cold. Then he stepped back, and the crowd went silent.

"All yours." He disappeared behind the curtains at the edge of the stage.

Selma looked out at the crowd. She couldn't remember what she was going to say or who they were. She didn't really care. She picked up the small black box sitting in front of her, tossed it over her shoulder, and walked away.

When she woke up, she was at her desk with the design she had been frantically working on when she dozed off. She swept the papers into the bin, went to bed, and didn't set her alarm for the next day.

Normally, Ed's chair sat by the window of his room in the retirement home. Today though, it stood on a golden beach, clear blue water lapping around its feet, while a warming sun shone down. His grandchildren dashed back and forth in the waves, laughing and splashing around. A newspaper lay in his lap, the crossword half complete.

His daughter appeared at his side and handed him a frosty glass of beer. "Here, Pa. It's been too long."

"It has. I'm sorry I didn't make it sooner, but Australia's such a long way, and travel gets harder the older I get."

"I understand." She kissed him on the forehead. "I'm sorry about before. They were arguments over nothing. I see that now."

"No, I'm sorry, it was all my fault."

She hugged him, and he hugged her back. They clutched each other so tight that it squeezed tears from his eyes, the happiest tears he'd ever shed.

A shadow fell across him, and he turned, expecting to see his son-in-law on his other side. Instead, a stranger stood there, dressed in a black suit, his tie loose and the top button of his shirt undone, exposing a small triangle of his pale skin to the blazing sun.

"What a beautiful ambition," the man said. "To spend your final days reunited with your family."

"It's all I've wanted for years," Ed said. "I didn't have the courage to reach out and make it happen. The dream keeps me going, but some days I'm afraid I'll never act on it."

"Let me take that fear away."

The man touched Ed's forehead, and his finger was as

cold as death. Then he walked out into the sea until he sank from view.

Ed looked at the children playing in the waves and realized that he didn't even know them.

When Ed's nurse walked in on him in the morning, she expected to see him holding his phone and his address book, trying to get up the courage for a call, like he did every morning. This time, he hadn't got out of bed.

Mr. No stalked through the last moments of dawn as the dreaming world lost its grip on LA. He found a night shift worker settling down to sleep, someone whose head he could rest in while he digested what he had consumed. It had been a very satisfying night.

CHAPTER SIX

The magical subway car came to a halt at the station for the Silver Griffins' LA HQ, hidden beneath the Griffith Observatory. The doors slid open, and Lucy stepped out, her Batman backpack over her shoulder and a Wonder Woman travel mug in her hand, full of steaming hot tea.

At the end of the station, Normandy, the gnome station keeper, was up a ladder and polishing the wall-mounted clock. It gleamed almost as brightly as the buttons on his uniform jacket.

"Good morning, Normandy," Lucy called.

"Good morning, Agent Heron." Normandy climbed down the ladder and walked over to her, tipping his cap in greeting. "Coming in for the day?"

"Hopefully not all of it," Lucy said. "I didn't sign up to the Silver Griffins so I could write reports and fill out requisition forms."

"No one does, but the forms need filling."

"Well, maybe, but it's hardly what I dreamed of."

Normandy chuckled. "Few jobs are. I got lucky."

"Really, this is your dream job?"

"Oh, yes." Normandy's smile lit up his face with a glow like summer dawn. "This position is every bit as prestigious to a gnome as working for one of the high magic libraries back on Oriceran and far more exotic. I saw enough grimoires growing up, but I never saw a cellphone in my life before I came here, and as for all the candy bars..." He shook his head in wonderment. "It's quite a world you have here, Agent Heron."

"I guess, when you put it like that." She took a paper bag out of her backpack and handed it to the gnome. "Speaking of sweet things, I baked cranberry biscuits, thought you might like some."

"Oh my!" Normandy's eyes went wide as he peered into the bag. "Thank you so much."

Lucy walked along the main tunnel from the station, up a set of spiral stairs, and out through a hidden door into the Observatory. It was still relatively early, and the place was quiet, with only a few tourists wandering around while staff set up for the day. She made her way past the pendulum, down an exhibition hall, and through another hidden door into the Griffins' HQ.

The receptionist sat behind his desk, reading a magazine about wands. Without looking up from the pages, he tapped a box on the desk. "ID."

"Really?" Lucy asked. "You don't know me by now?"

"Procedure."

It was never worth the fight. She tapped her wand to the box, triggering a green light. Then she put a single cookie down on the desk.

"You only get one because you make me do this every time."

"Thanks." He still didn't look up as he reached for the cookie.

Lucy headed onto the main office floor. Messenger pigeons fluttered overhead while witches and wizards sat at their desks, doing research or completing the admin that came with any large organization.

Lucy put a box of cookies down by the coffee machine in the corner, causing an immediate rush of agents from their desks. Then she took her seat across from her friend Jackie Kowal.

"Here, I saved some for you." Lucy handed Jackie a couple of the cookies.

"Awesome, I'll save these for later." Jackie set the cookies down next to her coffee mug. "You in for the morning?"

"Hopefully not that long. Why?"

"We have the meeting about refurbishing the break room, remember? Applegate finally approved the budget for it."

"So, what's the plan for the place? I mean, aside from throwing out that ratty old sofa."

"I say bigger sofas, make it properly relaxing, somewhere we can chill out in peace, but Jim and some of the other junior agents have been campaigning for a games console, and I don't see me getting a lot of quiet with that in there."

"Any other options?"

"As many as we have agents. Kelly wants it minimalist, but I think that's her way of making things uncomfortable so that we focus on work. Jenkins wants to put in vending machines, but I'm pretty sure that's so he can rig them with faults and odd contents, then use them to conduct experiments on all of us."

Lucy laughed. "I know the Special Equipment and Weapons crew are odd, but I don't think they'd go that far."

"Remember the psychedelic pigeons?"

"Okay, fair point, no Jenkins vending machines."

Kelly Petrie walked past, dressed in a smart suit and high heels. She gave them the curtest of nods.

"And a lovely warm hello to you too, Kelly," Jackie called, then lowered her voice and shook her head. "At least she's not in charge yet. That's when we'll really be in trouble."

"Kelly's not so bad," Lucy said.

Jackie raised an eyebrow. "You've changed your tune."

"All right, she is that bad, but we managed to work together on the Blight case. It turns out that sometimes we approach the work the same way. It's just that we get so caught up in disagreeing that we fight out of habit."

"Disagreeing with Kelly Petrie is the surest sign that you're in the right. I'd stick with it."

Sam, Roger Applegate's PA, scurried over to their desks.

"Aside from Petrie, you two are the most senior agents here, right?" Sam asked, face crumpled with worry.

"Sure," Jackie said. "What's up?"

"You should come to see."

Lucy and Jackie exchanged a look. Sam was normally unflappable, so this was a moment for the record books and a concerning one.

Sam led the two of them into Applegate's office, then

closed the door. Kelly was already in there, looking across the desk at Applegate himself. The regional manager stared vacantly at the monitor of his computer, hands lying idle by the keyboard. He was wearing his usual three-piece suit, but the tie wasn't straight, and his shirt was crumpled. Something flickered on the screen in front of him.

"I was asking Mr. Applegate if any new cases had come in today," Kelly said.

"Okay," Lucy said. So far, so normal, Kelly looking for extra work to suck up to the boss. "And?"

"Sir, do we have any new cases?" Kelly asked.

Applegate shrugged. "Don't know."

"Well, could you check?"

"Doesn't seem worth it."

Lucy felt a little of the alarm written over Kelly's and Sam's faces. Applegate might not be the hardest-working boss, but he always made sure to know what needed attending to, if only so that he could hand it off to another agent. What had gotten into him?

Lucy walked around the desk and looked at the monitor, which showed a video of cats playing.

"Is this work-related, sir?" she asked.

Applegate shrugged again. "It's cute. It'll do."

"Have you hit your head recently?"

Applegate shook his head.

"Been struck by any strange spells?"

He shook his head again.

"Maybe had an encounter with an unusual magical entity?"

He laughed quietly as the kittens tumbled over each other, then shook his head again.

"Maybe we should check that," Jackie said. She lowered the blinds on the glass wall, concealing them from the rest of the office.

"What are you doing?" Kelly hissed. "He didn't ask us to do that."

"He's not asking us to do anything. That's the problem."

Lucy pulled out her wand and cast a detection spell. A faint glow emanated from Applegate's head.

"There's some sort of magical influence here," she said, "but I don't recognize it. How about you lot?"

They pressed in close around Applegate, peering at the strands of magic. He didn't object, even when Sam leaned in, blocking his view of the playful cats.

"Means nothing to me," Jackie said.

"Or me," Sam said.

Kelly frowned, tilted her head from side to side, plucked at the strands of magic, then finally gave in. "I don't know either."

"One thing's for sure. He's in no state to run the Griffins." Lucy dismissed the spell and put her wand away. "One of us is going to have to take charge."

"Not me!" Jackie backed away. "I don't want to have to deal with everyone's complaints and demands and need for attention. You two have management training. One of you should take charge."

Lucy and Kelly looked at each other. This was about to get awkward.

"My vote is for Lucy," Jackie added.

Kelly scowled. "That's not how the Silver Griffins work."

"It could be. It's not like we have a procedure for when the boss goes temporarily brain dead."

"Actually, we do." Sam pulled out a phone and flicked through a document on it. "In case of the regional manager's incapacitation, and in circumstances where he can't nominate a stand-in, there are a series of factors that come into play, including time with the agency, seniority of rank, and managerial experience."

"Who does that put in charge?" Lucy was relieved to have the decision taken off their shoulders.

Sam held up the phone for all of them to see. "Agent Petrie is in charge."

Kelly beamed smugly. Lucy stifled a grimace, while Jackie wore hers openly.

"Well then, I'd better get started." Kelly pursed her lips. "Can we get Mr. Applegate down to the infirmary? I'm going to need his chair."

"Don't get too comfortable," Jackie said. "It's only temporary."

Lucy hoped that she was right.

CHAPTER SEVEN

In a network of rooms and tunnels underneath the Heron house, Ashley sat at a bank of monitors, watching the video feeds from the Mini Griffins. Her field agents, many only a year or two older than her, were out on patrol around their neighborhoods, looking for any sign of trouble.

"I'm bored," said Tommy, a ten-year-old based in West Hollywood. The view from his feed shifted as he lifted his cap so he could scratch his head. "It's been so quiet this week. No imps to chase, no shady artifact deals to expose. Not even another gang of bike thieves. I miss the good old days."

"The good old days of two weeks ago?" asked Mia, a twelve-year-old from Pasadena, who was picking up litter as she patrolled. "That's silly."

"Why? I can like things that happened before!"

"I think we at least have to become grownups before we start getting nostalgic."

Ashley leaned back in her seat, watching and listening. Tommy was right. It had been weirdly quiet this week.

Normally, the Mini Griffins would stumble across something in their patrols, whether it was an escaped magical animal or a crime they could report to the Silver Griffins. A few times, they had even tackled the criminals themselves. This week, nothing. LA's streets were as quiet as she had ever seen them, at least for magical activities.

"Let's stop early today," she said. "Save some energy for another day."

"What am I going to do for entertainment?" Tommy wailed. "I'm not allowed video games for two more days because of the state I left my room in, and there's nothing good on TV."

"I'm doing a live stream in an hour. You could watch that."

Tommy tipped his head on one side, slanting the view from his hat camera. "What are you streaming about?"

"How I built my mechanical pigeons."

"I'll pass. Gonna see if I can find any good Minecraft videos. If I can't play, at least I can watch."

One by one, the Mini Griffins switched off their cameras and microphones and headed for home. When the last monitor went black, Ashley got out of her seat and wandered down the tunnel to another part of the lair, where Dylan and Eddie lounged on bean bags.

"Again, again!" Eddie clapped.

"All right, one more time," Dylan said. He waved his wand and chanted a spell. Eddie's bean bag lifted into the air and spun three times while Eddie clung to it, giggling ecstatically.

"You're getting much better," Ashley said. "More controlled."

"I've been practicing a lot," Dylan said. "With help from Twylan and mom. The more variety of spells I master, the less likely I'll lose control when I have to cast something new. That's the theory, at least."

Ashley nodded. Sometimes she forgot how powerful her older brother was and how dangerous that power could be without proper training. She was used to thinking in terms of science and machines, not the wild wonders of magic.

She went to a corner of the room and picked up a box full of mechanical pigeons, all in different states of construction, from one that was separate pieces through to a completed automaton.

"What you doing?" Eddie ambled over, his movements wonky with dizziness, and peered into the box. Lifeless camera eyes peered back at him.

"I'm going on YouTube," Ashley said. "I'm going to talk about how I made these."

"Couldn't that lead to trouble?" Dylan asked. "Showing off your abilities like that."

"It's science, not magic, so I'm not doing anything the Silver Griffins would object to. I checked with mom."

"I guess that's okay then." Dylan levitated several bean bags at once, then dropped them in a row. He sighed. "It's not fair. You get to show the world what you can do while I have to hide it."

"Hiding's fun," Eddie said. "You wanna play hide-and-seek?"

"Sure, why not." Dylan stood. "Are you hiding first or seeking?"

"Hiding." The air around Eddie shimmered, and he

shrank down to a mouse, which scurried away down the tunnel.

"This could be challenging. There are some tiny spaces down here." Dylan smiled. "It'll make a nice change from practicing spells."

He hurried off in search of Eddie, leaving Ashley to carry her box into the computer room. She set it down next to her seat, then laid the mechanical birds out carefully in front of her so they were in order and each one within easy reach. She had already rigged a camera on a moving boom so that it could hang over each of the birds, letting her show her audience what she had done. These things were simple, with a little bit of thought.

She switched on a monitor and glanced at the time in its bottom right corner. Almost time for the show. She settled into her seat, switched on the cameras, and pulled up the custom software she'd created to control her video streams. As well as letting her shift easily between shots and control the sound, it let her anonymize the feed, fuzzing out her features and disguising her voice. That had downsides when it came to connecting with people through her channel, but she had reluctantly decided that it was for the best. She might not be doing magic, but she was creating some pretty amazing things, and there were people in the world who would try to steal them. A villain had tracked her down once before, and she didn't want it happening again.

With everything in place, she paused for a moment to rally her thoughts, then hit the streaming button. The TreeHouseGenius channel stirred into life.

"Hi," she said. "This is TreeHouseGenius, coming to you

live from the treehouse that isn't a treehouse anymore. Maybe I should change the channel name, what do you think? Comments are open, so let me know.

"Today, I'm going to talk about one of my most recent creations, this mechanical pigeon."

She picked up the complete pigeon and held it in front of the camera.

"This mechanical creature can carry messages and small objects to your friends and family. I made it using some of the principles we've talked about in previous videos, as well as some discoveries I made adjusting to this design. Getting the right materials was particularly important because it's hard for anything to fly when it's too heavy.

"As always, you can ask questions as we go along, and I'll try to answer them. First though, here are the parts that went into the pigeon…"

She started talking through her design process and the pieces that she had brought together for the pigeons. She had designed them for the Mini Griffins as a substitute for the live magical pigeons the Silver Griffins used, but she wasn't going to say that in the stream. After all, the Mini Griffins were a network of secret agents. It wouldn't be good security to give their existence away as mundane spy agencies did.

As she talked, questions started to pop up in the feed. She had thousands of followers, but not all of them could be there for a live stream, and even fewer had anything to say. Still, it was enough to keep her occupied, attention shifting between the devices in her hands and the chat bar on the monitor.

As she got near the end of her demonstration, the chat

went quiet. Knowing her dedicated viewers, they would be making notes on what they had seen and preparing to have a go at it themselves. Within a week, she would receive pictures of other people's imitations of her device, and that was one of the best parts about running the channel, seeing how it inspired others.

Still, she needed something to say.

"The other night at dinner, my family asked about what I dream of being when I grow up," she said. "It was fun to think about, so before I tell you my answer, what do you dream of being? Is there something you really want to do or someone you want to be like?"

Almost immediately, the comments started up again.

"I want to be like U!"

"Streaming channel + machine = life goals."

"Dreaming of 10,000 followers, 2 b half as good as u."

Ashley blinked, caught by surprise. There were other answers too, bands people wanted to be in or celebrities they dreamed of imitating, and some more action-oriented answers like going to the moon or winning a Nobel prize. Those were the sorts of answers she'd expected. It was the ones mentioning her that caught her off-guard.

"Some of you want to be like me?" she asked, her voice wavering at the thought.

"Totes!"

"For real!

"Yes! Yes! Yes!"

She took a moment to power up and launch one of the mechanical pigeons, buying her time to work out how she could react. She felt like she ought to say something, but she didn't want to come across as big-headed or to encourage them to keep dreaming so small. She was only a girl with some tools and a video channel. They could aim bigger than that.

"I never thought that people would want to be like me," she said at last. "I mean, I like being me, but what I do feels ordinary to me. It's what I do every day, so I never think of it as something you would dream of." She hesitated, lining the words up in her head. "I won't tell you what to aspire to or who to act like, but go read about some great scientists, like Ada Lovelace or Isaac Newton or Marie Curie. Those are the people I dream of being like, and maybe they'll give you something more to dream of too.

"I think I'll sign off there. Don't forget to hit like and subscribe, and I'll see you all soon."

She switched off the cameras and sat in silence, staring at the messages still filling the chat bar. Other kids wanted to be like her. She lived a life of magic and extraordinary machines, and that was still the strangest thing she had heard all week.

CHAPTER EIGHT

Lucy was standing by her SUV outside a Starbucks, sipping her tea and wondering what to do next, when the pigeon arrived. It landed on the roof of the Rivian and stared at her, cooing expectantly.

"You got a mission for me there, lad?" Lucy asked.

She set her cup down next to the pigeon, who seemed less than intimidated to be in the presence of a porcelain Wonder Woman, and untied the message from the pigeon's leg, then unrolled it to read:

Possible magical disturbance detected at candy store in Grand Central Market. Go at once to contain and cover up. RM Petrie.

It took her a moment to work out what the RM stood for. Apparently, Kelly was taking her temporary post as Regional Manager a little too seriously.

Its contents read, the message self-destructed by turning into a handful of worms, which drew eager cooing from the pigeon. Lucy set the worms down on the ground, and the bird hopped down to eat them while she got in her vehicle and drove away.

It only took a few minutes to reach the market, but it took nearly as long to find somewhere nearby where she could park. At last, she got out of the car and rushed into the market with her wand protruding from her back pocket.

The market was bustling with people, some of them shopping for fruit, veg, and fish, others looking for something they could eat right now. Even among that bustle, it was easy to work out where the problem was, thanks to the small crowd that had gathered toward the far side.

Lucy pushed her way through the gathering, apologizing and offering excuses as she went, sounding more English than she had in months. Having fought her way through to the front, she gazed at a scene of chaos. Colored candy lay scattered across the ground while other pieces flew through the air. Jars had been overturned, and one of them was rolling from side to side. The owner stood by the till and stared at the destruction, his face slack, with none of the outrage or protest Lucy would have expected from a man whose business was under attack.

"What are those things?" someone in the crowd asked.

"I think they're some kind of rat," a woman said.

"Don't be ridiculous. Rats ain't green or bright orange like that."

"They could be escaped lab rats. I saw this documentary on TV once—"

"That wasn't a documentary. It was one of those cartoons, one where the rats all—"

"I know what I saw, and I'm telling you—"

"Look, one of them's trying to steal a whole jar!"

Lucy rushed to block the way as a jar moved to the edge of the crowd. She bent to peer underneath and was unsurprised to see a troll, its spike of brightly colored hair pressed down by the container of illicit candy.

"Public health inspector," she called to the crowd. "I'll deal with this. There's nothing more to see."

"Why's public health hiring Australians?"

"That's not an Australian accent. It's New Zealand."

"No, it's Scottish."

"That ain't the point. The point is, why does it take an immigrant to catch rats."

"I'm English," Lucy said indignantly. "I'm here because I'm an expert in this particular type of rats. Now if you would get out of the way, I can—"

"I want to see these fancy rats," somebody said.

"I told you, they ain't rats, this Scottish lady's lying to cover up the truth, and I'm sticking around to prove it."

"They are rats, you'll see."

The crowd showed no sign of dispersing. If anything, it was getting bigger, thanks to the logic that told people that where others gather there must be something worth seeing. At least the noise covered Lucy's words as she leaned in and spoke quietly to the troll.

"Listen here, sunshine, I'm a Silver Griffin, and I'm in no mood to muck about. Why don't you and your mate come quietly, save us all a lot of bother?"

The troll set the jar aside, and for one brief, hopeful moment, Lucy thought that things were going to go smoothly. Then the troll started to expand, shooting up toward the ceiling. What had been a tiny, doll-like figure became a towering monster, muscles flexing and pointed teeth bared. Half the crowd screamed. The other half fumbled for their phones.

"Never was, never will be!" Lucy waved her wand, getting the spell off before anyone could take a photo. The crowd went still, every one of them staring vacantly at the air in front of them.

The troll wasn't so helpful. It swung a fist at Lucy, while behind it, a second troll expanded, shattering the candy jar it had been standing in.

Lucy ducked, and the fist swung through the air where she had been a moment before. She had to deal with this fast before the commotion drew more people.

"Refrigero!" A blast of icy magic shot from the end of Lucy's wand. It hit the troll, which froze in place, caught in mid-swing.

The other troll lurched toward her, trampling candy as it went. She cast the freeze spell again, but the troll ducked, and the magic flew wild. The troll stretched out its hands, trying to grab hold of Lucy, but she leapt clear, spinning around its side, and raised her wand again. The third shot of magic caught the troll in the chest and froze it in place.

Lucy looked around. She had two frozen trolls, at least fifty magically stunned bystanders, and only a few minutes before the effects started wearing off. She was going to need help.

She pulled out her phone and called the transport team at HQ.

"No time to mess around with vehicles," she said. "Can

you open a portal right now to the candy store at Grand Central Market, big enough to take an expanded troll?"

"We can try," said a voice at the other end of the line. "Hold on."

For a long moment, nothing happened. Lucy stood watching the still crowd, wary in case anyone else came close. Then a golden haze appeared in the air before solidifying into a portal.

"Perfect." Lucy shoved the nearest troll with all her strength, and it toppled over, falling straight through the portal. She had to drag the other one into place, leaving scuff marks on the floor, before she could get it through.

"All done," she shouted through the portal. The air fizzled, and the magic disappeared.

Lucy looked around. She was in time. People were starting to move again, looking at each other in confusion. With the memories of the preceding half-hour gone, they would have to piece together an explanation of what brought them to the candy store, but that seemed like a minor disruption compared with the forgotten troll attack.

The owner of the candy stall was one of the last people still standing staring vacantly into space. While he did that, Lucy went to clear up some of the mess, kicking away the troll tracks, dumping shattered glass and crushed candies into a bin, and tidying up the food that still looked edible.

"Do you... Did something happen here?" a woman asked as she tried to work out why the camera app was open on her phone.

"Not that I noticed," Lucy said.

"How come there's ice on the ceiling at this time of year?"

Lucy looked up at where the woman was pointing. Sure enough, there was a patch of ice caused by the spell she had missed the troll with.

"Must be a leak in an air conditioning system," Lucy said. "You know how these things go."

"Sure, yeah." The woman nodded uncertainly, then walked away.

At last, it was only Lucy and the store's owner. He no longer wore the utterly blank expression her spell had caused, but he didn't seem interested in what had happened like many of the others were. In fact, he didn't seem interested in anything at all, not even the damage to his stall. He simply gazed around him, watching people go by, and occasionally popped a toffee into his mouth.

"Are you okay there?" Lucy asked.

"Uhuh." The guy nodded.

"You don't have any questions or concerns, any worries about what's been happening?"

He shook his head.

"Well, okay then."

Lucy was about to walk away. After all, there were other cases to investigate, and if a human seemed disinterested in magical events, that was a good thing, right? Except that this guy was too disinterested, completely lost to the world. The trolls had smashed his jars, candies were missing, and he didn't care.

Lucy waved a hand in front of his face, and he smiled at her.

"Can I help you with something?" he asked.

"This store, it's yours, right?" Lucy asked.

"Sure."

"You must be proud of it?"

"It's okay, I guess."

"Have you owned it for long?"

"Sure, a while."

"And you love candy?"

"It's all right. Mostly just sugar, isn't it?"

The guy turned away, and Lucy took the opportunity to cast a magic detection spell covertly. Sure enough, a haze of power stood out like faint points of light around his head. Someone had interfered with his mind, as they had done to Applegate, but from what she saw here, Lucy couldn't tell who or how never mind how to fix it.

She put her wand away, bought a bag of gummy bears, and headed out through the market, which had returned to its normal level of activity. Shoppers made their way from stall to stall, some forceful and determined, others curious and inquisitive, but none with the slack expression of the candy store owner. That was a look that said the person wouldn't be doing anything of interest, wouldn't be getting excited or angry or passionate in any way. It wasn't an attitude that would stir up trouble, but that didn't mean it was good: a lot could go wrong when people stopped caring what happened to them.

Some magical was messing with people's minds, and it was Lucy's job to find out who.

CHAPTER NINE

Heather Fields stood at the front of the Underfoot Brigade's classroom. It wasn't what most teachers, or even most pupils, would have wanted from a school. Battered desks, mismatched chairs, and the room itself was a strange concrete chamber set off from a tunnel under the streets of LA. For a group of outcast teenage magicals and their nature witch teacher, it was a nearly perfect choice. It was certainly better than the old place, which still smelled of diesel fumes and soot after an attack by sentient smog.

"The freeze spell has a wide range of uses," Heather said. "That means you need to think carefully about how you cast it on each occasion. The power to hold an opponent in place is wildly excessive if you only want to cool down your drink."

A few of her pupils laughed, and though she figured they were humoring her, it was nice to hear. With the smaller class that was the portion of Underfoots with magical powers, it could sometimes be hard to get a feel for the mood in the room.

"To practice that, you each have a bottle of water," she said. "I want you to try to freeze it without creating frost on anything else nearby. Build up slowly until you get to the right amount of cold. When you finish, practice undoing your magic, then give it another go."

The results were inevitable. Within seconds, one pupil had frozen his desk to the floor, while another had barely got the first tiny chunk of ice to appear. Heather reminded herself that this was why she had value here.

Leontine, the crippled Arpak who was one of the Brigade's leaders, appeared through a door at the back of the room.

"Your visitors are starting to arrive," he said.

"All right then. Class, keep practicing as long as you like, but please don't freeze each other. Tomorrow, we'll explore the effect of freezing different materials. That's it for today."

Heather left the room and headed down the network of tunnels the Brigade had recently moved into. It was a different sort of space from the single vast tunnel that had housed them before. This one allowed more privacy, as well as room to get away from each other, which Heather thought was probably good for a bunch of teenagers.

She arrived at her room, a spacious storage chamber from an abandoned transit project. Although she preferred to spend her spare time out in the parks and woodlands around LA, she had decided that it was worth having a home down here, now that she spent more time with the kids. There was a bed, a desk, several chairs, and rows of plants sitting on shelves along one wall, as well as a couple of slender trees growing in tubs.

As she walked in, the bark on one of the trees rippled. Its slim trunk expanded and burst open. Mackam, a wiry wizard with a weather-worn face and a braided gray beard emerged into the room before the tree returned to its usual shape.

"Chief." Mackam nodded to Heather, then sat on the ground. The chairs were all occupied already, and several people were sitting on the bed. This looked like all of Heather's guests, not merely a few of them. The council of the Tolderai had gathered.

"Let's get straight to it." Heather looked around at the assembled representatives of her tribe of woodland wizards. "Nate, I'm impressed to see that you've earned a place on the council already."

Nathaniel Oakmantle, the newest addition to the tribe, blushed and pushed back a few blond strands that had broken loose from his ponytail.

"After my part in defeating the Choking Dread, some people thought that—"

"No need to justify yourself," Heather interrupted. "We're the Tolderai. We claim what is ours. Now what we need to claim for ourselves is a sense of purpose."

Some of the Tolderai nodded in agreement, while others looked bemused.

"We defend the trees," Mackam said. "Grow and nurture. Help the wild stay wild. We have all the purpose we need."

"No," Heather said. "That's our nature, our values, our sense of being. It's who we are, and it always will be. What we do has always been more than that. We've found specific battles to fight, forests to grow, places to protect.

"For centuries, our greatest purpose was to counter the Choking Dread. We fought it in the early days, then watched for its return, kept the memory of it alive, worked on plans and spells to fight it. It gave us drive and unity.

"Now the Choking Dread is gone. We defeated it, together with the Silver Griffins. Something else should take the place of that cause."

"Why?" Nathaniel asked. "Isn't it enough to look after the trees, to spend time in the forest, to be who we are?"

"You're too new to appreciate this Nate, but the rest of you, think about the other tribes we've known or the great tribes spoken of when we recite our histories around the campfires at the turning of the year. How many of them remain, compared with those that have dwindled? Without a concrete purpose, we risk becoming scattered and divided, fading into the background, disappearing from the memories of the world. I won't have that happen to us."

More of the council nodded now, Mackam among them.

"All right, you have a point," he said. "What's our purpose to be? What course do you want to set us on, chief?"

"It's not for me to decide," Heather said. "We need to find one together. That's why I've summoned you here so we can decide the future of our tribe."

A hubbub of conversation erupted as the witches and wizards all started throwing ideas around at once. Heather was about to bring order to the chaos when someone tapped her on the shoulder. She looked around to see Kix the gnome, one of the Underfoot Brigade, looking up at her.

"Sorry to interrupt your meeting," Kix said, "but Siltor's frozen to the wall, and we can't get him off."

Heather sighed. "All right, I'll come and fix it. Tolderai, keep talking."

She followed Kix back to the classroom, where a thick layer of ice fixed a teenage elf to the concrete wall.

"Who did this?" Heather asked.

"He did it to himself," Kix said. "He said he was going to do something really impressive with the ice. We all thought it was another one of his illusions at first, but then..." She tapped the ice. It was solid as a rock. "Normally, we'd get Twylan to fix a thing like this, but it's her first day learning about the Silver Griffins so she's not here."

"It's fine. I got you all playing with this spell. It's my responsibility to deal with the consequences." Heather laid her hands on the ice and cast the freezing spell in reverse. Cold flowed into her, and the ice melted, running down the wall and across the floor. Some of it dribbled down her arms, soaking the sleeves of her flannel shirt. At last, Siltor peeled away from the wall, shivering and clutching himself.

"What was the exercise I left?" Heather asked.

"Sorry, Miss Fields," Siltor said through chattering teeth.

"What was the exercise?"

"A small, controlled freeze."

"What did you do?"

"A big freeze that stuck me in place."

"And that was..."

"Stupid?"

"Right. Impressive but stupid, which is why we save the

impressive part until we know how to control a spell properly. I hope I'll see better behavior from you tomorrow."

She headed back to her room, leaving a trail of wet footprints along the way. She half-expected to return to a council divided, fighting among themselves over who had the best idea. Living in the wild, the Tolderai had developed wild ways, a harsh approach to surviving in tough environments, and they'd settled big decisions with fists on several occasions. Today, they talked civilly, even Mackam, although the aging wizard bounced from foot to foot and clutched the knife on his belt.

"Well?" Heather asked. "Have you settled on an idea yet?"

"We've talked about a few," Nathaniel said.

"All the ideas," Mackam said, eyes wide, voice intent. "So many ideas. So many futures, like the branch of a tree splitting and shooting off a hundred different ways."

"All right, someone tell me the best one."

"That's what we can't decide," Nathaniel said. "Everyone wants something different."

"Then someone tell me an idea, any damn idea, and we'll start from there."

"A forest!" Mackam shouted, leaping to his feet. "A vast forest, new lungs for this ravaged world. A canopy of green and the singing of birds, like this land once was."

"Maybe not this exact bit of land," Heather said. "But I take your point. Where would we plant this forest?"

Mackam shrugged. "Wherever land lies abandoned."

"I researched reforesting projects during my Ph.D.," Nathaniel said. "It's not that straightforward. The available land isn't always good to reforest, and even when neglected, investors who own the good land won't let you plant there because they're waiting for a more profitable plan. Then there are questions of which trees will be appropriate at what points, the supply of—"

"Okay, we get it." Heather waved him into silence. "Planting a vast new forest won't be simple. I don't think that comes as a surprise to anyone here, but at least we have the skills to make sure the trees grow once we get started. If we get started on that one. Now someone tell me another idea."

This time, Nathaniel tentatively raised his hand.

"Go on," Heather said. "Out with it."

"We could try working with the Silver Griffins, make supporting their work our grand cause."

There were dissatisfied mutters from around the room.

"Hear him out," Heather directed. "Keep going, Nate."

"Well, they know about us now. I know that's not traditional, and it's not what any of the tribe wanted, but we can't undo it. So, what I'm wondering is, could we make the most of it? Working with the Silver Griffins would give us a chance to help keep the magical world hidden, to protect those who need it, and to watch out for any magic that threatens the natural world."

"They write reports." Mackam practically spat the word. "They have..." A shudder ran through him. "...accounts."

"I take your point, Mackam," Heather said. "It's not our comfort zone. But then, when have we ever let comfort be an excuse? If we can live outdoors through icy winters, we can find the courage to face paperwork too. Nate raises some interesting points. Who else has another idea?"

Everyone started talking at once.

"All right, all right!" Heather shouted them back to silence. "Let me try a different question: has someone else's idea convinced anyone?"

This time, no one spoke.

"In that case, I have a proposal," Heather said.

"Ah, she does have a scheme!" Mackam grinned. "This was all a ruse to show us that the chief's ideas are best."

"Not at all. I propose that we try out some of these ideas, one at a time to see what suits us. Ideas are all well and good, but the proof of the plan lies in action. What do you say?"

A chorus of agreement filled the room. Heather smiled. It was time for the Tolderai to step out of the past and make a new future for themselves.

CHAPTER TEN

Twylan walked down the Griffith Observatory exhibition hall and stopped in front of an unremarkable, out-of-the-way stretch of wall. Even with dark glasses and a baseball cap hiding the magical glow of her eyes, she felt very conspicuous out in public like this, but she had her instructions, and this was where they had led her. She checked that no one was looking her way, then covertly tapped her wand against the wall and muttered a spell. A section opened, and Twylan stepped through.

On the other side was a reception room with a lone wizard sitting behind a desk. Aside from a computer monitor and an abandoned magazine, the desk held a box with two lightbulbs on the front.

"I'm here to see Mr. Applegate." Twylan took off her glasses and cap. "Um, I think I have an appointment for three o'clock. That is to say; I'm sure I have one. Twylan of the Underfoot Brigade."

The receptionist tapped on his keyboard and looked at something on his screen.

"Huh, so that's what this is," he said. "Hold on a sec." He picked up his desk phone and hit a button. "Sam? Yeah, I have the boss's three o'clock here. Some teenage witch... No, not that I've seen... Well, you'd know better than me... Okay, yeah, sure, whatever they think is best." He hung up and turned his attention back to Twylan. "Take a seat. Someone will be with you shortly."

There were a couple of sofas on one side of the room. Twylan sat on one of them and leafed through a fashion magazine on the coffee table. It was much more Kix's sort of thing than hers but was better than sitting with nothing to do except worry about making a good impression.

After a few minutes, a door opened, and a woman came in. She was quite tall, with a blonde bob, and wore the sort of trousers and blouse that sat at the midpoint of smart and practical. Twylan recognized her as one of Lucy Heron's friends.

"Twylan, right?" The woman held out her hand. "I'm Agent Kowal, badge number 782, but you can call me Jackie."

"Hi," Twylan said.

Jackie turned to the receptionist. "Can you calibrate the security to recognize her wand?"

"Really?" He glanced at Twylan's scruffy clothes and magic-scarred cheeks.

"Yes, really. She's going to be coming in and out for a while, and she might not always be with me."

Okay, sure." He pointed at the desktop box. "Put your wand on there, please."

Twylan did as instructed. The lights on the box's front flickered, one green and the other red. Both flashed on and off while the receptionist did something at his computer. Then the red light went out.

"All done," the receptionist said. "Have a nice day."

Twylan followed Jackie into a large open-plan office with witches and wizards at the desks and pigeons flapping past overhead.

Jackie sat at a desk and pulled a swivel chair over. "Here. Take a seat."

Twylan did. There wasn't much reason not to.

"So, Sam says that Applegate was going to prepare you for a life in the Silver Griffins?"

Twylan nodded. "He said that there are things I need to learn about before I apply. He's going to help me."

"Mr. Applegate isn't helping anyone today," Jackie said. "He's had some sort of magical accident, and our research people haven't worked out how to undo it yet."

"Oh. Should I come back another day?"

"No, you're all right, kid. We're keeping things going in his absence. The temporary boss—" Jackie emphasized the word temporary. "—isn't interested in this, and in fairness, she has a lot of other things to handle, so I'm going to show you the ropes instead."

"Thank you."

"Happy to help. I don't want us to lose a potentially promising recruit because Kelly fobs you off on some other chick who wastes your time with the boring stuff. So, did Applegate say what he was going to teach you?"

Twylan thought back to their fleeting conversations.

"I think it might have been about magical theory," she said. "He mentioned lending me books."

"Classic Applegate!" Jackie laughed. "Takes on responsibility, then finds a way to minimize the work for himself. If he didn't have books, he probably would have passed you to one of us instead."

Twylan wasn't convinced. Mr. Applegate had seemed nice and genuinely interested in helping her out.

"Do you always talk about him like this?" she asked.

"Oh, don't worry, this isn't me acting up because the boss is in some magical semi-coma. Old Applegate knows what I think of him, and that's why I'm never getting another promotion, but I'm okay with that. Fortunately, I'm damn good at what I do." Jackie got out of her chair. "Today, what I'm going to do is show you something worth seeing. Come on."

They walked out of the office, along a corridor, and down a set of spiral stairs.

"Pigeon lofts are that way." Jackie pointed up. "Special Equipment and Weapons over there." She pointed through a door leading off from the stairs. "We'll give both of those a look, but not before I've checked what madness Jenkins is cooking up this week."

Twylan tried to fix the words in her memory as she wondered who Jenkins was and what was so special about his weapons.

"Today, though," Jackie opened a doorway out of the stairwell. "I'm going to show you transport. Trust me. It's more exciting than it sounds."

They walked down another corridor, past several doors marked with runes and no entry signs.

"Quiz time," Jackie said. "Where does the power of the Silver Griffins come from?"

"From your magic."

"Bzzzzt, wrong answer! Though it is related, so I'll give you half a point. Think again."

"From the magical laws then? They let you tell people what to do."

"What makes people do what we tell them?"

Twylan thought hard about it. If magic wasn't the answer, was there some deeper power at work here, or was she thinking about the whole thing wrong?

"Come on." Jackie stopped in front of another door. "Once we walk through this door, it'll give the answer away."

Then it hit Twylan. "Trevilsom Prison. The fact that you can lock magicals away."

"Exactly!" Jackie flung the door open, and they walked through.

The room they entered was cavernous but not natural, with the sort of brick walls that Twylan associated with sewers from a century or more before. Along one side of the room was a series of separate compartments, each one with a cage door and lines of security runes on the arch above. Opposite them, a group of gnomes was sorting through crates, overseen by a wizard and a witch. The far wall drew Twylan's attention. It seemed simple, a blank space of undecorated brick, but it glowed with residue from long-term repeated exposure to magic.

Leaving Twylan to stare around, Jackie strode over to the magicals by the crates. She had a brief conversation with them, then returned to Twylan.

"We're all good to have a look around," she said. "You'll get to see the place in action shortly."

"This room is for portals, isn't it?" Twylan asked.

"Exactly."

"But why? I thought that the Silver Griffins could summon a portal anywhere."

"Portals take a lot of power, and they're not exactly stable, especially ones between Earth and Oriceran. Plus, creating one in a public space creates huge risks of exposure. So, we have the transportation department here, experts in portal magic, and a room set up to allow for larger, more stable portals. Most critically, we have a timetable for deliveries to and from Trevilsom."

"A timetable?"

"Of course. You think the guards there let portals appear on their premises whenever people want? Might as well give the prisoners the keys and tell them to let themselves out. So, we have a schedule for deliveries to Trevilsom and holding cells to keep the perps until then. We also have our schedule for deliveries by portal because it's a really handy way to shift stuff around."

Jackie led Twylan along the row of cells with their barred doors. Some contained boxes and crates, but two held trolls. As they approached, one of the trolls shrank to its smallest size and tried to squeeze through the bars. The runes around the cell's arch glowed, there was a flash of magic, and the troll flew back across its prison.

"Half-past," the wizard by the crates called. "Time for the Trevilsom run."

As if responding to those words, the blank wall at the end of the room glowed with a golden light, then turned into the black opening of a portal twelve feet high and equally wide.

"Wow." Twylan felt the power wafting off of it.

"Yep."

Jackie pulled her aside as a gnome approached, the wizard behind him, and unlocked the cells. One of the trolls walked meekly out, head hanging, and followed the gnome toward the portal. The moment the other troll stepped out, he transformed, expanding in seconds from six inches to ten feet tall. He swung a huge hand and slapped the wizard aside.

"Crap." Jackie whipped out her wand and fired a length of magical chain. The troll caught it around its arm, then used the chain to drag Jackie off her feet. The rest of the transportation team approached cautiously, hands and wands raised. The troll swung Jackie on the end of its chain and knocked them back.

Twylan pulled out her wand and pointed it at the troll. "Stupefacio."

A bolt of magic flew from her wand and hit the troll in the head. It blinked, stunned for a moment, then shook its head and advanced across the room, raising its foot over one of the prone gnomes.

"Stupefacio!" Twylan shouted, letting more of her power loose this time. The magic hit the troll so hard it staggered sideways, missing the gnome. Its mouth hung open, and it stared blankly at the portal for a second, then collapsed face down. There was a crash as it hit the floor.

Jackie pushed herself to her feet and prodded the troll with her foot. "Good work, Twylan. I can see why Lucy and Applegate want to make a Griffin out of you."

"Thank you." Twylan beamed. "What's next on the tour?"

CHAPTER ELEVEN

"This seems nice." Lucy looked down the menu. "I'm not sure what I expected from a Salvadoran restaurant, but it has me intrigued."

"Glad you approve." Charlie looked up from his menu, offering her that smile that always melted her heart. "I thought it would be nice to try something different while we have an evening to ourselves."

"You mean when we don't have Eddie demanding that everything is either cheese or pasta?"

"Or both. The perfect combination."

"For a little lad who's so adventurous in trying different animal shapes, he's very conservative when it comes to food."

"Give it a few years, and our kids will all be eating food we don't like, listening to music we've never heard of, and freaking us out with their terrible fashion choices. I'm happy to enjoy this period of calm while it lasts."

Lucy gazed across the small but bustling restaurant and out the window, not really seeing the people on West

Temple Street. Instead, she contemplated a future that was unsettlingly close and yet felt a million years away, in which her children became teenagers, with all the stress and turmoil that brought. Then she remembered the teenagers she knew, not the exaggerated ones on TV but the real ones in her life, and decided that there was no need for alarm.

"I'm not convinced the teenage years will be all that bad," she said. "The Underfoot Brigade are a lovely bunch, grounded and sensible despite everything they've been through. If they can stay balanced and emotionally healthy while living in the tunnels, I'm sure our children will be fine."

Charlie laughed. "You know that's not how teenage rebellion works, right? A comfortable home life never made anyone more cooperative toward their parents."

Lucy stuck out her tongue at him. "Let me hang onto my dreams, you monster."

She stuck the menu up between them, to more laughter from Charlie, and read again through the options on offer. It all sounded appetizing, but what was she after today— steak, chicken, maybe some of the *pupusas*?

"I might try the vegan sampler," Charlie said.

Lucy lowered her menu and stared at him in astonishment.

"You're not giving up meat, are you?" she asked. "And cheese? That could make cooking dinners for you and Eddie really difficult."

"Don't worry. I'm not going full vegan. I just thought I might cut back on the meat and dairy."

"Where's this coming from? You weren't worried about

the poor animals when we went around that farm with the kids. I've never seen Dylan so perturbed as when you called the piglet a bacon sandwich on legs."

"It's not about the cute animals or watching *Charlotte's Web* too many times. I've been talking with Max about how we can reduce our environmental footprint, and what we eat is one of the biggest issues. I'm going to see if we can buy more locally grown produce and eat less meat myself."

"Bless you, sweetheart, what a thoughtful thing to do," Lucy said. "Maybe I'll have that vegan sampler too. It looks like a good way to try as many dishes as possible, and I'm curious about the food here." She drew a deep breath, enjoying the smells that emerged from the kitchen. "Stomach-rumblingly curious."

A waiter arrived, and they filled the next couple of minutes with deciding on drinks and placing their order. Once they were alone again, Lucy reached across the table to take her husband's hand.

"It's funny thinking about what the kids will be like in a few years," she said. "I know that whatever we dream up, they'll be completely different and still brilliant, astounding us with who they can be."

"The future's never what we expect, is it?"

"Definitely not. When I was younger, I never imagined I'd wind up living in America or doing the job I do."

"I remember."

"You do?"

"Of course. That first day, in the National Gallery, you were so passionate about the art, but not in a clichéd eighteen-year-old way, going on about how you'd be a famous artist someday. You wanted to be a curator, caring for other creators' art, helping people to find the beauty in it."

"I can't believe you remember that, after all these years! I must have sounded like such a bore."

"Not at all. It was one of the things I loved about you from the start. You were passionate, but you wanted to lift other people, not make yourself important. You care more than anyone I know."

"Well, I definitely care about you." She leaned across the table and kissed him, then hurriedly sat back with flushed cheeks as the waiter arrived with their drinks. "Thank you."

"No problem." The waiter smiled at them like they were a surprise cute cat picture popping up on his Twitter feed, then hurried off to serve another customer.

"I feel terrible," Lucy said. "You remember exactly what I had to say a decade and a half ago, and I can't even remember whether we talked about your life goals. But you wanted to work with computers, right, or you wouldn't have been studying them?"

"Working with computers covers a multitude of sins," Charlie said. "Back then, people were barely thinking about the sort of work I do now. The cloud has become massive in the past decade, and the possibilities are still massively underexplored. It's safe to say that life caught me by surprise too."

"It's been a good surprise, right?"

"Of course! I got you and the kids. Surprises don't get any better than that."

"No, but your job, it is the sort of thing you want to do, isn't it?"

"Sure. I enjoy it. The problem-solving side is satisfying, and I'm helping people out."

"There's a but behind that sentence, and I don't mean the cute little one you're sitting on."

Charlie laughed and sipped his Corona. "I'm glad you approve, as you are now this butt's main audience."

"I feel like you're dodging a question. What did you want to do with your life before we met?"

"Like I said, I wanted to work in IT. I guess it's just that I had dreams about running my own business. That's something you have to build up to. It takes time to generate the idea and save up the money so you can take a chance on it. That way of living isn't exactly secure and stable. Once Dylan came along, the certainty of a paycheck mattered more than chasing some half-formed dream."

"You shouldn't have to give up on your dreams for us! What sort of business was it going to be?"

"Not a clue." Charlie laughed. "I mean, I had plenty of ideas, but which one I was following changed with the days of the week. Most of them weren't practical, and the ones that were have probably all been done by other people by now. That's the thing. Technology doesn't sit still while you do."

Lucy looked down at her drink. "I feel bad now. You gave up your dreams for me."

"That's all they were, dreams. Idle ideas I talked about with my buddies. I wasn't going to be the next Bill Gates. Besides, I traded it all in for the woman of my dreams. That's a win by any standard." He ran a finger along her cheek, then tipped her chin up so that they were looking each other in the eyes. "You're the last thing I see before I fall asleep at night and the first thing I think of when I wake up in the morning. I dreamed of being a millionaire because that's an easy thing to imagine, but I could never have dreamed of meeting someone as wonderful as you or being as happy as you've made me."

Lucy blushed and pressed his hand against her cheek.

"All right. I'll accept it. Remember, I have a stable job now, and we have savings in case things go wrong. If you come up with a dream for your business again, one you think would work, you're going to follow it, and the kids and I will be here to cheerlead for you every step of the way."

"All right." Charlie raised his glass. "It's a deal. Here's to dreams of the future."

"To all our dreams coming true." They clinked glasses and gazed into each other's eyes, as happy as they'd ever been.

CHAPTER TWELVE

Gruffbar slowed his Harley and turned off the street through the open doors of Gunther's auto shop. The place was full, cars and bikes taking up every spare space. Half a dozen mechanics, some of them human and some disguised magicals, were busy at exposed engines or sticking out from underneath vehicles with parts and tools lying scattered around them. Bangs, clangs, and the *hiss* of welding accompanied the smells of gas and motor oil. It was good to be home.

A spot by the wall gave Gruffbar enough space to park his bike, with the added advantage of being out of the way. He dismounted, grabbed his bags, and headed for the steps to the first-floor office at the back of the building. As he approached, Gunther emerged from his office. He held a pen, which looked tiny between his part-ogre fingers, and an expression that Gruffbar could only assume was surprise contorted his face.

"Wasn't sure you'd be back," Gunther said. "Riding out of town like that, with everything that was going on."

"Well, here I am. It turns out that Florida is mostly just swamp, and I need to be in a proper city. Business looks good."

Gunther cast an evaluating gaze around the shop floor, taking in the steady activity of a flourishing business. He nodded slowly.

"These new clean air regulations been good for us."

"Really? I would have thought that would mean people were driving less, spending less on their cars."

Gunther shook his head. "Some, maybe, but the ones who want to keep driving, they've got to get tuned up, maybe more than that, get their cars so they're still legal."

"Huh. Who'd have thought that the green movement was good for you." Gruffbar hefted his bags. "I should get back to work. Got to reach out to clients again, let them know that I'm in town."

"About that…" Gunther scratched the back of his neck and stared down at the floor.

"What? Have some of them been around and you didn't call me?"

"No, it ain't that. I rented out the office to someone new." Gunther shrugged apologetically. "Like I said, didn't know if you was coming back."

"That didn't take long."

"Good office space is at a premium. That's what my rentals guy says."

"What you have is not good office space."

"All right, out-of-the-way office space for magicals is at a premium. That good enough for you?"

"Good enough is the perfect description. I'll go talk

with your new tenant, see if we can't sort something out between us."

Gruffbar stomped up the steps and kicked the office door open. It slammed against the wall, shaking the room and almost knocking over a tall and poorly balanced potted plant. The place still held all his furniture: the rescued desk, the secondhand seats, the lone filing cabinet in one corner, and the one good chair that he had sat in, but which was now occupied by a Willen in a vest.

"Can I help you?" She looked at him down her long rodent nose.

"Yeah, you can get out of my seat."

"I think you'll find this is my office."

"I think you'll find that I was here first, and now I want my office back."

"I've paid rent. This is my place now."

Gruffbar pulled a handful of bills from his pocket, weighed them between his fingers, then tossed them onto the desk.

"That's six hundred and fifty. I know how much Gunther charges for this place, so it more than covers you. Now get out."

"This isn't just about the money. I need a space. I've started giving out this address. You're going to have to find somewhere new."

Gruffbar set his bags down, pulled out a cigar, and lit it using a chunky metal lighter. A gray-blue streamer of smoke drifted from the cigar's glowing tip.

"I'm a lawyer, not a hoodlum," he said. "But I can pick you up and fling you out that door if I have to. So, take the money, get out of my chair, and we won't need to have any trouble."

The Willen's eyes darted back and forth between Gruffbar, the cash, and the office door. She was an entire foot shorter than Gruffbar, only able to face him head-on because the seat boosted her, and she had to see that she wasn't going to win this one.

"We got off to a bad start," she said. "We don't have to carry on that way. You want to cooperate. You want to make me happy."

Her eyes spun, and Gruffbar felt a fog start to settle over his mind.

"Oh no, you don't." He grabbed her by the neck and slammed her face into the desk. "You save that hypnotism shit for whatever sort of customers you're conning here."

Her eyes stopped spinning, and she thrashed around instead, trying to break free. The bills fluttered from the desk and across the floor.

"This is assault!" she exclaimed. "Let me go, or I'll call the Silver Griffins!"

"If you wanted the Griffins' attention, you wouldn't be working out of a back room office like this. If you wanted to strike a deal, you definitely shouldn't have started by messing with my brain. Nobody touches my thoughts but me."

"Okay, okay, I get it." The Willen stopped struggling. "Let go and I'll leave."

Gruffbar released his grip on her neck. She slid off the desk, straightened her vest, and cleared her throat.

"I should get my files."

"Sure. I don't want them."

The Willen opened the filing cabinet's bottom drawer, took out a single cardboard folder, and slid the drawer shut. As she headed for the door, she looked around and sighed.

"This would have been perfect for what I had planned."

"Don't forget your rent money." Gruffbar pointed at some of the bills lying on the floor.

The Willen scowled, then stooped and gathered up the cash scattered like discarded candy wrappers around Gruffbar's feet.

"You're a real asshole, you know that?" the Willen said.

"The realest of assholes. Remember that next time you need a lawyer. You don't always want a good guy on your side in court."

Clutching her file and a fistful of crumpled money, the Willen headed out the door and away.

Gruffbar walked around the desk and settled down in his chair. He'd been thinking about this chair for half the journey from Florida. He loved the feeling that came with sitting in the saddle of his bike, feeling the engine thrum and the wind whip past as he roared across America, but it couldn't match this chair for sheer comfort. The cushioning gave way in just the right places while holding firm in others, not simply a passive piece of furniture for him to sit on but something that supported and eased him.

Oh yes, it was good to be home.

He sat back and put his feet up, blowing smoke rings at the ceiling, relishing the moment. Still, he couldn't quite relax. After all, he was back in LA for a reason, and it had nothing to do with office furniture. He needed to make sure that someone dealt with Mr. No.

He took out his phone and scrolled to a contact he hadn't been sure he would ever use. As a lawyer working on the magical side of the street, he inevitably had to be aware of the Silver Griffins and their activities, and sometimes he had to get clients out of trouble with them. Still, he tried to keep direct interactions to a minimum. When someone had given him this number, he'd logged it in case, not because he expected to need it any time soon. Now the just-in-case moment had arrived.

He took out another phone, a burner, typed the number in, and hit the call button.

"Hello, S. and G. Enterprises," said a voice at the other end of the line. "How can I help you?"

"I know that's the Silver Griffins," Gruffbar said. "I want to tip you off about a magical threat."

"Please hold the line, sir. One of our agents will speak with you shortly."

The mindless *plink* and *plonk* of hold music replaced the call handler's voice. Gruffbar gritted his teeth. He loved almost every sign of civilization, from elegant oil paintings to crumpled soda cans rusting in the street, each one reflecting the ingenuity and artifice of its creators. Still, even he couldn't stand hold music.

After thirty seconds that seemed to stretch into a torturous eternity, a voice emerged.

"Thank you for waiting. Do you have some information to share?"

Gruffbar lowered his voice into something rougher and deeper than his usual tone. He didn't want anything connecting this call back to him.

"There's a monster in LA," he said. "A tall, dark figure

stalking people's dreams, stealing their aspirations. It will leave them as husks, alive but without purpose."

"I see. Could you tell me the names of the victims?"

"I don't know. I don't know if there are any yet, but they're coming."

"I see, sir. Does this menace have a name?"

Gruffbar frowned. The tone of the Griffin's voice said that none of this had convinced him.

"He's called Mr. No," Gruffbar said.

"Like in the James Bond film?" The disbelief was increasingly clear.

"Not like in the film, that's Dr. No, this is Mr. No."

"Of course. Completely different."

"You have to believe me. This creature is a menace. You have to stop him."

"Well, could you tell me how you know any of this so we can confirm it?"

"No." Of course, he couldn't tell them. It wasn't for him to share the shame of what had happened to his clan, how Mr. No had wormed his way in and picked them off one by one, without ever being noticed. More than that, Gruffbar couldn't have people thinking that he cooperated with the Silver Griffins. The damage that would do to his professional reputation didn't bear thinking about. "I can't tell you how I know, but this information is good. I've seen him firsthand."

"Seen him here in LA?"

"No."

"But seen him recently, and he was on his way here?"

"Yes. In a dream."

"Uhuh. Well, tell you what, sir, would you like to leave some contact details so we can follow up with you?"

"No. No details. This is anonymous."

"That's what I thought. Tell you what, next time you want to make us waste our time chasing after nothing, maybe make it a bit more convincing?"

The speaker hung up. Gruffbar glared at the silent burner phone, then snapped it in two and crushed the parts into little pieces. It didn't seem likely that they'd try to trace the call after a conversation like that, but he could never be too careful.

So much for the anonymous tipoff. He would have to find another way to get through to the Griffins.

CHAPTER THIRTEEN

"Eddie won't settle down," Charlie said as he walked into the kitchen, rubbing his temples.

"Still?" Lucy glanced at the oven clock. "It's hours past his bedtime."

"Don't I know it."

"Let me give it a try."

Lucy went through to Eddie's bedroom. It had a mural of a jungle on one wall and a scattering of toys across the floor. Eddie lay in bed, under Transformers sheets, making a pair of plastic dinosaurs fight each other. A dream catcher spun on a string above his head.

"Roawor!" he bellowed with surprising volume for such a small boy. "I'ma eat your head." One of the dinosaurs battered frantically at the other, plastic teeth banging off the back of an equally solid neck. "Roawowowor!"

"Eddie, sweetheart, it's time to sleep now," Lucy said.

"Not sleepy."

"I think you are really, and you'll realize that once you chill out."

"Don't wanna."

"Eddie." Lucy folded her arms and put on a stern voice. "What have I said about this before?"

Eddie mumbled something and knocked his dinosaurs together.

"What's that?" Lucy asked.

"Need to sleep so I can play tomorrow."

"That's right. Now, why don't you put the dinosaurs down and read a book? That'll keep you entertained if you're not sleepy."

More importantly, it would lead to him dozing off if he was tired, which he had to be by now. Lucy went to his bookshelf and picked one that hadn't been out in a while, hoping that the novelty of the pictures would keep him entertained.

"How about this? It's all about nocturnal animals, ones that come awake at night. You can find out if you're like them or if you need your sleep."

"Okay." Eddie set aside the dinosaurs and accepted the book. Then he stretched up his arms. "Hug?"

"Always." Lucy leaned over and hugged him tightly, then kissed him on the top of the head. When he let her go, she set the book carefully in his lap and headed for the door. "See you in the morning, sweetheart."

Charlie was in the bedroom when Lucy went through and halfway ready for bed.

"It's gone quiet," he whispered. "Did you soothe the savage beast?"

"I gave him a book, which will calm him down. With the amount of energy he used today, he should be asleep in minutes."

"Great thinking."

Lucy changed into her pajamas, went to the bathroom to brush her teeth, then joined her husband in bed. She curled up next to him, sticking her head up under an arm that was holding up his e-reader.

"What are you reading?"

"Technical manual for some new software we're installing at work."

"Wow, thrill a minute stuff."

"Things were hectic in the office. This is the first chance I've had to sit down and read it all week."

"Well, I wouldn't want to spoil your reading time." Lucy kissed him on the neck. "Unless, of course…"

She kissed him on the side of his chin, then the cheek. Charlie grinned and set the e-reader aside.

"Unless what?"

"Unless there's something else that—" Lucy was interrupted by a piercing sound and a fluttering. "What was that?"

"I don't know, but let's not worry about it." Charlie kissed her on the forehead, then on the tip of her nose.

The fluttering continued, and there was another piercing whistle.

"Whatever it is, I'd better go deal with it." Lucy flung off the sheets. "Don't want it waking up the kids."

She followed the fluttering down the hallway to Eddie's room. When she looked in, the bed was empty, the book lying abandoned on the pillow. A large bat was flapping in circles around the room.

Lucy groaned.

"Eddie, is that you?" she asked.

The bat flapped closer and let out a shrill whistling sound.

"The whole point of sonar is that it's supposed to be silent," Lucy said.

The bat opened its mouth again, and this time no sound came out.

Lucy walked over to the bed and looked at the book. Sure enough, it was open on a page about bats, showing a whole swarm of them flapping around a cave. Instead of rest, Eddie had found inspiration in his book.

"Eddie, it's too late to be playing," Lucy said firmly. "Come back to bed, please."

The bat flapped around her head some more.

"Right now."

The bat made its way to bed with slow, reluctant wing-beats and settled on the pillow next to the book.

"You can't sleep like that," Lucy admonished. "Get into your shape, please."

The air shimmered, and Eddie turned back into a little boy.

"Good book." He patted the pages and yawned.

"I'm sure it's great," Lucy said. "Now it's time to set it aside and sleep." She closed the book and set it on the floor next to Eddie's bed. "You can read more in the morning."

"Okay." Eddie rolled over. "Goodnight, Mommy."

"Goodnight, sweetheart."

She switched off the light and walked out of the room, then crept down the hallway, past the doors of the other kids' rooms, and into her bedroom. Charlie lay with his eyes closed and his e-reader abandoned next to him, making gentle snuffling sounds.

"Are you still awake?" Lucy whispered as she slid into bed. His lack of answer was an answer in itself.

Lucy picked up the e-reader. She wasn't interested in Charlie's instruction manual, but he had plenty of other books on there. She found a biography of Jimi Hendrix and read the first chapter before her eyelids drooped, and sleep started to take hold. After setting the e-reader aside, she switched off the light and rolled over, ready for a good night's sleep.

A howl burst out of the night.

Lucy sat bolt upright. All sorts of things howled, and many of them were bad news. She grabbed her wand off the nightstand and hurried into the hallway, looking around warily and listening for clues to approaching danger.

There was another howl, drawn-out as if the creature was testing the limits of its voice. She followed it to Eddie's room and peered inside.

The cutest coyote pup she had ever seen lay in Eddie's bed, staring up at the dangling dream catcher. It had skinny little legs, a fluffy body, and the sort of face that would have made a Disney animator proud, with wide dark eyes and triangular ears that stuck out sharply from the top of its head. When Lucy appeared, it looked around, then leapt out of bed and ran over to jump up and down at her feet.

"All right, Lassie," Lucy whispered. "I get it, you're utterly adorable, and Timmy's stuck down the well."

She stroked the coyote's head, and it licked her hand.

"You know you couldn't get away with that as a human, right?" Lucy said.

The coyote took a few steps back, lowered its hindquarters, tipped its head back, and opened its mouth wide.

"No!" Lucy snapped. "No more howling, Eddie."

The coyote froze, staring at her with those deep, dark eyes, silently begging for one more chance to show off what it could do.

"No, you'll wake up Ashley and Dylan. This is far too noisy for the time of night, and you're supposed to be in bed."

She pointed at the crumpled duvet and abandoned pillow.

The coyote walked slowly to the bed with its ears drooping and head dangling.

"Don't use that card with me. You've had all day to play around, as a boy or a bat or a coyote or whatever else you wanted to be. Now it's time to sleep."

The coyote hopped onto the bed and curled up around itself.

"Back to human, please."

The air rippled, and the coyote turned back into Eddie in his pajamas. Lucy pulled the duvet over his shoulders, tucked him in, picked up the animal book, and crossed the room to set it back on the shelf. Eddie watched this last part sadly.

"Good book," he said.

"I'm sure it is, and you can read more of it tomorrow."

Eddie shook his head. "Night book with night animals."

"If you say so. Right now though, you should sleep."

Lucy wondered if non-magical moms went through trials like this. Did their kids get up in the middle of the night to play soccer or watch cartoons or whatever kids did when they weren't science geniuses or magically empowered? Did little boys who couldn't turn into animals spend the night doing impressions of monkeys and bears and wake their parents up that way?

She crept back to her bedroom, set her wand on the nightstand, and climbed into bed. The sheets were a soft, warm embrace, lulling her to sleep. As she closed her eyes and laid her head on the pillow, she could feel unconsciousness calling out to her. The soft, fuzzy world of sleep reached out with welcoming arms, and...

There was a *thud*. Then another. And another. Something was crashing around somewhere in the house. Lucy had a good idea of who and where it was although not what shape it would take.

She ought to get up. If she didn't, Eddie might wake the other kids, making them tired and grumpy tomorrow. He was a lost cause, but she only wanted to deal with one exhausted child at a time. The problem was that her bed was so comfortable, and she had been on the verge of dozing off. She really didn't want to get up.

A *crash* followed another *thump*.

Lucy nudged Charlie. He made an indistinct noise and rolled away from her. She nudged him again.

"What?" he said sleepily.

"Eddie's up and playing. I've been to deal with him twice. It's your turn."

"I was sleeping."

"And I'm trying to. Now go."

"Ugh." Charlie flung off the sheets, slid his feet into his slippers, and walked out of the room.

Lucy pulled the sheets up over her head and tried to ignore the noises coming through the house, but she wasn't quite as sleepy as she had been a moment before. They'd disrupted her perfect drift into the dream realm, and now she couldn't quite doze off. It didn't help that those noisy *thuds* kept coming. What on earth was Eddie playing at this time?

A few minutes later, quiet descended. Charlie walked back in, kicked off his slippers, and got into bed. He wrapped an arm around Lucy, and she curled in close to him.

"Did you know that some kangaroos are nocturnal?" Charlie said.

CHAPTER FOURTEEN

"I should have known you'd be a cocktail bar kind of guy."
Sarah looked across the table at Ellis.

It was deep into a summer evening, the sky shifting
through the warm colors of sunset out across Echo Park. A
waiter had been around the tables, setting a lit candle on
each one, creating an intimate glow around the center of
the table. Ellis could have kissed the guy for adding that
little touch of magic although that wasn't who he wanted
to kiss tonight.

"Honestly, it ain't exactly my normal choice, but traveling around a lot, you learn to adapt."

Ellis looked around. He'd picked the place to be conve-
nient for Sarah, to suit what he knew about her tastes, and
based on some hefty Internet research. A mezcal-oriented
cocktail bar would never usually have crossed his radar
except for something to rush past while chasing a suspect.
Still, there was something cozy about the place, its rosy
decor matching the sky outside, and he'd found a corn

whiskey and bourbon cocktail that was more to his tastes than the other offerings on the menu.

"You've even adapted your drinking," Sarah said. "You're normally more of a beer guy, right?"

"Proper beer, none of your Budweiser nonsense."

"Of course. Cocktails don't count as nonsense?"

He shrugged. "When in Rome, do as the Romans do. I figured they probably do a better job with cocktails than beers here."

Plus, he hoped to impress her with his sophistication and to show that they might have something in common. It was a while since he'd been on a date, but he remembered that as the sort of detail you were supposed to get right.

"I figured I'd try to find somewhere you would like, and a lot of your nights out seem to involve tequila or mezcal places."

"Ah, the dangers of social media, it's so easy to get pigeonholed." Sarah laughed. "I'm not the mezcal fan. That's all about Jackie."

"Oh." Ellis blushed and looked down at his drink. He'd thought that he'd made a perfect choice, but apparently, he'd made it for the wrong woman. "Sorry. We can go somewhere that's more to your liking."

"No, it's great!" Now Sarah blushed. "Sorry, I didn't mean to say that I don't like it here. It's just that my social life gets a bit dominated by Jackie sometimes. You've worked with her. You must have realized that it's easiest to let her have her way."

"I didn't exactly take the easy path."

"That explains why she kept complaining about you." Sarah laughed.

"She did?" He wasn't surprised, but now he was worried at what Jackie might have said.

"It's okay, nothing that would put me off. Obviously, I mean, here we are."

"Obviously." Ellis nervously laughed as he was about to take a drink. The cocktail dribbled down his chin and stained his red tie brown. "Dagnabbit!"

He froze in the process of mopping at the spill with a napkin. Sarah was laughing at him.

"Did you just say dagnabbit?" she asked. "I thought that was reserved for cartoon prospectors and old people on TV."

"My grandma had some strong opinions on swearing, so I had to find other ways to vent. Once you get into a habit like that, it's kinda hard to break."

He tensed up, defensive at her laughter and frustrated at how he was making a fool of himself. He took another long drink, careful not to spill it this time.

"Sorry, I shouldn't laugh. Honestly, it's kind of cute."

Cute was at least better than some of the alternatives, and with Sarah sitting there in a floral print dress, a poster girl for every hope a summer's night could present, he was willing to cling onto any kind of hope. Ellis glanced at his watch.

"Our ride should be along any minute. Are you ready for some dinner?"

"That would be lovely." Sarah finished her drink, brushed her red hair back over her shoulder, and got up from her seat. Together, they walked out onto Sunset Boulevard.

"So where are we going?" she asked.

"Somewhere I guarantee you won't have eaten before."

"A new restaurant?"

"Kinda."

"Intriguing." She smiled at him. "I like a man of mystery."

A car pulled up in front of the bar. There was a gnome at the wheel, an unseasonal combination of a scarf, hat, and shades allowing him to pass for human to a casual observer. "Ride for Ellis?" he asked.

"That's us." Ellis opened the back door of the cab for Sarah. "Ma'am."

"Such a gentleman."

She got in, and he closed the door behind her before getting in on the other side. The car pulled out into traffic, then immediately pulled off onto a smaller side road.

"This leads to a restaurant?" Sarah asked. "It must be very out of the way."

"That's kinda the idea."

The cab driver looked all around.

"No one to see us," he said. "Switching illusions."

He waved his hands, and the air throbbed with magic. The cab vanished from around them, leaving them sitting on a flying carpet suspended a foot above the back street.

"Oh wow!" Sarah laughed. "That's definitely different."

"Invisibility field on," the cab driver said. "And we're away."

They lifted into the air, floating above the streets of LA. Sarah clung to the carpet as the air rushed past. People and cars became dots beneath them, and the city spread out in every direction, a landscape filled with the shining stars of neon lights.

"Okay, this is cool," Sarah said. "Very *Aladdin*."

"*Aladdin*?"

"You know, the Disney film. A whole new world! Boy takes girl on a magic carpet ride, sings her a song about how wonderful things can be."

"Oh. I thought I'd come up with something new." Ellis's heart sank. Nothing about this evening was going the way that he'd planned.

"Wait, you've never seen *Aladdin*?"

"That's Disney, right? Grandma had opinions on Disney. She didn't approve of talking mice or racist old businessmen."

"I can see where she's coming from on part of that, but still, no Disney? You never saw *Sleeping Beauty* or *The Lion King*, or that version of *Robin Hood* where he's a fox?"

"Not a minute of it."

"How sad."

An awkward silence fell. It was hard to carry on a conversation about something one of them knew nothing about, and Ellis was feeling the weight of his ignorance, especially regarding how a magic carpet might be a romantic cliché. So much for setting up a dream date.

No sooner had that thought hit than the carpet trembled, and the driver let out a worried noise.

"What's the matter?" Ellis asked.

"Just an old enchantment wearing thin," the driver said. "Nothing to worry about. We're nearly there anyway."

The carpet shook, and frayed threads fell away from the sides. They were losing height. The driver frantically waved his hands through the air as he tried to pull the magic together.

"This doesn't feel like nothing to worry about," Ellis said.

"It's fine, it's fine, it's fine," the driver said as threads flew off in every direction and the carpet shrank around them.

"No, it ain't."

Ellis pulled out his wand, then grabbed hold of Sarah and the driver as the last of the carpet disintegrated.

"Volant!"

Magic held them up, floating a hundred feet above Griffith Observatory.

"Which way?" Ellis asked through gritted teeth as he strained to hold them in the air.

"There." The driver pointed to high ground north of the observatory.

Ellis twitched his wand, and they floated toward where the gnome had pointed. Soon they landed beside a picnic table on a deserted trail. There was a cloth on the table, with fine crockery and cutlery set out and wine in an ice bucket. Candles at the corners of the table offered illumination.

The gnome hurried off, leaving Ellis and Sarah alone.

"Wow, this is quite something." She took a seat.

"Not something out of Disney?"

"Not that I remember."

Ellis sat across from her and straightened his jacket. Maybe this part would work out.

"The flowers are a lovely touch." She brushed the red roses sitting in a vase at one end of the table. "They match your tie."

He had no idea what to say to that. Red roses were

supposed to be romantic, right? Except that anything red would match his outfits, so did that send a weird message, like he was trying to do something subliminal? His stomach got knotted up along with his thoughts.

"It's quite a view." He gestured toward the city lights below them.

"One of my favorites," Sarah agreed.

A sinking feeling came over Ellis. "You come up here a lot, huh?"

"Quite a lot, usually running with Jackie and Lucy."

So much for a unique and special night. It had all seemed so impressive in his head, but everything he'd picked was either mundane to her and unraveling before his eyes. At least the food should be good. He'd picked his chef carefully.

An elf in a tuxedo appeared, a white towel draped across her arm, the image of a professional waiter.

"Chef Delrinen sends her apologies," she said. "She suffered an injury while foraging in the forests of Oriceran, and has sent an apprentice to cook your dinner in her place."

"I get it," Ellis said. "Accidents happen." He wasn't too worried. The apprentice to a celebrated chef should be a professional in their own right.

A dwarf in a big white hat appeared from behind the waiter and waved sheepishly at them. "Hi."

"This is Harlow Downdelver," the waiter said with a weary sigh. "Chef Delrinen's new apprentice."

"New?" Ellis asked, an increasingly familiar sense of disappointment settling over him.

"New." The waiter managed to make the word sound like a curse.

"So, uh, I'm afraid the soufflé fell flat," Downdelver said. "But it should still taste good. The fish, on the other hand, isn't as fresh as I thought."

Of course, the food had gone wrong. Everything else had. It was time to cut his losses.

"Let's skip to the dessert," Ellis said.

"There was supposed to be a dessert?" Downdelver asked.

Ellis sighed. So many fine plans. So much disappointment.

"There, there." Sarah patted him on the shoulder. "It was all a lovely thought."

CHAPTER FIFTEEN

The decor in the Silver Griffins' break room wasn't as old as the LA office itself, but it felt that way. The tables were wobbly, the seats worn, and stuffing leaked out of the sofa like guts from a giant squashed bug. The coffee pot had a thick dark crust around its rim, and most of the teaspoons had gone missing sometime in the early 2000s.

Today, the place was crowded. It was hard to get every single Griffin to come into the office when there was an annual report or a speech from a senior wizard who had flown in from out of town, but the fate of the break room was something that everyone could acknowledge was important.

"Everybody, settle down," Kelly said from the front of the room. "We won't get anywhere while you're all talking at once."

It was an exercise in futility. With dozens of witches and wizards chattering excitedly to each other, her voice was lost in the hubbub.

"Seriously, sit down and listen," Kelly snapped. Still, no

one was listening. When the boss took charge, people went quiet because he made sure that they got pay, pensions, promotions, and the equipment they needed to do their jobs. Kelly wasn't the boss. She was just a stand-in, someone filling the gap while Roger Applegate stared vacantly at a screen all day.

"This is ridiculous," Kelly muttered. "I thought they wanted to sort this out?"

"I've got it." Jackie climbed up on a chair and raised her voice to a shout. "Shut up, the lot of you!" In the ensuing silence, every pair of eyes turned her way. "Kelly's in charge, so keep quiet and listen until she says otherwise. That way, we might get the place fixed up this century."

She jumped down off the seat and gestured from Kelly to the rest of the room.

"Thank you, Jackie." Kelly surveyed the assembled magicals. "And thank you, everyone, for coming. Based on the meeting last week, it's clear that everyone has a different idea for how our break room should be, both functionally and aesthetically. Rather than leave anyone disappointed, we've come up with a plan that incorporates something for everyone. Today, we're going to put that plan into action."

She smiled and paused, waiting for the appreciation to wash over her. It didn't arrive.

"As I say, something for everyone," she said. "You all get your way. Is that cool with you all?"

There were shrugs and some murmurs of assent. This was supposed to be Kelly's big moment of success, the part of being the boss where everyone would love her, but instead, they seemed indifferent. She tried not to let her disappointment show.

"All right, here's how it's going to work." Several tables had been pushed together in the middle of the room, and she unrolled a diagram on there. "This shows what we're doing where in the room and who asked for each part. You'll each be responsible for the bit you requested to make sure it works out right. Rather than bring in workers, we're going to do it by magic. Some things, like vending machines and the game system, are out in the office so you can levitate them in. For basic furniture like the seats, we'll use spells to spruce up what we have, and the same goes for the walls and floor. Decoration by spellcraft, playing to our strengths. Does that make sense?"

At least this time people nodded and said yes.

"All right, let's get to it!"

Kelly took a step back, smiling.

"Get to it? That's all the coordination you're going to give?" Jackie looked at Kelly and raised an eyebrow.

"They have the plan. They know what they're doing," Kelly said.

"Do they know what the others are doing?" Lucy, who had been sitting quietly on the sofa, came to look at the plan. Details crowded it, each for different people to deal with.

"I'm running our whole office, all our investigations," Kelly snapped as a vending machine levitated into the room. "Did you want this to be the thing I put most effort into?"

"No, but..." Lucy ducked as a couch sailed through the air, slammed into the flying vending machine, and crashed to the ground. "I'm not sure that a free-for-all is the way to get this done."

The vending machine had reached its spot at the back of the room, and immediately hit a problem, as the counter it was replacing hadn't been removed yet. Toliver Jenkins, his wand extended to hold the machine in the air, looked around for help, as other Griffins bustled around him.

"Nigel?" he called. "Come help with this." He stumbled as someone backed into him, carrying an armchair, and the vending machine wobbled in the air. "Nigel, where are you?"

Behind him, people were decorating. Blue paint spread across one wall, pink over the one joining it. Directed by magic, it made a perfectly smooth layer, but where the colors met, they melted together into an unfortunate purple that reminded Lucy of a bruise.

"Nigel!" Jenkins shouted, not the only person raising his voice. Off to one side, Jim, Sam, and the receptionist were arguing about how best to set up the games station. "Come here, Nigel!"

"I'm on tables!" Nigel shouted from the far side of the room.

"You're my assistant. Get over here and assist."

"I have my work."

"That's no excuse in the lab. What makes you think it will work here?"

"We're not in the lab."

"We're at work."

"You're not the boss of me."

"That's exactly what I am!" Jenkins waved his arm angrily around, and the vending machine flew through the air, almost hitting a senior wizard in the head. "Sorry, my bad!"

Another argument was underway around the sofa where Lucy had been sitting. One person was in charge of seating for that corner while another handled decoration. Both felt that the sofa's style was part of their job, and they had very different opinions on it. They both repeatedly waved their wands, using magic to transform the sofa to their taste, and it stuttered between shapes and colors like a piece of badly planned animation.

By now, Kelly stood surrounded at the diagram in the center of the room, frantically trying to settle jurisdictional disputes and questions about what parts of the plan meant. She clutched her head with one hand while the other hand waved around, directing Griffins in their work.

Jackie sidled up to Lucy. "Are you enjoying this as much as I am?" She watched Kelly's stress mount.

"Not really," Lucy said. "I just want a nice break room. I thought you did too."

"Oh, I do, and I'm going to sabotage that games system the minute anyone looks away to make sure we get somewhere peaceful. It's still fun to watch the chaos, especially when it's Kelly's chaos to struggle with."

"This is a difficult situation. We should probably give her more help."

"Being in charge is all Kelly's ever dreamed of. She wished this on herself."

"It could as easily have been one of us if Applegate had set out the hierarchy differently. We'll both suffer if our colleagues fall out over this, so I think we should help sort it out."

"You're as right as you are reasonable. I give in. Let's be good people."

While Jackie went to clear space for the vending machine, Lucy headed for the ever-changing sofa.

"What's the problem?" she asked.

"We need something that looks stylish," one of the bickering Griffins said. "To fit the decor of the place."

"Stylishness doesn't matter," the other one said. "It needs to be comfortable. This is our rest space, not a showroom."

"There's nothing restful about an ugly room."

"There's nothing relaxing about an uncomfortable couch."

"You both make good points," Lucy said, trying not to slip into the tone she used when settling disagreements between the kids. "We can have any sofa we want, seeing as we're magicking it up ourselves, so is there one that would look good enough and be comfortable enough to make you both happy?"

"I suppose we could do something like..." One of the sofa Griffins waved her wand. The existing shape of the sofa extended and puffed out.

"And if we want it to go with the new walls..." The other one waved his wand, and the color darkened a little.

"Or how about..."

Lucy stepped back. She didn't need to approve the final design. She'd set them on the path to cooperation, and that would do.

The noise in the break room was starting to settle down. In one sense, everything they set out to do was finished. They'd revamped the chairs and tables, though in a bland and mismatched style. The dirty walls had a new coat of paint although they were all different colors and didn't go together. The vending machine was in place, as was the games console. Both were a little awkward to get at, and they'd lost some space to fit them in. It was a bit of everything, and as a result, it was deeply, uninspiringly "all right."

The other Griffins were coming to the same conclusion, and after all the anticipation at the renovation, "all right" was a disappointing place to end up. Nobody could complain—they'd all got something they wanted, and they'd been listened to. Would they be any more enthusiastic about the place than they had been a week before? Lucy doubted it.

Kelly stood in the middle of the room, her hair all messed up on one side, the plans for the room crumpled in her hand. There was a frantic twitch to her eyes, and people were backing away from her stiff grin.

"Thank you, everyone," she said. "I'm sure we can all agree that this has been a success, can't we?"

They had the good sense to nod and murmur their assent.

"Great, then we can get back to work. Thank you all for a job well done."

Kelly walked out. A few at a time, the other Griffins followed her until only Jackie and Lucy remained.

"You're not going to wreck that games system, are you?" Lucy asked.

Jackie shook her head. "I'll buy some headphones for it instead, then glare at anyone who plays without them."

"That should solve it."

"Makes you miss Applegate's guiding hand, doesn't it?"

"It makes me appreciate how much work he does."

"How much work he delegates, you mean."

"I guess, but at least he delegates well. Do you think Kelly can get the hang of that?"

Jackie shrugged. "Time will tell."

CHAPTER SIXTEEN

Heather shifted uncomfortably in her seat. Offices were too formal, too lifeless, too full of everything she most despised about urban living. Even when they had plants in them, those plants were usually either fake or sickly because offices suited plants even less than human beings.

"You want to help the Silver Griffins?" Kelly asked.

Dressed in sturdy boots, well-worn jeans, and a flannel shirt, Heather felt completely out of place facing a woman dressed in a sharp suit and heels, with matching lipstick. That outfit proclaimed a sort of authority that Heather seldom acknowledged but held sway over her and her tribe as long as they tried to function in LA. She was facing everything she most disliked about the hierarchies of magic, and though she was the one offering to help, she felt like she was asking a favor. Everything was out of line.

"That's right." She masked her discomfort behind a firm nod. "We need to be useful. This is a way to do that."

"How many Tolderai are we talking about?"

"That many." Heather pointed through the glass wall—

why make a wall at all if you were going to use glass, unless it was for a greenhouse—to where a dozen witches and wizards stood near the door to reception, under the supervision of the nervous-looking receptionist. "For now. There are more out in the world, but I haven't brought them yet. This takes organizing."

"It will take some organizing on our side as well, as I'm sure you can understand. We weren't expecting a sudden influx of support like this. We'll need time to work out what to do with you."

"Well, what were your people going to do today?"

"Patrol the city looking for magical trouble and respond to contain any incidents we hear about."

"Then we'll help with that."

"I can't have you charging off to tackle magical crimes on your own." Kelly fought to keep the panic out of her voice. She barely had a grasp over what her regular agents were doing. The thought of managing a bunch of wild and undisciplined forest witches made her whole body tense.

"Then we'll work with your agents. They can show my people how to deal with magical crime."

"That could work..." Kelly bit her lip as she considered the easiest way to contain this problem while she looked for a long-term solution. "All right, we'll pair you up with agents and get you into the field. Let's see what you're capable of."

"I hate these damn contraptions." Mackam clung to the inside of the car's passenger door as Jackie raced through the mid-morning traffic. "Noisy, ugly, smelly things."

"Sounds like you have a lot in common," Jackie said as she steered east out of the heart of the city, through Monterey Park.

Mackam threw his head back and laughed. The beads in his braided beard clattered against each other.

"Ha! I like that. But there's only space in the world for one of me, and there are millions of these infernal contraptions."

"It would be good to see less traffic," Jackie agreed. "But you try taking people's cars away, even after all that business with the smog, and you'll see how unpopular you can become."

"I don't care about popularity."

"You surprise me."

Jackie turned right off I-10, then continued a little farther before pulling into the parking lot of a shopping mall.

"More abominations," Mackam said.

"If you think human civilization is so awful, why do you want to help out around here?"

"Everyone is awful. That's why they need me to tell them how to be better."

"I can't argue with that."

Mackam glared at the security cameras overlooking the parking lot.

"Always watching," he snarled. "It shouldn't be allowed."

"It certainly makes our job more difficult."

"Then let me fix the problem."

Mackam muttered something and flicked his wand. Sparks showered from the cameras as they all shorted out.

"You can't do that," Jackie said. "We're supposed to prevent magical disruption to mundane society."

"That's not disruption. It's making their lives better. Now the man can't see what they're doing."

"The man stops kids breaking into cars while people are shopping."

"Where are these thieving children? I'll teach them the hard value of honesty."

"Maybe later. For now, put your wand away, and let's go see what all the fuss is about."

At Jackie's coaxing, Mackam put his wand into the pocket of his camouflage pants, and together they walked into the mall. The place was weekday morning busy, no families or huddles of teenagers keeping themselves entertained through commerce, but with shoppers on specific errands hurrying back and forth. The eateries were mostly empty, which suited Jackie. The fewer people who were around, the less likely that this incident would cause a big problem.

In one corner of the mall, something had pulled a section of floor tiles, and a heap of dirt and broken concrete lay next to them. Someone had set up fencing around the hole, but it looked more like the top of a nine-teenth-century mine shaft than a modern protective barrier. A nervous-looking security guard stood nearby.

"Are you with the police?" the security guard asked as they approached. "I called hours ago."

"We're outside consultants, helping the police," Jackie said. "Was it like this when you arrived this morning?"

"Uhuh. We weren't expecting any work, and the guys down there, they won't even come out to explain themselves, just keep shouting up at me about how they've staked a claim. I think they might be crazy."

"We've got this. Why don't you go check on the rest of the mall?"

Jackie jumped down into the hole, and Mackam followed. They found themselves in a dirt tunnel only four feet tall, its roof and walls held up with wooden beams. From down the tunnel, a dwarf approached, a pick in his hands.

"You can't come down here," he said. "You've not got protective gear."

"You can't dig here," Jackie said.

"Why not? We heard that the land shopping malls are built on is full of wealth, and no one was mining this one. Complete waste of a rich seam."

"They don't mean that there's literally treasure under here, only that retail real estate is a good investment."

"Yeah, right. That's clearly a cover story. Why build a grand place like this if not as a working mine?"

Jackie shook her head. There was no talking with some people.

"It doesn't matter," she said. "The point is, we're with the Silver Griffins, at least I am, and we're telling you to shut this down."

"I have rights. You can't do this to me!"

"Oh yes, we can!" Mackam leapt forward, wand out. There was a flash of magic and roots burst from the earth, binding the dwarf to the wall. Before Jackie could say anything, the Tolderai raced off along the tunnel, seemingly unrestricted by having to run at a crouch.

"Mackam, come back here!" Jackie shouted. "We don't just charge in."

It was too late. She heard crashes and thuds, the hiss of magic, shouts of alarm, and rushing footsteps. The best she could do was damage limitation, so she pulled out her wand and ran after him.

As she ran down the lamp-lit tunnel, she found dwarves lying around to left and right, some bound in roots, others frozen in place. From ahead, the noises continued, but now the tunnel was rougher, and it was heading uphill. There was a crash, dirt and tiles slid across the ground, and a pool of brighter light appeared.

Jackie put on an extra burst of speed, bounded up a heap of rubble, jumped over a stunned dwarf, and emerged once more into the shopping mall. The security guard and a handful of customers were staring in amazement as one last dwarf was wrestled to the ground by a selection of potted plants while Mackam waved his wand and giggled.

"Never was, never will be!" Jackie shouted, getting off the spell before anyone could leave. The onlookers froze, and Mackam turned proudly to Jackie.

"Got them all," he said.

"You certainly did," Jackie said. "But this is not how we do things."

"Why not? They were the ones making trouble!"

"We could have explained things to them, quietly talked them out of there. As far as anyone up here knew, that hole would have been some emergency drain repairs. Now..." She sighed and pulled out her phone. "I'm calling transportation to pick up the dwarves. You and I have some serious clearing up to do."

It was late in the day when Kelly and Heather met again in Applegate's office.

"Thank you for your help today," Kelly said, her tone frosty, "but we won't be making use of your services in the future."

"Why not?" Heather asked. "Don't you need more people?"

"More people, yes. More chaos to clear up? No."

"They did good work. Mackam captured dwarves running a rogue industrial operation."

"Mackam nearly gave away the existence of magicals to the inhabitants of Monterey Park. He started a fight with a band of dwarves in a shopping center, was seen by a dozen people, and wasted hours of our people's time clearing up."

"Mackam's always been hot-headed, but he'll learn."

"He wasn't the worst. One of your people attacked a tree surgeon working in a public park. Another one almost strangled a renegade wizard with the roots of his oak."

"You said he was a renegade. You're supposed to stop them."

"Stop, not kill!"

They sat staring at each other in tense silence.

"We can do better," Heather said at last through gritted teeth.

"Maybe, and if any of your people want to apply to be Silver Griffins, to go through the full vetting process and the training that follows, we'll find out if that's true. However, one day of your untrained assistance was one day too many."

"I see." Heather got up out of her seat. She was angry at the Tolderai for their behavior, upset with herself for not foreseeing this, and most of all mad at Kelly for casting them aside so quickly, without even a chance to make good their mistakes. Still, now that the Tolderai were known to the magical world, they had to stay on the good side of the Silver Griffins so she had to keep her manners. "Thank you for giving us a chance."

"Thank you for trying to help."

That "trying" was the last patronizing straw. Heather stalked out of the office and back to her people.

CHAPTER SEVENTEEN

Lucy lay on the bed, still dressed and with her wand in her hand. Next to her, Charlie was already under the covers and soundly asleep. She would get changed soon and join him. She needed a moment first to gather what energy she had left, so she could stand up long enough to clean her teeth.

It had been a long day. First, she had looked for evidence about Applegate's crippling demotivation, with little luck. Then there had been a disastrous trip out to contain a band of teenage shifters, in which she was assisted by one of the Tolderai, leading to several badly hurt shifters and a lot of awkward questions. Then there had been the work of clearing that up and talking Heather down from her fury about how Kelly dealt with the whole thing. Without Applegate to take charge, she, Kelly, and Jackie had to stay late to deal with the aftermath of their Tolderai day—processing casualties and prisoners, checking that others thoroughly cleared up magical crime scenes, putting in place the extra details that would ensure that a cover story stuck. She'd gotten home hours after dinner was over and found that Eddie had sneaked out of bed to play at being a crocodile in the living room. By the time she had him in bed and not gnashing at his pillow with rows of pointed teeth, she was completely exhausted. The only comfort was that the next day couldn't be as bad. Could it?

As she replayed the day in her head, her mind drifted, and sleep crept in.

Lucy stood in darkness.

No, stood was the wrong word. There was nothing solid beneath her feet to stand on. She floated in darkness although she couldn't sense empty air beneath her or see a drop where she might fall.

Her wand was in her hand, more solid and certain than anything else in the world. Its gold bands glowed, and worn lumps on the dark wood seemed to reflect that light. Power pulsed through it.

"What is this?" Lucy asked. "Where am I?"

No answer came back to her, but she didn't need one. The thought appeared in her mind, not a mere idea but a certainty, solid as stone or as a mother's love. She was asleep, and this was where her mind went when consciousness departed.

"Did you do this?" she asked the wand. "Are you why I'm aware of it all?"

Again, there was no answer, except for the one that

already existed inside her head. The wand was opening a path for her into the dream realm.

"I'd rather sleep," Lucy said. "You know, get some rest. If I let go of you, will that happen?"

The wand went cold at those words.

"Don't like that idea, huh? Well then, why don't you show me around while we're here."

Lights glowed in the darkness. They had always been there, bright and shining, yet invisible to her until she looked. Four million brilliant points of life, the minds of LA.

One of the points of light was right in front of her. As she watched, it unfurled like a flower whose petals were grown from memory and imagination. She drifted forward and into the dream.

She found herself standing inside a computer, or at least that was what it looked like. Rows of circuit boards towered to the right and left, connected by wires made of a neon glow. The air swirled with floating letters and numbers, like spells cast by electricity.

In the middle of all this electronic activity, Charlie sat at a desk, typing on an invisible keyboard. He wore his "Kiss the Cook" apron with nothing underneath, and his hair stuck up like a troll's. Off to one side, a five-man band in nineties slacker fashions played indie rock. In front of Charlie, a ball of cheese hung suspended on a string of salami, caged in by rows of slim green beans.

"Don't abandon me like this," the cheese said, its outer layer parting to reveal an unsettlingly human mouth. "I've always been there for you."

"Me too," the salami said.

"I know," Charlie replied. "I'm not judging you, but I have the future to think of, right guys?"

"Don't you go and cut your hair," the band replied in unison.

Lucy looked down at her wand.

"This isn't my dream, is it?" she whispered. "It's his."

Charlie looked at her and smiled.

"I'm writing a new program for the cows," he said. "To make them fart less. Methane is a greenhouse gas."

"Thanks for sharing, sweetie."

Lucy kissed him on the forehead, then took a step back, and Charlie returned to typing on his non-existent keyboard while the cheese pleaded for freedom, or possibly for him to eat it. It was hard to tell.

"I feel creepy, watching my husband's dreams," she said. "Can we try someone else?"

The dream receded, and she hung in darkness again. She picked a distant light at random and pointed at it. It rushed toward her, and she was inside it.

This time, the dream was about cats. Hundreds of cats, thousands of cats, all of them gathered around a young man in the middle of his living room.

"Here's a treat for you." He held out a tiny biscuit, which one of the cats took. "And one for you, and one for you, and one for you…"

"This doesn't seem too weird," Lucy said. Then she looked down and realized that the man was pulling the biscuits from the flesh of his leg. "Okay, I take that back. This isn't just weird but gross. Let's try another one."

This time, instead of returning to the darkness, she sensed the other dreams around her from inside this one.

She didn't need to see those bright points. They were always there, right beyond her touch, and she could reach for them whenever she needed to. Now that she paid attention, she sensed that they each had a different tone. Some were brighter than others, some calmer. Some throbbed with anxiety while others pulsed with excitement.

Lucy reached for one that glowed with something like pride. As her wand touched it, she was drawn across, from one dream to another.

This dream took place in a concert hall, in front of an audience of thousands. It would have been enough to fill Lucy with a deep sense of anxiety, but that wasn't the feeling that came to her. Great pride and satisfaction filled the air, spreading out from a young woman who sat with her eyes closed in a chair on the stage, playing the cello. The fingers of one hand moved up and down the strings while the other drew the bow back and forth, playing a tune that made Lucy's heart soar.

"It's beautiful," she whispered, a tear forming at the corner of her eye.

A tall, thin figure stalked onto the stage. His bald head was pale above his black suit. When he reached the cellist, he paused and tilted his head, like a bloodhound sniffing at a trail. A tremor of unease ran through Lucy but was lost in the joy that the music brought. Everything would be well. This woman's music and her long-dreamed rise to stardom would see to that.

Then the man touched the cellist's forehead with a slender finger. The music grew quieter, the cellist's movements slower and less ambitious. Her eyes opened, and she looked blankly at the audience, who faded away. After a moment, the cello slipped from her hands, not even making a *thud* as it hit the floorboards, just fading into nothing. She pulled a TV remote from somewhere down the side of her seat and pointed it into the distance.

As the grandeur of the concert hall became a cramped, nondescript apartment, Lucy's heart broke. The young woman had so much potential, so much vision for her future, and she was letting it all go.

The tall black-clad man looked up as if hearing the scream Lucy wanted to utter. His eyes shone, his gaze fixing her in place.

"Well." His voice made her feel like spiders' legs were creeping up her spine. "Who do we have here?"

He had been far away from Lucy In the concert hall, but in the confines of the apartment, they were only a few feet apart.

"So much power," he said. "So much potential. And your dreams…" He stroked the air in front of her face. "Oh, so delicious."

A pointed pink tongue snaked out to lick pale lips.

"Get away from me." Lucy tried to step back, but the apartment wall was in the way.

"No space to run," the man said. "As if anyone can run from me."

He raised a single finger and reached out toward her forehead.

"No!" Lucy shouted.

She raised her wand and cast chains to bind the man, but they passed straight through him. She cast a freezing spell, but it melted in the air. She summoned vines from the earth beneath the apartment floor, but they withered at his feet, and all the while that pale finger came closer and closer.

"Such limited imagination," the man said. "You'll never trap me like that. I am a master of this place, and these…" He kicked at the fallen vines and meltwater around his feet. "Trifles. Whereas you, you are a fountain of something richer, something I long to taste."

That finger touched her forehead, and a chill ran through Lucy.

A pulse of power burst from her wand, a spell that she hadn't cast but that seemed to come from the wood itself. It flung her and the slim man apart. Then the world around her burst like a soap bubble, and she tumbled end-over-end through the darkness of the dream world.

Lucy woke with a start. She was still lying on her bed, wand in hand, her clothes plastered to her with sweat. When she glanced at her phone, she saw that less than twenty minutes had passed.

"What was that?" she whispered in fear and amazement. "Who was that?"

Beside her, Charlie mumbled incoherently, then rolled over and went back to sleep.

Lucy got up and crept through to the kitchen to make herself a calming cup of tea. It didn't matter how tired she was. After seeing what her dreams could hold, she wasn't ready to sleep yet.

CHAPTER EIGHTEEN

Ellis stepped inside the pub and immediately felt at home. There was a big wooden bar, brick walls, old-fashioned ornaments, and a nice long row of beer taps. The atmosphere of cozy familiarity embraced him like a blanket. Then he saw Sarah sitting near the end of the bar, and his mood got even better.

"Howdy," he said, taking a seat next to her. "This is a mighty fine place you've picked. Not at all what I was expecting."

"It has the phrase 'public house' in its name. Surely that gave you a clue what sort of place it would be?"

"I stopped trusting bar names when I saw how few Irish people ran Irish ones."

Sarah laughed. "Fair point, but this time you would have been okay." She smiled as the barman approached. "This one's on me. What are you having?"

Ellis perused the beer taps, asked the barman a couple of questions, and settled on a locally made pale ale. Sarah ordered a white wine.

"That's part of why I wasn't expecting this," Ellis said. "You don't come across as the craft ale type."

"I'll give anything a try once or twice, but after our last date, I thought I'd keep things low-key and unadventurous today."

Ellis blushed almost bright enough to match his tie and looked down at the bar.

"About last time," he said, "I'm sorry for the terrible dinner and for making you part of a magic carpet crash."

"You don't need to apologize. You tried to do something amazing, and if it didn't work out, you still get points for effort."

"Thanks."

Their drinks appeared, and she held hers up. "Here's to a quiet evening."

"Here's to that." Ellis clinked glasses, then took a sip of his beer. It didn't chase away all of his nervousness, but it at least made things a little easier.

"So, what's the plan for the evening?" he asked. "If we're staying low-key, I assume you ain't gonna whisk me away to some fancy restaurant with bow-tie waiters and those tiny servings."

The way she had dressed matched that assessment. Sarah looked damn good in jeans and a top that brought out the green of her eyes, but she wasn't going to get past the door of anywhere fancy. Ellis was more than okay with that.

"There are a few nice places around here if we want to grab a bite," she said. "Mostly though, I thought we could have a couple of drinks and get to know each other better."

"I like the sound of that. So, tell me, how did a nice witch like you become a doctor?"

"Same way anyone does, big student loans and a lot of hard work."

Ellis laughed. "Okay then, let me ask the right question. Why did you become a doctor?"

"Same reason anyone does, I wanted to help other people. That and I was good at biological sciences but couldn't wrap my head around the humanities, so I was never going to make much of a politician."

"Would you have wanted to?"

"Not really. It looks like a nasty business, constantly putting the other side down. I think it would stress me out too much."

"This coming from a lady who holds other people's lives in her hands on a daily basis."

"Maybe not daily, but yes, I do see the irony. How about you, why did—" She paused and frowned as her handbag buzzed. "Sorry, I'd better check this." She took her phone out.

"You on call?"

"Not officially, but my magical patients don't have anyone else to turn to." She answered the call. "Hello?"

Ellis focused on his beer and tried not to listen in while Sarah talked to a potential patient on the other end of the line. It was hard when all he wanted to do was look at her, but the beer was good, and that was a comfort. After a couple of minutes, Sarah hung up.

"I'm really sorry about this," she said, "but I'm needed."

She put her phone back in her bag, then put some cash on the bar to cover their drinks. Ellis's heart sank. Two dates, two nights gone wrong. Things were starting to look cursed.

Sarah hesitated, looking less sure of herself than she had a moment before.

"Normally, I'd suggest we rearrange for another day, but you might not be in LA much longer, right?"

"Really depends on whether I can hunt down my monster."

"In that case, do you want to come with me? This next bit won't be much fun, but we can carry on our date afterward. I know it's not what you were expecting, but it would be nice to salvage something of our evening."

"Sure thing." Ellis drained the last of his beer and got off his stool. "I'll stand around an operating theater for hours watching folks get sliced up if that's what it takes for five minutes more with you."

Sarah laughed. "It shouldn't be that bad, but the thought is appreciated."

They headed out into the street, and Sarah flagged down a cab. Moments later, they were in the back seat, leaving the heart of the city.

"I'd ask how your work was going, but..." Sarah nodded to the driver. No talking about magical investigations in front of ordinary people.

"I'd ask the same thing, but I figure I'm about to see it firsthand. Let's try a different topic. You watch anything good lately?"

"Yes, but you probably won't know it. I found this Welsh detective show—"

"You mean *Hinterland*?"

"You know it?"

"I don't understand how that detective looks so pissed all the time when the scenery's so stunning."

"Beautiful but gray…"

They talked about TV shows until their ride pulled to a stop on a residential street.

"Thanks." Sarah paid the driver and got out, followed by Ellis.

"Thought we'd be going to a hospital," he said as the car drove off.

"Magical case, remember? A lot of my patients can't go to the hospital."

Sarah opened a gate next to one of the houses and walked through. In the yard were three teenage magicals, all of whom looked faintly familiar to Ellis, an Arpak, and a gnome standing over an elf on the ground. The elf's legs were both twisted around in pretzel-like loops. One of the Arpak's wings appeared to be mechanical.

"Oh, Siltor." Sarah knelt next to the elf and ran her hands along his legs. "What on earth happened?"

"I was trying out a new illusion, but the magic went wrong." The elf swallowed and touched the top of one of his twisted legs, then flinched back. "It all turned real somehow. Can you fix it?"

"Yes, of course, but we'll need to do this carefully." Sarah unlocked the door to her house and switched on a light. "Ellis, could you help them bring him in?"

Together with the Arpak, Ellis carried Siltor through the house to a back room, which Sarah had set up like a doctor's surgery. The surfaces were white and sparkling clean, the cupboards glass-fronted, filled with instruments and pill bottles. They laid Siltor on an operating table in the center of the room while Sarah fetched a large bottle, some cloths, and a pair of scissors.

"First things first," she said, her tone serious, "we're going to have to ruin those pants."

"What?" Siltor looked at her in alarm.

"There's no way we can take them off while your legs are like this, and I can't get at your legs with the pants on, so…"

Sarah swiftly cut the material off the blushing elf to the amusement of his friends. They looked less amused when she handed them each a cloth soaked in a strange-smelling liquid from the bottle.

"I'm going to start a spell," she said. "While I do it, I need you to rub this ointment into his legs."

"Into his legs?" The Arpak looked as awkward as only a teenager could. Siltor himself looked mortified.

"Oh, get over yourselves." The gnome held her cloth out and ready. "It's not like we have to rub his junk."

The Arpak blushed but held his cloth ready.

Sarah waved her wand, and the magic started. While Siltor's friends rubbed ointment into his legs, she followed their movements with magic. Where the spell and the medicine combined, his limbs slowly straightened, shifting into something more like a normal pair of pasty teenage legs. At last, Siltor sat in his underpants and t-shirt, clutching thighs that gleamed from the ointment.

"Thank you so much, Dr. Smith," he said.

"I'm happy to help." She held out another bottle. "Your legs are going to feel strange for the next few days. Rub this on in the morning and the evening or get someone to do it for you. It'll prevent any residual muscle knotting from becoming a permanent problem."

She took a pair of worn tracksuit pants out of a cupboard, and Siltor put them on. They barely reached halfway down his shins, but at least his blushing went down.

"Back to the tunnels, all three of you," she said. "Next time, be more careful what you cast."

The teenagers headed out, and Sarah closed the door behind them. Then she looked at Ellis, and the two of them could no longer hold back their laughter. They laughed and laughed until Ellis was leaning against a counter to hold himself up.

"That poor dude," he said. "First his legs, then getting half-stripped in front of his buddies."

"I felt awful," Sarah said, "but what else was I going to do?"

"I don't know how you kept a straight face."

"It's not the most embarrassing state I've seen a patient in. Not even top ten."

"Really?" Ellis raised an eyebrow.

"Oh, you'll hear those stories soon enough. But first..." Sarah picked up her purse off the counter, then tilted her head on one side as she looked at him. "I was going to suggest we go out to find some dinner, but didn't you say that you've never seen *Aladdin*?"

"That's right."

"Then how about we order some takeout, open a bottle of wine, and I introduce you to a whole new world?"

Ellis smiled. "That sounds perfect."

CHAPTER NINETEEN

Mr. No stalked through the void between dreams. He was a shadow of a shadow, a thing made of magic and dark impulses, a being that should not have existed. That was why he had to exist—there was nothing so foul that the imagination couldn't conjure it into the world and no more powerful imagination than the collective unconscious of dreams.

Mr. No wasn't prone to obsession. The dreamscape was so rich in potential, the inner world of humans and magicals so rich and varied that he didn't need to fixate. He could simply roam, see what caught his eye, and then picked off a particularly tasty morsel when it was at its most vulnerable. Opportunism was so much more straightforward than having a plan.

Sometimes, though, it was worth paying attention, worth pursuing that special someone to their home in their head. Someone like the witch he had seen the previous night, standing around in a musician's dreams. So, Mr. No strode through the dreamscape of Los Angeles, hunting for Lucy.

He stopped in the head of a young director, just starting with adverts and music videos. A promising talent, like the previous night's cellist. Was that what the witch was after? To see the dreams of the inspired and the creative, to treat their subconscious as a place of entertainment? She wouldn't be the first, and she wouldn't be the last. A dreamer's wand could open up a cinema more vivid than any in the world, an art gallery more dazzling, a concert hall more stunning in its talent and its scope.

Still, the dreams of creatives weren't always creative visions. Tonight, the video director was stuck in a closed-loop, reliving a childhood spelling test over and over, excruciated by the memory of getting every answer wrong. It was awkward, not entertaining. If the dream witch were looking for entertainment, then she wouldn't find it here.

Mr. No moved on. He spent time in the heads of painters and photographers, DJs and videographers, the lead singer of a rock band, and the lead soprano of a classical choir. Nothing. No living thing in any of those dreams except for the dreamers themselves.

His pursuit wasn't merely about hunger although that played a part. Mr. No's appetite wasn't like other people's. It wasn't about what he needed to keep him going, but about what he wanted, what he desired. Once a longing was inside him, it became like starvation to deny it. The thing he thought of had to be his. So it was with the witch. The minute he'd seen her, he knew that she would have to become a meal.

It was more than that. She was another wanderer in the

realm of dreams. There weren't many of those, certainly not in this country in this year. Their rarity made them curious, but their very presence made them a threat. The dreamers themselves could not fight back, but if someone else took up residence inside their heads, that person could become a menace to Mr. No, especially if that person displayed the sort of power that the witch had done. Mr. No could not risk leaving such a threat in the world. To do so would be to risk making himself the hunted instead of the hunter, which would simply not do.

Going to creatives wasn't achieving what Mr. No wanted. He would have to try something else.

He stepped out of dreams and into the darkness around them. The witch had shown strong energy, a distinctive strand of magic. Could he sense that?

There was no need to close his eyes. This was the dream world, and if he thought of his eyes as closed, that was how they would be. Besides, there was no real sight here, only what the imagination filled the visual gap with.

With his other senses shut off, Mr. No allowed an awareness of the dreams to wash over him. His mind brushed across each one in turn, gaining an understanding of the dream and the dreamer. Each was unique in its gifts, its tastes, its aspirations. Each created a special world within itself.

His mind brushed across one, and he stopped. That was it, not the witch herself, but something like her. Something that would sate this particular hunger. A mind with as much power and potential, whose future greatness he could gobble up, swallowing those sweet aspirations like so much candy.

He opened what passed for eyes and stepped into the dream.

The dream was about the past, the sort that could only exist in the subconscious of someone who cared about history. Details were exquisitely, accurately imagined, but jumbled together by the chaos of the unconscious. Spanish treasure ships, their timbers creaking and sails straining before a storm, reared above the beaches of Normandy in 1944, where knights and Nazis fought for the fate of the world.

The dreamer himself stood at the bow of one of the ships. He was a boy, perhaps twelve years old, tall and skinny with dark, unruly hair. His features were like those of the witch. Her son, probably. That would explain why his power and his personality felt so much like hers.

As Mr. No watched, Dylan scrambled down a rope from the treasure ship. Instead of landing in the water, he landed dry on the beach because physical space didn't matter in dreams. What mattered was symbolic space, the transition from one state to another. If the journey was the point of travel, then many dreams missed the point.

Dylan strode up the beach. The knights and Nazis had turned into diggers, each man and woman carrying a spade or a pick.

"Here." Dylan pointed to where the stone top of a pyramid peaked out amid the steel tank traps. "This is where we'll find the tomb."

A spade appeared in his hand, and he started digging, along with the people around him. Sand flew, and the ground level descended around them in defiance of physics and full accord with dream logic. Soon, a whole pyramid lay exposed, its stone doors hanging open, revealing a long, dark chamber beyond.

"This is it." Dylan waved a flaming finger to light his way, an excited grin on his face. "We're going to find the treasure."

"What sort of treasure?" Mr. No asked, standing beside the boy.

"Magical treasure," Dylan said excitedly. "There's an ancient staff full of spells no one knows anymore. I'm going to save it for the Silver Griffins, teach people those spells, and learn new things about ancient Oriceran."

"Fascinating." Mr. No raised a single slender finger. "You sound truly inspired."

"There's nothing better than history," Dylan said. He frowned. "Do I know you? You don't seem like anyone I know."

"Oh, I'm not. I am, like the artifacts you're hunting, utterly unique."

"That's cool."

"It really is."

Mr. No placed the tip of his finger in the middle of Dylan's forehead, and Dylan's face went slack.

It took several minutes to drain the fantastical dreams and aspirations from Dylan Heron, and Mr. No relished every moment of it. He had never tasted a mind so delicious, so rich in power and potential. By the time he finished, he felt bloated, so stuffed with wonder that his mind could hardly hold it.

As Dylan's dreams faded to gray mundanity, Mr. No stepped back into the void between dreams.

"Oh, yes," he said to himself. "That will do very nicely, for a while, at least."

Charlie knocked on Dylan's bedroom door.

"Hey, buddy, it's time to get up."

Buddy the dog, hearing what sounded like his name, yapped excitedly around Charlie's feet.

"Not you, Buddy." Charlie bent to pat the dog's head. "Though I should probably be careful with the 'B' word, huh?"

He opened Dylan's door, walked in, and drew back the curtains.

"Come on, lazy bones," he said. "Time to get up, or you won't have time for breakfast before school."

Dylan slowly sat up and swung his legs over the edge of the bed. Charlie frowned. Was this the beginning of the teenage behavior he'd not at all been looking forward to? An unwillingness to get out of bed seemed like it could be the start, but Dylan wasn't complaining. He was reaching for his clothes, and if he did it without any enthusiasm, well, no one was excited to face the world every day.

Charlie went into the kitchen and carried on making pancakes. The rest of the family were at the table, waiting for their breakfast. After a few minutes, Dylan slouched in and took his seat with them. His hair was unruly, which wasn't unusual, but his clothes were unusually untidy.

"Here we go." Charlie dished up pancakes onto every-body's plates. "Tuck in."

The others topped their pancakes with berries and

maple syrup and attacked them with enthusiasm. Dylan ate his dry, slicing pieces off and transferring them to his mouth mechanically, seldom looking up from the table.

"Are you all right, sweetheart?" Lucy asked.

Dylan nodded without enthusiasm.

"I found something you'll like," Charlie said. "A chance for kids to volunteer on an archaeological dig. Is that something you'd like to do during the summer vacation?"

Dylan shrugged.

"Real archeology, getting your hands on some history. Isn't that what you always wanted?"

Dylan shrugged again. Lucy reached out and touched his forehead, and he flinched from the slight cold of her hand, but he didn't seem to have a temperature. She exchanged a look with Charlie, and this time it was their turn to shrug. Whatever had come over their eldest child, it didn't seem urgent, and they weren't going to fix it at the dining table. They got back to their breakfast, fortifying themselves to go out and face the day.

"Look." Eddie dangled strips of pancakes as if they were tentacles. "I'ma jellyfish." The air around Eddie started to shimmer.

"No magic!" his parents exclaimed in unison.

Dylan kept eating his plain pancakes.

CHAPTER TWENTY

"I will never admit this once we're past this door," Jackie said, "but you're about to see the coolest room in the whole building."

Twylan read the sign next to the door: "SEW."

"Do they make costumes for you?" she asked. "I don't remember seeing anyone in a uniform, except that gnome at the station, and is it even a uniform if you're the only one wearing it?"

"Not sewing, S E W: Special Equipment and Weapons department. This is the realm of Toliver Jenkins, our in-house mad scientist, and he comes up with some amazing things. Though again, you tell him I said that, and I'll call you a liar, we clear?"

"Uhuh." Twylan couldn't imagine attacking the world with the head-on force that Jackie did, but she was at least getting used to being around her. "This all sounds exciting."

"Don't say that sort of thing in there. You'll only encourage him."

Again, the words sounded alien to Twylan, who worked hard at encouraging the rest of the Underfoot Brigade, but she kept that thought to herself and followed Jackie in as the stainless steel blast door swung open.

"Jenkins!" Jackie shouted down a corridor with a bend at the end. "Is it safe to come in, or are you going to blow us all up in some idiot misfire?"

Jackie's voice normally carried pretty well, but this time it was drowned out by the sound of angry guitars and a voice that was closer to growling than to singing.

"Told you he was a madman." Jackie leaned close so Twylan could hear her. "He thinks this noise is music."

They walked down the corridor, past a cluster of tiny sprites that had got caught in a magical net.

"Should we let them out?" Twylan asked.

"They're trapped for a reason. I don't know what it is, but do you think it's a good idea to meddle?"

Twylan shook her head.

"Sorry," she said to the sprites. "I'll come back for you if I'm allowed."

Then she followed Jackie around the corner and out into the main chamber of the Special Weapons and Equipment lab. It was a wide-open space, a hundred yards long and nearly twenty high, its concrete walls decorated with bullet holes, charred patches, and places where the concrete seemed to have melted from within. At the near end of the room, a pair of speakers as tall as Twylan trembled as they blasted the place with death metal. At the far end, two men in lab coats stood peering at something on the floor.

"Jenkins!" Jackie shouted.

Neither man looked up.

Jackie stepped through a door into an adjacent office and pulled a cable from the back of a stereo system. The music abruptly stopped, and the two men looked around.

"Who are you?" called the one with the close-cropped ginger hair.

"She's with me," Jackie replied as she re-entered the testing range.

"Agent Kowal!" The man grinned and waved. "Come help us settle a dispute."

Jackie and Twylan walked down to join the men. They were standing over the remains of something that might once have been a crash test dummy but was now as thin as a slice of pizza.

"How would you describe the state of John Doe here?" the ginger man asked.

"Very dead," Jackie said.

"Could you be more precise?"

"I'd call him flattened."

"See?" Jenkins looked smugly at the other man, who was younger and had a nervous twitch.

The nervous man hesitated for a moment, then looked at Twylan. "What do you think?"

"Well, he is quite flat." Twylan crouched to get a closer look. "In a lumpy way, not like he's been in a press, more like someone beat him with a hammer. I think pummeled describes it better." She lifted one of the dummy's hands, and the attached arm fell to pieces. "Maybe even pulverized?"

"Good words," Jackie said. "We don't use pulverized enough around here. I change my vote."

The nervous man smiled slightly and held out his hand. With a sigh, the ginger man handed over a dollar bill.

"I suppose we can adjust the catalog description," he said. "Now, what can I do for you ladies today?"

"Twylan's learning about how the Griffins work," Jackie said. She indicated the ginger man. "Twylan, this is Toliver Jenkins, head of Special Equipment and Weapons." She gestured at the other man. "This is his assistant, Nigel something, or idiot number two as I think of him."

"Pleased to meet you." Twylan shook hands with both men.

"Your eyes." Jenkins peered at the magic that crackled like lightning across Twylan's cheeks. "Is that natural, or do you take a supplement for it?"

Twylan looked away, uncomfortable at the mention of her deformity.

"Don't be an asshole, Jenkins," Jackie said.

"I was asking about—"

"Yes, yes, yes, you're just a poor scientist, too distracted to learn social skills, yada yada bullshit. If you can build this crap, you can work out not to ask a question like that."

Nigel stared at Jackie, wide-eyed in wonder, while Twylan wished that she could vanish into the floor. A long, awkward moment passed.

"Sorry," Jenkins said. "That was rude of me. Can I make it up to you by showing you something cool?"

"Um, I guess," Twylan said.

"Great, then come this way."

They all followed Jenkins to one side of the room, where an assortment of odd devices lay piled on a table.

"These are all our latest creations," he said. "Most of them still in the testing phase. Let's see. We'll start with…"

He picked up a wooden disk the size of a coaster, with a rune inscribed on each side, then skimmed it across the floor to the middle of the room. Nigel handed Twylan a remote control and set a toy car down in front of her.

"Drive over it," he said.

Twylan thumbed the controls and sent the car out across the room. When one wheel hit the wood, the disk sprang into the air, the runes flashed, and the car turned into a bunch of mistletoe.

"Runic landmines," Jenkins said proudly. "We're working on a variety of trigger mechanisms and outcomes, but this pressure-sensitive floral display is the Hodr model.

"Next up, Agent Kowal, why don't you try a little of this?"

He handed Jackie a bottle of what looked like a bright orange sports drink.

"Is this going to make me sick?" she asked.

"Not at all."

"Hm." She sniffed at it suspiciously. "Smells all right."

"The flavor is spiced apple and raspberry, but taste is hardly the point. Please, go ahead…"

Jackie sipped, then swallowed a couple of good glugs.

"Say, that's not bad. You might have a future in soft drinks." She frowned and pressed a hand to her chest. "I thought you said it wasn't going to—"

She belched. The air ignited as it came out, becoming a

long spray of fire. Jackie flung the bottle away and grabbed Jenkins by the lapels of his lab coat.

"Why the hell would you make that?" she asked.

"Why wouldn't I?" he asked. "It's so much fun."

He picked up another bottle, this one green, and guzzled half the contents. The others stepped back as he belched a stream of freezing air, from which snowflakes swirled.

"That has to be the most pointless thing you've ever invented," Jackie said.

Nigel shook his head, and Jenkins frowned at him.

"What do you mean by that, Nigel?" Jenkins asked.

Nigel pointed at what appeared to be a pillow.

"This?" Jackie picked the pillow up and peered at it. The cloth felt odd, and the pattern of it made her head spin. "You're saying the drink isn't even your worst idea this week?"

"Agent Kowal, I tolerate your dismissive attitude, but I will not have you denigrating our fine work." Jenkins snatched the pillow from her hands. "This is one of the best magical devices I've produced in weeks, maybe even months, and I don't say that lightly. Look, my stitching has improved since that unfortunate incident with the spider silk parachute."

He ran a finger along the edge and smiled.

"What does it do?" Twylan asked. Based on what she had seen so far, she assumed there would be some sort of attack, perhaps razor-sharp feathers bursting out to stab anyone hit with the pillow.

"This allows us to insert objects into the nocturnal imagination. Do you want someone to dream about a knife? Then put that knife inside the pillow and have them sleep on it. The knife will appear in their dream. Want to give them a mid-sleep snack? Sandwich in the pillow, sandwich in the dream. I tested that one myself."

"That sounds like it could be messy," Twylan said.

"Nigel's right. It's completely useless," Jackie said.

"To the likes of you and me, perhaps," Jenkins said. "Think of the therapeutic potential though. Is a young child having nightmares? Then insert their most comforting toy into their dream to soothe them through. Perhaps a trauma victim has recurring nightmares of their attack. We can equip them to fight back or give them a reminder that none of it is real, breaking the cycle of distress."

"I don't think that's how trauma works."

"So, the exact application needs some refinement, but the principle is sound. I need to find a magical therapist to work with me in refining my methodology. Sadly, there aren't many, and they're very busy."

"So right now, it's useless?"

"As all devices are at the start. It's down to human ingenuity to make them useful."

"There's certainly a lot of ingenuity here," Twylan said. "Thank you for sharing it with us."

Jackie shook her head at the encouraging words, but she smiled a little too.

"Thank you," Jenkins said. "It's good that someone appreciates our efforts. Now, would you like to see our wands and charms while you're down here? If you become a Silver Griffin, you'll draw from our armory, so you should see what you're getting into."

"Yes, please," Twylan said.

Jenkins led her into the next room.

"Don't worry, Nigel," Jackie said as the two of them followed. "We all know your boss is mad."

Nigel smiled at her.

"He is," he whispered. "Some days, that's half the fun."

CHAPTER TWENTY-ONE

Charlie was out working, and Lucy was busy in the kitchen, so Ashley opened the door to Sofia and Lance, Dylan's best friends from school.

"Hey, Ashley," Sofia said. "How you doing?"

"I'm okay," Ashley said. "Have you come to play with Dylan?"

"We mostly wanted to check that he's okay. He seemed kind of weird at school today."

"Like, totally lethargic." Lance slumped his shoulders and hung his head in an exaggerated impression of how Dylan had been. "Doing nothing, saying nothing, just sitting there. We were worried he might be sick."

"Mom was worried about it too." Ashley lowered her voice to a conspiratorial whisper. "She took his temperature and felt his belly, but couldn't find anything, so she took him to the doctor."

"What did the doctor say? Was he all, like, 'this is the Mongolian yak plague, we must give him an IV drip, stat!'"

Sofia rolled her eyes. "Ignore him. He started watching medical shows, and now he's like a walking script for an emergency room drama."

"An actor has to practice his craft!"

"Not right now he doesn't. Ashley, what did the doctor say?"

"He couldn't find anything wrong either. He said to try feeding him different things, make sure he gets rest and exercise, and come back if nothing changes."

"This is why you need medical dramas," Lance said. "Real doctors are boring. Anyway, can we see Dylan?"

"Sure, he's watching TV. It's kind of all he does at the moment." Ashley frowned. "I don't like it. We used to do interesting things together."

Sofia and Lance exchanged a look. They knew that the Herons weren't an ordinary family and that "interesting things" could involve all sorts of magic. They also knew that, technically, they weren't supposed to know about these things, which made asking questions awkward.

Ashley led them into the living room, where Dylan was slumped on the couch, watching cartoons. Next to him, Eddie was also watching. While Dylan's gaze seemed distant, barely taking in what was happening on the screen, Eddie watched with a feverish, obsessive intensity, leaning forward so that he could better focus on the action, hands clenched in his lap.

"Smash!" Eddie shouted as they came into the room. On screen, a pair of robots were flinging each other around a brightly colored cityscape.

"Hi, Dylan," Sofia said. "How are you doing?"

Dylan looked up, nodded briefly, and turned his attention back to the TV.

"I'm okay," he said.

"You missed band practice," Lance said. "It was a cool one too. We're learning this old Beatles song, and it has a bit that's all like…" He positioned his hands as if playing his guitar and made a passable imitation of a guitar solo. "You should come next week."

"Okay."

"Okay you'll come along, or okay you're hoping I'll shut up now?"

"I can't really be bothered with band. It's too much effort."

"But you love band! You get to play your trumpet."

Dylan shrugged. "Trumpet's okay, I guess."

"See?" Ashley whispered.

Sofia rummaged around in her crowded backpack, then pulled out a comic.

"Here." She placed it in Dylan's lap. "That's the new Ms. Marvel. It's really cool. There's this bit with Spiderman in it, and… Well, I won't spoil it, but you should read it, like, right now."

"Hey, why didn't you show me that?" Lance asked. "I like Ms. Marvel."

"You don't take proper care of my comics. Besides…" She jerked her head toward Dylan, who hadn't touched the comic.

"Oh, yeah, right. Take a look, Dylan. Is it cool?"

Dylan shrugged, indifferent. Eddie, on the other hand, had opinions about all this conversation.

"Too much talking," he said. "Can't hear cartoons."

Sofia glanced at the screen. It didn't seem like there was a lot of dialog going on although that wasn't really the point.

"Maybe Dylan could come out with us," she suggested, "then we can leave you and the cartoons in peace."

"Yes." Eddie tugged on Dylan's arm. "Go play."

"I'm okay here." Dylan shrugged his little brother off.

Eddie frowned, but he lacked the words to express his frustration adequately, and besides, another exciting part had come up in the cartoon. He leaned forward to watch.

Something more was needed to get Dylan off the sofa. Sofia decided that it was time to bring out the big guns, the sort of trip that she would normally never suggest, but that was perfect to pluck at Dylan's enthusiasm.

"We were going to ask my mom to drive us up to the Autry Museum," she said. "Go see all those old baskets and paintings and things."

"We were?" Lance asked. His tone changed as he saw the waggling of Sofia's eyebrows. "Oh yeah, right, we were. All those old things, can't wait to see them."

He grinned, and they all stared expectantly at Dylan. He didn't say anything.

"So, you want to come?" Sofia asked.

Dylan shook his head. "I'm not really interested in old stuff."

"You have shelves full of books on old stuff!" Lance exclaimed. "Your favorite shows are on the History Channel. When we went on the school trip to the tar pits, you were the only person the teachers had to tell to speed up because you were slowing the whole class down reading all the signs."

"I guess."

Lance flung his hands in the air. "I give up!"

Sofia leaned down to whisper to Ashley.

"Isn't there something you can do?" She wiggled her fingers. "You know, with the magic?"

"I don't do magic," Ashley shook her head. "Ooh, but I have something exciting!"

She hurried off and returned a minute later with a model of a dragon a foot long.

"Look, Dylan," she said. "I finished making Smaug the Second."

She placed the dragon in the middle of the living room floor, then took a few steps back.

"Smaug," she said, "fly."

The dragon flapped its wings. The beat grew quicker and stronger with each moment until the dragon was hovering in the air, wings beating furiously and tail swaying from side to side.

"Pretty cool, right?" Ashley asked.

"So freaking cool!" Lance stared at it.

"Did you make that?" Sofia asked, amazed. "You're some kind of *Iron Man* tech genius."

"I don't really like Iron Man," Ashley admitted.

That got Eddie's attention and a shocked look from him.

"Iron Man is best!" he said and leaped off the sofa, arms spread wide as if flying. He made rocket noises and zoomed around the room while the dragon hovered in the air.

"What do you think, Dylan?" Ashley asked.

Dylan looked up briefly.

"Cool." He said the word without any passion as if he was fobbing the moment off.

"Fine." Ashley gave an order, and the dragon flew forward a couple of feet, blocking Dylan's view of the TV. "What do you think now?"

"It's still cool." Dylan didn't seem bothered that he couldn't see the TV properly. He just stared at the dragon with the same indifferent gaze with which he greeted everything else.

"How about this?" Ashley said. "Smaug, flame!"

Fire burst from the mouth of the dragon and almost hit the curtains.

"Smaug, stop!" Ashley said in a panic.

The dragon closed its mouth and dropped to the carpet.

"Can I have a go with that?" Lance asked.

"Not now," Sofia said. "We're here for a reason, remember?"

Eddie, still hurtling around the room on imaginary thrusters, came to a stop in front of them. It had finally registered in his brain that something was going on here, something more than just watching cartoons or getting in the way of watching cartoons. The others seemed unhappy, and he didn't like that.

"What you doing?" he asked.

"We're trying to get Dylan to come outside and play," Sofia said. It was a near enough approximation of the truth for dealing with a three-year-old.

"Oh." Eddie pulled a thoughtful face. "Okay."

The air shimmered around Eddie. A moment later, an adorable, fluffy puppy stood in his place.

"That's amazing!" Lance stared.

"So cute." Sofia ruffled the fur on the top of the puppy's head. "Who wouldn't want to play with an adorable little pup like you?"

The puppy bounced across the carpet and up into Dylan's lap, where it sat staring at him, tail twitching back and forth, tongue hanging out.

"Hi, Eddie," Dylan said. He patted the puppy's head absent-mindedly.

"We should take him for a walk," Sofia said. "Throw sticks and things. You want to come?"

"No, I'm okay."

Buddy, having heard the word "walk," scurried into the room with his tail wagging. He looked at the other dog in confusion for a moment, but this wasn't the first time Eddie had turned into a puppy, and it raised his hopes for a good run around outside. He barked and jumped up on the sofa, then licked Dylan's face. Still no response.

The air around Eddie shimmered again. This time he turned into a monkey, leapt down to the floor, and grabbed Dylan's hand, trying to drag him out of his seat. Dylan let him pull him up but then stood there, still without the slightest hint that he cared what they did next.

"Seriously, man," Sofia said. "What is up with you?"

Dylan shrugged, a gesture that was now becoming so frustratingly familiar that she almost wanted to punch him. Still, he was her friend, and she was here to help him.

"How about if we go for a walk? Exercise might liven you up."

"If you want."

They headed for the door. Sofia didn't have high hopes, but this was better than nothing. Whatever was wrong with her friend, she hoped that it passed soon because this wasn't at all like the Dylan she knew.

CHAPTER TWENTY-TWO

Gruffbar stood in a gallery of the Los Angeles County Museum of art, looking at a huge canvas that filled most of the wall in front of him, an abstract piece of dark, sketchy lines across a pale background. To him, art was like a well-constructed building, a finely tuned motor, or the smell of traffic fumes—a reflection of civilization and all it could achieve, of how magicals and mundane humans could master their world. It made life feel worthwhile.

A lot of dwarves that Gruffbar knew didn't like the sort of art on display in this gallery. They preferred the concrete symbolism of realist work, whether it was a statue of one of their ancestors or an embossed door depicting the history of a clan. To them, traditional art better represented what made dwarf culture strong and what could add strength to any culture: tradition, respect, a true and accurate depiction of the historical past.

He could understand that impulse, but he felt like it got things backward. What were dwarf runes if not a form of abstraction? What was a well-designed tunnel system if not an abstract figure of beauty carved through earth and solid stone? Sure, traditional art could be great, but so could this stuff if you took the time to enjoy it. It wasn't only about the obvious things that the art showed you. It was about the thoughts and feelings it evoked.

Today though, he didn't have time for that. He hadn't come to the museum on his initiative but tailing Lucy Heron. Trying to tip the Silver Griffins off by phone call or anonymous email hadn't worked, as no one took what he said seriously. A more direct approach was needed. He didn't want to talk to a group of Griffins, who might decide Gruffbar himself needed more intense questioning and perhaps a cell in Trevilsom, but if he got one on by themselves, he could get away if things went wrong. If he could get to one of the smarter, more influential ones, there was a better chance they would act on what he knew. So, he had followed Lucy here on her lunch break, and now he stood down the gallery from her while she looked at the images, waiting for a chance to talk to her alone.

At last, the couple of Korean tourists who had been standing near Lucy moved on. Gruffbar walked over and stood next to her as if he was one more art fan looking at the work.

It was weird being this close to her. He had worked for several clients who had run afoul of Silver Griffin Agent 485, the famous Lucy Heron, but his encounters with her mostly boiled down to a research file, which he had been building up since his days working for Zero. Here in her presence, he was aware of her magical power in a way he hadn't been before. It was unmistakable to someone with his experience around magicals, an aura that said this was someone who could change the world or change him in very bad ways if she wanted to.

He swallowed, trying to keep his cool, and looked up at the painting. It was another abstract piece, oils this time, blobs of color piled up in layers so thick that he could sense their roughness just looking at them. The colors were chaotic, even distressing in the way that they mixed the dark and the bright.

"You can feel the tension in the piece, can't you?" he asked.

"Absolutely," she said. "There's a strain to it, the brightness calling you one way, the darkness the other. I suppose that's life for some people."

"Is evocation enough, though? I wonder whether a piece like this provides anything new when we've already had the likes of Pollock and Rothko."

"I wonder why you've been following me all morning."

Gruffbar cursed in the confines of his head. He thought he'd been careful, but apparently not careful enough. No point lying now, though. After all, he'd been on the verge of telling her the truth.

"I need to talk to someone from the Silver Griffins," he said. "I chose you."

"There are better ways to do that than stalking agents."

More tourists walked in, chattering to each other. Lucy walked down the gallery, away from them, and Gruffbar followed, neither looking directly at the other. Instead, they stopped in front of another painting and stood gazing at it as if they were merely two more art fans discussing inspiration and technique.

"I know you, don't I?" Lucy said. "From a case."

"You might have seen me when I was working for Zero."

"Ah."

"I'm a lawyer, not a gangster. My clients are sometimes criminals. That doesn't mean that I am." He was, and he knew it, but that wasn't a topic for this conversation. "Today, I'm on your side. I want to share information about a threat."

"Hm." Lucy tilted her head on one side, subtly shifting her view of the painting. "Why would I listen to you? Given your clients, this is probably a way to take out the competition."

Gruffbar hesitated. He would certainly consider reporting an enemy to the Griffins if he thought he could do it without endangering himself. There might be honor among thieves, from time to time, but there was also a brutal pragmatism necessary to survive on the wrong side of the law. That wasn't the important thing, though. What mattered was convincing Lucy of what he had to say.

"This isn't a professional thing," he said. "It's about self-preservation. There's a powerful magical loose in LA, one that nearly destroyed a lot of people who were close to me. Before you say it, no, not the sort of people I associate with now, the ones you might think deserve to be destroyed. These were ordinary dwarves. Things nearly went very badly for them, and things could go very badly for the citizens of LA now. I don't want to see that happen again."

"Because this magical might get you while he's here?"

"That's one reason, but there's this too." Gruffbar pointed at the painting in front of them. "And all of this." He gestured around the gallery. "If this magical isn't stopped, there won't be any great works of art, or music, or literature in the future. No grand achievements. No space flights or journeys to the depths of the ocean. No updated sports cars or new skyscraper towering over the rest. Civilization will settle where it is now. It'll stop reaching for anything higher."

"This is all very ominous, but it's also very vague. You haven't said anything yet to convince me that there's a real threat."

Here it was again, the point that Gruffbar had got stuck on before. How could you convince people that a threat was real when they could only see it in dreams, a space of imagined and non-existent things?

"This is going to sound fake," he said, "but this creature lives in dreams."

He paused, waiting for her to scoff at him.

"Is he tall and pale?" Lucy asked. "Dressed in black?"

Gruffbar stared up at her. "You've seen him?"

"I don't exactly know what I saw or what it means. Tell me about him."

"His name is Mr. No. He lives in dreams. As far as I can tell, that's the only place he can live. The real world is inaccessible to him. That's a strength, not a weakness because it means that most people ignore him or don't believe in him, and even if they want to fight back, they don't know how. The only way that my people got out safely was by making a deal, and most people won't have anything to make that worth his while.

"He lives in the dreams we have while sleeping, but he feeds on the other sort of dreams, people's hopes and aspirations. He gets into their heads and sucks that out. The passion. The enthusiasm. The commitment to get a thing done. It all goes away, leaving them with no desire to do anything beyond drifting through life. Most won't go so far as to starve to death, but they won't strive for anything either, not to maintain relationships or build a career or make art. They'll just drift, hollow shells of themselves.

"The bigger the dreams, and the bigger the person's potential, the tastier they are to Mr. No. The dreams of young artists and engineers, yearning to make something great, and with the drive and skills to achieve it, those are really tasty to him. Same for a passionate politician, a brilliant teacher, a magical with great power and the will to do something with it."

"Dylan," Lucy whispered.

That name rang a bell, something from the files. Gruffbar remembered a young wizard in the cave beneath La Brea, using powerful magic to beat Gruffbar and almost stop his escape.

"Your son," he said. "Mr. No got to him?"

"I think so." Lucy ran her hands over her face. "He definitely got to my boss, and he tried for me, but I got away."

"Wow. Not many people can do that."

"I still don't know how I did it." Lucy touched her back pocket, where her wand was. "But I'll find a way to deal with him again."

Gruffbar wondered for a moment if he should explain the trap he had used against Mr. No when he was younger. However, that was a tool the Silver Griffins could use against him and his clients, and he was loath to equip them like that. They would find a way of their own, probably. If not, if it looked like they would lose, he could tell them, but only as a last resort.

"Is there anything else you can tell me?" Lucy asked.

"Only that you should act fast because the longer you leave this, the fewer people you'll have with the will to fight alongside you."

"Once they lose their dreams to him, can people get them back?" she asked, her voice cracking at the horror of what this represented for people she loved. "Or is that it, forever?"

"Your son can recover if you beat Mr. No." Gruffbar didn't know how true that was, how long the ambitions remained intact inside Mr. No, but it seemed like the best thing to motivate her.

"Thank you." Lucy drew a deep breath. "I should get back to work."

"Sure. I'm going to stick around for a while, enjoy the art. If we're going to stop seeing new wonders, I want to make the most of the ones we've got."

"Check out the modern Islamic art section. There are some really interesting things there."

"Thanks. Good luck, Agent Heron. I think you're going to need it."

CHAPTER TWENTY-THREE

Mr. No perched in the darkness between dreams, contemplating the tiny bright lights that were millions of souls drifting through the void of sleep. How many of them, he wondered, were children? How many were retired? Those were two groups he mostly avoided. Children needed more time to mature, to develop aspirations that were truly inspiring or truly odious. True, they might dream big, but it was in the late teens and into adulthood that those dreams crystalized, matured, gained nuance and substance, became something worth his time. It wasn't until then that you found the next Taylor Swift, or the next Mussolini, people with great or terrible vision. As for the elders, they still had dreams for the future, primarily hopes for their children and grandchildren, aspirations for the generations to come. Those were more diffuse, less concentrated and powerful. They would do for a snack, but they hardly set his taste buds ablaze. No, it was in the full thrust of adulthood that he found most of his meals.

Of course, there were exceptions. The Heron boy had

been as delicious as he was young. Such immense raw power and such grand, focused ideals. He knew what he wanted from life in a way that few twelve-year-olds did. Or he had known.

There was no Dylan Heron to be had tonight though, at least not in the dreams that Mr. No had peered into. The world was a flatter, more disappointing place this time.

Still, he had to eat. He touched a dream and stepped inside.

Immediately, he regretted his random choice. The woman was having a nightmare, and that, from Mr. No's point of view, was an immensely tedious thing. When they were afraid, people forgot their dreams and aspirations. They were too busy facing the crisis before them.

In this case, the woman was being chased. Why the thing chasing her was a giant chair, Mr. No didn't know. It probably reflected some deep-rooted anxiety or childhood trauma. However, his interest in the mind wasn't that of a psychiatrist or counselor, and he had little desire to understand the inner turmoil of his prey. Perhaps she even feared the psychiatrist's couch, and that was why furniture was after her. Who really cared?

What mattered was that true nightmares were a trap. There was a barrier around them that stopped the dreamer from escaping until the nightmare ended or some moment of desperate will burst them through. As long as that barrier was in place, anyone else in the dream was trapped too. Mr. No sat down, crossed his legs, and waited, watching as the chair chased the woman down the street. How dull her terror was, how disappointing her screams and tears.

At last, the nightmare reached its climax. The chair leapt on the woman, slamming her into the ground. It opened a mouth full of wooden teeth. She screeched in panic, and the teeth closed in, and—

The dream burst, finally disintegrating under the pressure of the woman's fear. Somewhere in LA, she would wake up sweating amid tangled sheets, perhaps awakening a disappointed lover. Mr. No simply found himself back in the void.

He looked at the other points of light scattered around him. This time, he would be more careful. He reached out, plucked one from the firmament, and held it up between his thumb and forefinger. He rolled it back and forth, expanding it to the size of a large marble, and brought it to his eye to peer inside.

That was more like it. A football player on the field, dressed in the full padding and helmet of his sport, armored against the world. It reminded Mr. No of warriors' dreams long ago, fierce men and sometimes women dressed in metal and self-belief, wielding shining swords or the hefty weight of axes. Now it was all guns and jet planes, the sheer visceral weight of those old combats transferred to the sports field instead.

The player began his dash down the field, and Mr. No joined the crowd watching him. Around them, the empty imitations of an audience cheered and waved their hands in the air, but he didn't join.

The problem was that this young man dreamed so small. Here he was, on the field of his high school sports ground when he could be dreaming of anywhere. That reflected a lack of drive. Where was the professional stadium with its bright lights, or better yet an international crowd? Why stick with realism? He could have been playing in space or in front of every would-be lover who had ever turned him down. Instead, he dreamed mundane, to fit with mundane ambitions. Not unsatisfying, but after the Heron boy, not enough.

Mr. No stepped back through the crowd and into the next dream over. This one was surreal: talking clouds, flying buildings, maple syrup running down the street. It didn't matter how powerful or ambitious the dreamer was. Catching them in a moment like this would only lead to a muddled, bland meal. He opened a gap between two pink elephants and stepped out.

Back in the void, Mr. No looked around for a suitable dream from a suitable dreamer. Some stood out, burning brightly amid dimmer glows. The most intense often reflected the most passionate dreamers. Mr. No cupped one in the palm of his hand and looked into it.

This was more like it. A chess champion, his unconscious muddling together his last match and a scene from a drama series, so that a local sports hall gained features from a dramatically lit Soviet building. A crowd that was half people in slogan-covered t-shirts and half gray-bearded men in suits and ties watched as the game played out.

The chessboard reflected the dreamer's obsession. The pieces were those of a real set, with no extra additions or changes of rules for the dream. Every last pawn was beautifully carved, and if they had faces that watched with glowing eyes as he pushed them around the board, at least they didn't move about of their own free will.

The face of the young man's opponent kept changing as they played. The visages were old and young, male and female, shifting smoothly from one to the next. Mr. No recognized one or two from other dreams, which probably meant that they were famous, for all that it mattered to him. The power and ambition that drove people to fame interested him, not the trappings of celebrity.

Mr. No stepped out of the crowd and over to the board. The pattern of pieces meant nothing to him, but it clearly meant something to the players, who were staring at it intently.

"Are you winning?" Mr. No asked.

"I think so." The dreamer jumped his knight forward over the heads of the pawns. "Although it's going to be close."

"Do you always win?"

"No, I'm not that good yet, but one day I will be."

Mr. No grinned and stretched out his finger.

"At least, I hope I will be," the young man added.

Mr. No hesitated. The dreamer had seemed so certain a moment before, with the kind of conviction that Mr. No relished. He didn't want some watered-down version of that. He wanted the real thing.

"Just hope?" he asked. "Not know?"

"Isn't hope enough?" The young man shrugged. "It's not like I'm going to make a living off this. It's only chess."

He slid a rook forward, taking his opponent's bishop.

Mr. No frowned. What had seemed to hold such potential was turning into disappointment. Still, he needed something to keep his energy up.

The flickering opponent moved his queen. The

dreamer grinned, made one last move, and sat back, arms folded. His opponent sighed and knocked his king over, accepting his defeat.

In the dreamer's moment of triumph, Mr. No touched his forehead and sucked all that glory away.

It was fine. Not a bad meal, as these things went. But as the dreamer slumped in his seat, the beautiful chess set replaced by one of cardboard and plastic, the competition hall by a dining table, Mr. No couldn't help feeling disappointed. He had eaten so richly before. This was bitter in its mundanity.

He needed something more.

He emerged from the dream and looked into another—an aspiring actress at an audition. He watched her for a moment, waited until they offered her the part, then reached in to take those hopes of Hollywood glory. It tasted of mediocrity, of soda adverts, and a decade in soap operas—a watery, weak ambition.

He stepped into another dream and another, gobbling down the cut-throat promises of a rising politician and the verbose internal monologue of an aspiring screenwriter. They were all fine, but nothing more, and as their dreams faded into the real world, Mr. No sat alone and disappointed in the world of dreams.

How could he find something as rich and wonderful as the Heron boy?

Of course, the mother, the one he had been looking for. She was a powerful witch, as powerful as her son, and though her ambitions seemed mundane—love, motherhood, a mid-level career—her aspirations for the world around her were far grander. She wanted everyone to be safe and happy, no matter who they were or where they came from. How did she manage to dream so strongly of such a boring thing? He didn't understand, but he knew that he had to find out.

He looked around. She should have shone out, but something was hiding her, keeping her safe as part of the background. That wand. Still, it could only disguise her, not keep her from Mr. No forever. Every dream was accessible to him.

Four million dreamers in LA. It would take a little while, even focusing on the brightest dreams, but he would find Lucy Heron.

He reached out, scooped up a handful of dreams, and started looking through them.

CHAPTER TWENTY-FOUR

Lucy walked into the house and headed straight for the kettle. It had been a long day again, and she needed a cuppa to keep her going through dinner and into the evening.

"Hi, honey." Charlie waved to her from the dining room, where he sat at the table with a scatter of papers and two other guys.

"Hi, sweetheart," Lucy said. Then she did a double-take as she realized who Charlie's visitors were. One, dressed in a sharp three-piece suit with a pocket square that matched his tie, was Max Petrie, Kelly's husband. The other one, wearing camouflage pants, a tight black t-shirt, and a pair of wraparound shades even though he was indoors, was Ringo Fuller, third-rate bounty hunter and first-rate pain in the neck.

"Hi, Lucy." Max looked up from the papers with a smile.

"Hey, 485." Fuller touched the rim of his sunglasses with two fingers.

"Hi, guys." Lucy tried not to let her bewilderment show. "What are you doing here?"

"Great things, I hope," Max said. The warmth of his smile helped to counter Lucy's concerns. From the few encounters she'd had with Max, he seemed like a genuinely lovely, friendly guy, to the point where Lucy didn't understand how he'd ended up with the stuck-up and scheming Kelly. "I should let Charlie explain."

"Tell you what, you guys carry on without me for a few minutes," Charlie said. "I should talk with my wife."

He came through to the kitchen, took the lid off a plastic tub, and held it out to Lucy. The sweet smell of chocolate wafted out.

"I made brownies if you want one," he said. "They're not as good as yours, but I wanted something to offer the guys."

"Thanks." Lucy took one. She was proud enough of her baking to admit that he was right, these weren't as good as when she made them, but she appreciated the effort. She took a sip of her tea, then lowered her voice so the others wouldn't overhear. "So, what's all this?"

"You remember that talk we had the other day about our dreams and what we wanted to do with our lives?"

"This is about setting up your own business?"

"Only if you're okay with it."

Lucy smiled and hugged him.

"Sweetheart, if you want to follow your dreams, I'm with you every step of the way." She glanced into the other room. "I just wasn't expecting it to be with this company."

Charlie laughed. "Sorry about that. I hoped we'd be done by now so I could talk to you about this after dinner instead of ambushing you with my guests."

"Speaking of dinner, I should put some on." Lucy took a

big pan out of a cupboard and started filling it with water. "You keep talking. I'm all ears."

"Really? Because I could have sworn I saw a nose and kissed some lips at one point."

"Very funny. I mean I want to hear all about your grand plans."

"Well, do you remember I got talking with Ringo before about how polluting his van is?"

"That monstrosity with the eagle on the side?"

"Don't call it that in front of Ringo. He's very proud of that van."

"But it's... Never mind. Go on." She put the water on the stove to boil and took a tub of Bolognese sauce out of the freezer, something she'd set aside for busy days like this.

"Can I help?" Charlie asked. "Seeing as I'm in here anyway."

"That's okay, I've got it. Do you want to invite Max and Ringo to eat with us?"

"That's very sweet of you." Charlie kissed her on the forehead. "I think I've thrown your plans enough for one evening. Besides, dinner will give us a good motive to get this meeting finished."

"So, the business is about cleaner cars?"

"Right! Well, Ringo and I have been talking about how we could use magical technology to clean up exhaust fumes. Obviously, we can't do it for mundane drivers, in case they start asking questions, but a lot of magicals drive these days, and after Blight's pollution attack, we think a lot of them will be willing to pay to clean up their act."

"So, you'd be making magical clean air filters? Is there money in that?"

"There are grants we can apply for, money set aside by Wood Elves, or government departments that know a little about magic. Max thinks there's enough out there to get us started, at least."

"That's fantastic. How is this going to work?"

"Do you want to come and see?" He gestured into the dining room.

"Sure, why not. This pot won't boil if I stand here watching it."

She followed him to where the others were sitting at the table, going through their heaps of papers.

"I think we can share our trade secrets with Lucy, right?" Charlie asked.

"Sure, why not," Ringo said.

"It would be rude not to," Max agreed. "Especially after we've hijacked your house as our temporary head office."

"Great." Charlie spread a series of diagrams across one side of the table. "These are the initial designs that Ringo and I have worked out."

The diagrams showed a variety of different devices, including a pipe with runes engraved around its inside, an engraved ring that could fit around an exhaust, and a round box full of filters, circuitry, and storage devices that could hold spells. Lucy understood what most of the magical components were, though not the technology or how it all fitted together.

"So, these are purifying runes." She peered at one of the diagrams. "This is to convert ash into water, or maybe not quite ash, but something like that."

She flipped a page, revealing a picture of an imp sitting inside a box under a car, eating dust from a rune-inscribed bowl.

"Is that a trash imp eating pollution? I mean, it's certainly novel, but how will the imps feel about it?"

"If they're not interested, we're not interested," Fuller said. "I spend enough time chasing monsters as a bounty hunter. I don't want to make it part of this too."

Charlie grinned. "We sift the crud out of the fumes, turn it into something safe or feed it to some creature that lives off dirt and pollution. None of the changes will be so intrusive that they could mess with the engine, at least not yet. We need to prove this works on a large scale before we risk wrecking anyone's engine."

"If you and Ringo came up with these, what's Max's role in the business?" Lucy asked.

"They brought me in for the legal work," Max said. "You never want to go with second best on lawyers, and business and environmental regulations are my sweet spot. Charlie asked me for a little advice at first, but when I heard what they were working on, I said that I'm all in. We need to clean up the world, and this is a great way to do it."

"He's way more than just our lawyer," Ringo said. "Tell her about the other plans."

"We might be getting ahead of ourselves there, guys."

"No, tell her."

"Tell her."

"Tell me!"

"Okay, okay, okay." Max fished a briefcase out from under the table and took out another bundle of papers, this one bound along one edge. "This is something I came up with over the weekend, a potential business plan for Stage Two."

Lucy took the plan and leafed through it. In between the main text, there were pictures of factories and equipment she didn't recognize, lists of laws and regulations, and an assortment of maps, some of which she knew from a previous case were pollution maps of LA. At the back were tables full of financial calculations.

"You did all this over the weekend?" She sounded impressed.

"I got overexcited, and Kelly was busy with Griffins' stuff, so I had time spare."

Lucy couldn't imagine getting overexcited by something like this. She also couldn't work out what it was all saying. "Could you give me the Cliff Notes?"

Max held up one of the car filter diagrams.

"This stuff is fantastic," he said. "It could make a real difference. However, most of the biggest sources of pollution are industrial, which means that's where we can make the biggest difference and the most money, as better regulations force companies to clean up.

"So, instead of making this all about cars, we make those into a proof of concept. We use them to demonstrate that we can remove the pollutants at their source. Then we use that to secure more funding and scale the technology up. We start selling magical-owned businesses a way to be cleaner. This is how we save the world."

Lucy smiled at Charlie. Here he was following his dream and using it to make the world better in ways she never could. She couldn't think of a time she had ever been prouder of him.

"This is fantastic," she said. "Does it mean you'll be giving up your job?"

"No, it's a side project, for now at least," Charlie said. "Maybe one day…"

"I hope that day comes soon, if only so that Fuller here stops being the world's worst bounty hunter and gets out of the Silver Griffins' way."

"Hey, I'm a Level Three!" Fuller said. "There are a lot of bounty hunters worse than me."

"As boasts go, that's not great. Seriously, this is fantastic. I really hope it works. Now, I need to get back to making dinner, which means we'll need this table soon."

She headed into the kitchen while the men cleared up their papers, excitedly talking the whole time about what they were going to achieve. It was still weird hearing Fuller's voice in her house and seeing Kelly's husband hanging around. Still, if this was what would let Charlie chase his dreams, Lucy was with him every step of the way. Once she had made dinner for the kids, of course.

CHAPTER TWENTY-FIVE

Ellis had his phone out and the magical tracking app up as he walked into a hotel near the airport. He was pretty sure he'd stayed in this hotel before although he couldn't be totally sure since they started to blur together after a while. That was one of the downsides of all this traveling. Sooner or later, you had a day when you couldn't even remember which city a hotel was in, never mind whether you'd stayed there.

Not that it mattered. He had a room in a whole other hotel. He'd come to this one tracking down his target.

The image on the screen showed him the Wilderghast standing over a bed in a blandly decorated hotel room. There was an inoffensive art print on the wall, a large TV facing the bed, and on the bed itself, a man was sleeping. He looked like he was probably a traveling executive or someone in sales, and he'd fallen asleep wearing his shirt, suit pants, and socks, probably intending to catch a power nap between a flight and a meeting. Even a few minutes of sleep could be enough for a Wilderghast to seize its opportunity.

The creature stood over the man, one skeletal hand emerging from its gray robes, power running from that hand into the man's head. He frowned in his sleep, twitched, and flung a hand up as if fending off some invisible attacker. The nightmare had begun.

Ellis followed the app past the hotel lobby, into an elevator, and up to the fourth floor. Three doors down was the room he was after. He checked that no one was around, then tapped the lock with his wand. It *clicked,* and the door swung open.

The Wilderghast looked up as Ellis walked in and let the door fall shut behind him.

"Howdy," he said. "Remember me?"

The Wilderghast hissed and raised one hand to point at him, but the other still hovered over the hotel guest's head. The man was writhing now and making distressed murmurs.

"I'd say we should settle this peacefully," Ellis said, "but we both know that ain't gonna happen."

He pointed his wand at the Wilderghast, but before he could get a spell off, it flung one at him. He countered it in a flash of blue light, but another one was coming, the Wilderghast keeping Ellis on the back foot. He flung himself to the floor, narrowly missing the second attack.

The Wilderghast cackled and leapt up onto the bed. It stood with one foot on each side of its victim, robes swaying, a hand still pressed against the man's forehead. The Wilderghast kept the nightmare in place, using it as a power source, draining off his fear to fuel its magic. It had grown either stronger or smarter since the last time Ellis faced it, and either way, he was off to a bad start.

"Contego!" Ellis snapped, throwing up a magical shield as the Wilderghast shot another spell at him. The magic burst against the protection, leaving him safe.

Ellis rolled under the bed, then quickly out the far side. The Wilderghast tried to turn while keeping the hand on its victim's head, an awkward maneuver that bought Ellis a vital moment.

"Incarcero exspiravit." A net of magic sprang from the tip of his wand and expanded to become a glowing cage surrounding the Wilderghast. "Got you."

The Wilderghast cackled and thrust a hand between the bars of the cage. This time, its magic hit Ellis flat in the face at nearly point-blank range. He staggered back, then yawned as a great wave of tiredness swept over him.

"Oh no, you don't," he said, but his eyelids were drooping, his limbs growing heavy. He slumped into a seat in the corner of the room. "Not gonna… not gonna…"

Like that, he was asleep.

In his dream, Ellis walked down a wood-paneled corridor with a thick red carpet beneath his feet. On the walls were the heads of monsters he had defeated mounted on plaques, like something out of an aristocratic country house somewhere in merry old England. There were crossed wands over the doorway at the end of the hall.

Sarah was walking with him, her arm through his. She smiled and asked excited questions as he explained what the different creatures were and how he had captured them. Each time, an image of the story appeared in the air in front of him, a fragment of memory, a memento of his career. He had done a lot of good work, and it felt great to share all of that with Sarah. Sure, he was showing off, but she didn't seem to mind.

They stopped in front of a frog-like monster with a long, dangling tongue.

"This one got mighty messy," Ellis said. "That tongue can stretch to a dozen feet, and let me tell you. It's not fun to be licked by it."

The air in front of them glowed, and the appropriate memory appeared, Ellis fighting the frog creature in a swamp, its tongue wrapping around his legs and pulling him over.

"Oh no!" Sarah exclaimed, leaning closer as she clutched his arm.

"Don't worry," he said. "It worked out all right in the end."

He was vaguely aware of someone else walking through the door and down the corridor toward them, a tall, slim figure dressed in black. The slim man walked around behind them while the memory played and stopped on the far side of Ellis from Sarah.

"You must be very proud," the tall man said in a voice like a razor scraping over stone.

"I am." Ellis was still smiling despite the creepiness of the guy's voice. "This is everything I've done before..." He turned to point at the other wall, where empty wooden shields were waiting to take future heads. "...and that's what I'm gonna do in the future."

"Well, it's certainly bolder than some of the things I've seen recently. It might do, even if it's not what I'm after. I assume this isn't literal though, that you don't want a country mansion with corpses on the walls?"

Ellis laughed. "No, sir. I want her to be proud."

He patted the dream vision of Sarah on the hand, and she smiled.

"Are you here for the hunting trophies?" she asked.

"In a manner of speaking," the tall man said, and he raised his hand, one finger stretched out.

The light flickered, and shadows crept in from the corners of the corridor. The slim man frowned.

"What is this?" he asked.

"I don't know," Ellis said as a sense of disquiet grabbed hold of him. "But I don't like it."

The frog creature leapt down off the wall. It wasn't just a head anymore. The whole monster was there, its long tongue lashing around like a whip.

"Get behind me." Ellis put himself between Sarah and the danger.

"Interesting," the slim man said. "Maybe this is part of the dream, your chance to save the girl and play the hero once more."

"No, this ain't what I want."

Another monster jumped down from the wall, and another, and another. They surrounded Ellis, dozens of them, hundreds even, a decade's worth of monsters and villains he had fought. Whichever way he turned, there were more of them, closing in with fangs and claws and glowing eyes, reaching for him, snatching Sarah away. She screamed, but when he turned to look for her, he couldn't see where she had gone.

"Sarah?" he shouted. "Sarah!"

Now it was only him and the monsters closing in and the slim, dark-clad man standing off to one side, frowning.

"Get back!" Ellis said, panic rising. He should have been able to fight back, but he didn't have his wand, and he couldn't remember his spells, and he'd forgotten how to fight, and, and, and...

"How tedious." The tall man reached into the shadows and pulled something out. A Wilderghast, its gray robe frayed and its bony fingers twitching.

"Let me out of this," the tall man snapped.

"Can't," the Wilderghast hissed.

"Then stop it at once."

"Shan't."

"Do you understand what I am?"

The Wilderghast's robes rippled in something like a shrug.

"You ruined a perfectly good meal," the tall man said. "Look at this. It's turned from bold dreams to fearful drivel."

"Don't care."

In the middle of the corridor, the monsters were closing in. Ellis couldn't see past them anymore. Their claws tore his clothes and scratched his skin. The frog's tongue wrapped around his throat. His heart hammered in terror.

"If I can't have him, you certainly can't." The tall man pressed his palm against the Wilderghast's face. There was a flash of icy white light, and—

Ellis woke with a start. He sat slumped in a hotel room chair, the Wilderghast standing over him, the tips of its skeletal fingers pressed to his face.

Ellis whipped his wand up and pressed it under the creature's chin as he straightened. "Incarcero exspiravit."

This time, he flung all of his power into the spell. Driven by the fear and frustration of his nightmare, it wrapped itself tightly around the Wilderghast, so tight that the bars pressed right against its skin. The cage pinned its arms to its sides, and though it twisted its wrist and frantically tried to get a hand free, the creature couldn't get its magic out.

Ellis pushed the bound monster off him onto the floor. Exhausted, he slumped in the seat. His heart was still pounding, and he felt like he had gone five rounds fighting off a gorilla. That had been all too close. The Wilderghast had gotten inside his head, filled it with terrible monsters out for revenge and that creepy guy in the suit. If he hadn't managed to snap out of it, the creature would have kept it going, draining off the power of his fear, until he had a mental breakdown or a heart attack.

There was a groan from the bed. The room's other occupant looked like he was about to wake up.

Ellis took out his phone and quickly found the number for the Griffins' transport team under Griffith Observatory.

"I have an entity I need to transport out right now," he said. "Can you provide a portal?"

"One second…"

There was a moment of static on the line, a crackle of distant magic, and a golden glow in the air, followed a moment later by the dark opening of a magical portal. Ellis grabbed the prone Wilderghast and flung it through.

"All done," he said into the phone. "You can close it."

There was another burst of static, then the portal disappeared.

"Thanks." Ellis hung up.

With a groan, the hotel guest sat up in bed.

"That was the worst," he moaned. Then he noticed Ellis. "What are you doing in my room?"

"Wait, is this not my room?" Ellis looked around, making a face of exaggerated confusion. "Sorry, they all look the same, you know?"

CHAPTER TWENTY-SIX

Lucy picked up the magic jar off the counter in the dining room. It was rammed full, brimming over with colored slips of paper and dollar bills. Looking at it made her smile, remembering all those moments when one of the kids had done something they shouldn't have, but that was cute or amusing in its way. Like Eddie turning into a bunny and hopping across the table, or Ashley enthusiastically presenting a robot at dinner and trying to use it to serve the peas. It reminded her too of how sharp her kids could be, catching those moments when she or Charlie stealthily or absentmindedly used magic over a meal. The kids always looked so pleased with themselves when they caught their parents out, and those moments hammered the rules home.

Now it was Saturday morning, with the house in a state after a week of both she and Charlie stretched thin by work. The time had come to settle the account on all those magical misdemeanors.

"Do you think this will work with Dylan the way he is?" Charlie asked.

He looked as concerned as Lucy felt about their son's recent lethargy. She wrapped an arm around his waist and squeezed him tight.

"I hope so," she said. "If not, better to deal with it sooner rather than later."

"All right then, let's do it." Charlie fixed a smile in place and raised his voice. "Kids, family meeting!"

Ashley emerged from her room with a screwdriver in her hand. She popped it in her pocket, sat at the dining table, and folded her hands in front of her, attentively waiting.

To Lucy's surprise, Dylan came next. He moved without enthusiasm, but there was no resistance either. He didn't drag his feet or try to avoid the meeting, merely came in, sat, and stared blankly at the table. His slumped state upset Ashley, who looked at her brother with concern, then looked down at the table while sucking on the tip of her finger.

Lucy squeezed her daughter's shoulder. "Don't worry. It'll be all right soon."

"Really?"

"I promise."

Ashley smiled.

"Eddie!" Charlie shouted. "Where are you?"

"Batman's on!" Eddie shouted from the living room. The dramatic dialogue and exaggerated musical cues of a cartoon backed up his words.

"Batman will still be there when we've finished. Now switch him off and come here please."

There was a dramatic sigh. Then the TV fell silent. A moment later, an owl flapped into the room and perched on the back of a chair next to Ashley.

"Is that allowed?" Ashley asked. "I know we're not eating, but we are together at the table."

"I'll allow it this time," Lucy said. "But Eddie, please change."

The air around the owl shimmered and turned into Eddie, who slid down the chair into his seat.

"This jar is full," Lucy said, "so it's time to settle up."

She tipped the jar up. Dollar bills and slips of paper fluttered across the table. Some had jammed together near the bottom, and Lucy had to bang on the container to make them all fall out.

"This could take a while to sort," Lucy said.

"It doesn't have to." Charlie waved his wand and said a few magic words. The papers swirled into the air, spun as if in a whirlwind, and separated into four neat stacks: a pile of notes in front of each kid and a heap of dollar bills in front of their parents. Eddie's was by far the largest.

"I win!" He grinned.

"Do you know what you win?" Lucy asked. "Chores!"

"Oh." Eddie's face fell.

"You made your choices," Charlie said. "Now you have to pay the piper."

"Don't want pipes."

"It's a figure of speech."

"Don't want figure."

Charlie sighed. "I mean that if you didn't want extra chores, you shouldn't have broken the rules."

That was a point that Eddie couldn't argue with. He

picked up his stack of paper and riffled through it, looking at the colors of the notes and the "E" he had carefully drawn on each one. Given how much fun he'd had turning into different animals, it had been worth it.

"We have a lot of chores that need doing, and I've made a list of them." Lucy unfolded a piece of paper. "Each time you complete a chore, one of those notes goes in the recycling bin. Once all the notes are gone, you can go back to enjoying your weekend."

"What if someone doesn't get through them all today?" Ashley eyed Eddie's notes.

"Then that person will spend Sunday doing chores as well."

"What?" Eddie looked appalled. "Sunday is Superman day!"

"Then you'd better get your chores done so you can watch Superman."

"What chores?"

"First up for you, tidying away the toys in the living room. Ashley, can you do some vacuuming, please? Dylan, the bathroom needs cleaning."

"What if one chore is bigger than another?" Ashley demonstrated a scientist's interest in precision and a small girl's interest in making sure she got a fair share.

"I'll let big chores count for more than one note. If you're worried about getting your weekend back, you should start cleaning now, not waste time fussing here."

"What about you and Dad?"

"Well, we said this was going to pay for Halloween candy." Lucy picked up the pile of dollar bills. "Halloween is still a long way off, so how about if, instead, your dad goes to the shops and spends it on some treats we can share once you've finished the chores?"

Ashley and Eddie both perked up at that idea, and they nodded eagerly. Dylan sat expressionless, staring at the sheet of chores.

"All right then, let's get to it!" Lucy clapped.

Ashley and Eddie sprang into action, racing off to their chores. Lucy worried that Dylan might not even do anything, but he got out of his seat and calmly headed for the bathroom.

"Maybe this will be good for him?" Lucy whispered to Charlie. "Something to get him motivated."

"Maybe." Charlie picked up the cash. "Right now, I feel motivated to go get some candy."

He headed out, leaving Lucy in the dining room by herself. She arranged the kids' stacks of notes next to the chore list, where she could keep an eye on it all and took out some paperwork she needed to do for work. She was about to get started when there was a crash from the living room.

Lucy hurried through to find Eddie, in the form of a monkey, putting a lamp back in place with his tail. His arms were full of toys, but the floor was almost clear, the things he had been playing with over the past few days piled up in boxes beside the sofa. The lamp didn't look broken so she decided that it was best not to say anything. She didn't want to put him off when he was doing something useful.

In the hallway, Ashley was sitting with a screwdriver in

her hand. She'd taken the case off the vacuum cleaner and was rummaging around inside.

"That doesn't look like getting the job done, sweetheart," Lucy said.

"I'm making the machine more efficient," Ashley said. "That way, I can do the cleaning quicker. I'll save time over the lifetime duration of the chore and make it easier for next time."

Lucy couldn't argue with logic like that, and she trusted that her daughter actually would make things better, so she moved on without further comment.

In the bathroom, work was progressing nicely. The sink was clean, the mirror shone, and Dylan had moved on to cleaning the shower. This wasn't what Lucy had expected from him, and it filled her with hope. Maybe he was coming out the other side of what Mr. No had done to him.

"That's some great work you're doing there, sweetheart."

"I guess." Dylan shrugged. "Might as well do it."

"Imagine how lovely the house will be when we're all done."

"I guess."

There was that shrug again. It hurt to see him like this, indifferent to what was happening in his life. She would have preferred for him to argue, to talk about all the better things he could have done with his weekend if it meant she had the son she knew.

She went back to her paperwork while the house bustled around her. From time to time, one of the kids would come in and tell her that they'd completed a task. Eddie and Ashley took great delight in dropping a slip of paper in the bin each time, while Dylan accepted his reward and his next chore with equal indifference. By the time Charlie got home, most of the house was clean and tidy, and the kids had moved on to the back yard, where a rabbit-shaped Eddie plucked up weeds between his teeth while Dylan mechanically swept the patio and Ashley carefully cut the dead heads from flowers.

"Wow." Charlie dropped a bag of candy onto the kitchen counter and looked around. "We should do this every weekend."

"Sadly, we're almost out of credit." Lucy pointed at the stacks of notes. There was only one left for Ashley and two for Dylan although Eddie still owed plenty of work. "Unless you want to trust Eddie's talents for every chore around here. He has a lot of enthusiasm now he's got started, but I can't see him cleaning the oven properly, can you?"

"Maybe not. So how is he ever going to work off that debt?"

Lucy flicked through the pile of notes. "Maybe we could make some of these quietly disappear. He's done a lot of work, and I think he'll remember this next time he thinks about becoming a parrot during dinner."

"It would be harsh to hold a three-year-old to the same standard as the rest."

Lucy dropped half of Eddie's remaining notes into the bin, then set the others back on the table. "We can't totally let him off."

Charlie rattled the bag. "I think all of this good work has earned a snack break. What do you reckon?"

"I think you should go call the kids in, and I'll put the kettle on for us. Candy won't be enough to see me through the day."

CHAPTER TWENTY-SEVEN

The Tolderai stood at the back of the group of volunteers, trying to look as ordinary and inconspicuous as they could. That was fine for some of them. Heather's jeans and flannel shirt or Carol's long green skirt and loose blouse fit in among the sort of people who came out to spend their Saturday getting closer to nature. Others stood out more. Despite being persuaded to leave his beloved knife at home, Mackam was still a distinctive figure with beads shining in the braids of his long gray beard and a gleam of madness in his eyes. A middle-aged father instinctively steered his kids away from them, muttering something about getting closer to hear the instructions.

If her strange new volunteers unsettled the woman leading the replanting project, she didn't show it. She smiled at everyone as if they were the finest people she'd ever met.

"Thanks for coming out today folks," she said, "and for sacrificing your Saturday to such a good cause. My name's Anna, and I'll be leading you today. As you know, parts of

Griffith Park have grown pretty barren, and we lost a lot of the more delicate plants to damage from the recent smog. That's why it's so important that we undertake these replanting projects to bring this wonderful part of our city back to life.

"It's great to see more of you than ever before. Don't worry if you're new. We have all the tools and materials you need, and I'll show you what to do. If you're uncertain about anything, ask another member of the group. We're a friendly bunch, right guys?"

The side-eye some of the volunteers gave the Tolderai only slightly muted the sound of assent.

"Okay," Anna said. "Follow me. Let's go plant some trees!"

The Tolderai followed the rest of the volunteers. Heather's spirits rose from being out in nature instead of down in the tunnels or around the built-up parts of the city. She felt reinvigorated, ready for the hard work of planting and the harder work of dealing with people.

She grabbed Mackam's arm as he veered away. "Nobody's going to ambush us," she said. "We don't need anyone scouting the flanks."

"You never know." Mackam's eyes darted back and forth. "You have to keep your guard up. Start getting lazy and they'll pin you down. That's how you end up dead."

"We're here to plant trees, not fight a war. Try to keep that sort of talk to yourself."

Mackam scowled but fell into line. There weren't many people in the world that he would obey, but Heather had earned her place as chief, and following her lead nearly always went well.

"She said that she would tell us what to do." Mackam glared at the back of Anna's head. "Impertinent idea. We know how to handle nature a hundred times better than them."

"Remember, she's never met us before. Stay polite, do as instructed, and she'll soon realize she can trust us with plants far more than these mundanes."

A man with gray streaks in his hair turned briefly to give her a curious look. Heather forced herself to smile, an uncomfortable expression that didn't seem to make the man any happier. She needed practice at this.

They arrived in a dip between two ridgelines. Someone had brought a truck up across the rough dirt. In its bed were tools, saplings, trays full of seedlings, plastic sacks full of compost, and a big barrel of water with a hose attached. Anna handed out spades and gardening forks.

"The first step is to prepare the ground," she said. "I've marked out plots where we're going to plant. Please pick one and dig through the soil there. Break it up as much as you can and set aside any large stones.

"Now, is anyone feeling strong and ready for a special task?"

"I'm strong as an oak!" Mackam declared, puffing out his chest.

Anna looked at the wiry older man, but if he wasn't what she had been after, that wasn't going to put her off.

"Great simile." She laughed. "Could you help me distribute the compost while the others dig?"

Soon, the Tolderai were hard at work, digging alongside the ordinary humans. Heather found herself working with a young family, the kids picking at the dirt with trowels while the adults did the hard labor.

"It's good to bring young to these things," she said, trying to spark a conversation.

"Thanks." The mother smiled. "We want them to understand the importance of nature. Imagine how cool it'll be if they can come back here when they're older and sit around under full-grown trees they helped to plant."

"Children should understand nature. It's dirt and sweat and blood, not just the pretty pictures in books."

"Um, maybe." The woman laughed uncomfortably. "These two are a little young for that red in tooth and claw stuff though. We're more about the adorable little bunnies right now."

"The bunnies that hawks and foxes will hunt before their bones feed the trees? Nature is a wonder."

"I might see if Anna has something the kids can help with." The woman took her children's hands to lead them hurriedly away.

Heather smiled. That seemed to have gone well. She could see other Tolderai talking with the people around them, and if some looked unsettled, at least others looked fascinated. Nature shouldn't be an easy thing to face. If the Tolderai could open some eyes to that, they would be doing good work here beyond merely helping plants to take root.

Anna appeared and set a sapling down. She smiled at Heather, who forced a smile back. She approved of this woman with her fragile beauty and gently determined demeanor.

"You're friends with Mackam, right?" Anna said.

"Yes."

"Is he…" Anna's expression went through some contortions that Heather recognized as a struggle for the tactful form of words.

"Be direct," Heather said. She had no patience for other approaches and only used them herself resentfully.

"Is he well, psychologically? He's been saying some odd things, and I'm sure they're well-intentioned, but people are a little unsettled by him."

Heather looked at where Mackam stood by one group of diggers, a bag of compost at his feet and a feverish expression on his face. He was gesticulating wildly, his beard swaying as he spoke, and the listeners were shifting away from him.

"Has he been talking about government surveillance?" she asked.

"Among other things, yes."

"I'll deal with it."

Heather strode over to Mackam.

"…which is why you wear the foil under your shirt, not wrapped around your head," he was saying. "To keep the radio waves out."

She grabbed him by the arm and dragged him away from his bewildered audience.

"What are you doing?" she snarled.

"Enlightening them! What are we for if not to save these people from their ignorance?"

"This is our chance to do something useful, helping the ordinary humans to make their city better, encouraging them to care about their world more. We can't do that if you scare them off with your crazed rantings."

"I'm not crazy! I'm the only one who fully sees the truth."

"Even the tribe won't listen to you when you get like this. What makes you think it's suitable for them?"

"Maybe they're more open-minded than you fools. How will I know if I don't try?"

Heather was all clenched up inside. She could feel people watching her, could feel her frustration like a burning in the back of her head. But getting into a stand-up row with Mackam right now wouldn't help. He had to be managed. That was part of a chief's job.

"What if some of them work for the man?" she said. "They could report you as soon as we finish here."

Mackam's eyes went even wider than they already were.

"I hadn't thought of that. I should be more careful, listen to them, watch for signs of the other side's agents."

"Exactly. What better way to do that than by quietly distributing the compost?"

"You're right, chief. Thanks."

Mackam slapped her on the shoulder, then hurried back to his task. Heather returned to digging her patch of dirt, breaking up the soil, clearing out the weeds and stones, adding compost to enrich it ready for the plants. It was satisfying work, the physical labor grounding her in her body, connecting her to herself, and she had soon prepared a larger plot than anyone else. This would certainly do as a new purpose for the Tolderai. Reforesting America, one urban planting project at a time.

"Great work, Heather." Anna patted her on the arm and Heather smiled her first genuine smile of the day.

"Thanks. Are we ready to plant now?" She knew they were, but she also realized the importance of letting other people preserve their authority. It was all part of fitting in.

"Absolutely. I get the feeling you know what you're doing already, right?"

"I have some experience with trees."

"Great. Plant the sapling somewhere near the center of your patch, then the other seedlings around it. I'm sure I can trust you to get that right without me."

Heather beamed as the other woman walked away. Yes, this work would be good for the tribe and her.

She dug a hole for her sapling, loosened its ball of roots and dirt, then carefully lowered it into the space.

"That's it." She covertly released a small trickle of nurturing magic into the soil. "Grow here. Become strong. Help make our world better."

She patted the soil down around it, then turned to fetch her tray of seedlings. Her gaze went to another plot, where Carol was setting small plants into the ground. As she patted the soil down around each one, its flowers unfurled, revealing bright blooms. The people she was working with gasped and cheered, drawing the attention of others.

Heather muttered a curse and spat to ward off bad luck, but it was too late. She had told the Tolderai not to use any magic that others would see or that could draw attention. What was Carol doing?

Then she remembered that Carol usually lived in an isolated community, out in the wilds of Alaska. The people there were used to her presence and probably took the small miracles of growing things for granted. After all, it was amazing that anything grew amid the frost and snow. Here in the city, things were very different.

Too many people were watching now. They wouldn't forget this. The Tolderai couldn't simply explain it away, especially since the tree in the center of Carol's plot had also started to unfurl unexpected leaves.

Heather rushed over, put a hand on Carol's arm, and hauled her to her feet. "We have to leave," she said. "All of us."

"But what…" Carol finally noticed the onlookers and the way they were responding to her plants. "Oh."

"Wow!" Anna had come over and stared in amazement at Carol's plot. "That's quite a green thumb you have there. How did you do it?"

"It's a secret," Heather said. "And now we have to leave."

Her heart sank as she saw Anna's expression, but excuses or apologies risked a conversation, which chanced her saying something that would make everything worse.

"Come," she called.

The Tolderai broke away from their work and followed as Heather and Carol strode away. Behind them, the other volunteers gathered around the blooming plot, talking about super fertilizers, old farming tricks, and sleight of hand, trying to work out how she had done it.

Once they were out of sight, the Tolderai found a tree and transported away one by one. Heather was the last one left, looking back the way they had come. This had seemed so promising, but like working with the Silver Griffins, it hadn't suited her people in the end. She would have to accept her disappointment, and they would have to try something else.

CHAPTER TWENTY-EIGHT

Lucy stood in the living room doorway, leaning against the frame and smiling as she basked in the sight of her kids gathered together on the couch. Dylan and Ashley, tired from a hard day of chores and coming down from their post-candy sugar rush, sat watching a show. Eddie, who would normally have been as eager as anyone to watch TV, lay with his eyes closed and one arm wrapped around Buddy, the boy and the dog both fast asleep. Lucy didn't know how Eddie had gotten hold of her wand, but he clutched it in his tiny fist, with Buddy's paw on top, and she didn't have the heart to take it away when they looked so peaceful.

Charlie hugged her from behind, the warmth of his touch adding to her contentment. "Look at the little guy. He's exhausted."

"Hardly surprising. He's never done such a hard day's work in his life."

Charlie chuckled. "Very true, and he even did a passable job of some of it."

Lucy elbowed him in the ribs. "Don't be a jerk. He did really well at pulling up those weeds, and it would have taken far longer to tidy the edge of the lawn without help from a mole's paws."

"Should we move him to bed, or maybe wake him up so he'll sleep properly later?"

"No, leave him for a while. He's earned this."

"I wonder what he's dreaming about."

In the realm of dreams, Eddie's and Buddy's minds brushed against each other, connected through Lucy's wand. Together, they dreamed.

In the dream, Buddy was still a bloodhound, like he had been before Dylan accidentally transformed him. He loped along, ears flapping, nose twitching, relishing the map of scents that was the world.

What a world it was. Somewhere in the distance, he smelled uncooked sausages. It was like the glorious day when he was still a puppy, when Charlie had brought home a long, old-fashioned string of links from the butcher, then left them out for a minute while he went to answer the door, not realizing that Buddy could reach the kitchen counter. That had led to the tastiest few minutes of Buddy's life and some of the most entertaining as Charlie had chased him around the house, trying to rescue what remained and stop Buddy covering everything with sausage meat.

His mouth watered at the memory.

"Buddy dog!" Eddie appeared beside Buddy. As often

happened in his dreams, Eddie was a robot, but Buddy recognized him. Eddie giggled as the dog licked the metal of his hand.

Buddy's head turned. He sniffed the breeze. He could still smell sausages, but something else as well, something suspicious. He growled and pointed his nose past the trees on which candy and dog treats grew toward a row of shops.

"We look," Eddie announced.

Together, they walked toward the buildings. The shops were all familiar ones. There was an organic butcher that Charlie sometimes took them to, except that it wasn't inside a market now but had a street-side place. There was the candy store, with a six-foot gummy bear waving from behind the counter, and a toy store with remote control helicopters and cars whizzing around outside, and all the most exciting video games playing on screens in the window.

Buddy's nose led him past all the shops and out the far side of town. There, a group of gnomes had gathered. Buddy quite liked gnomes, they were a good height for patting him on the head, but these were bad gnomes. He could tell because they smelled of tar and sulfur. With the gnomes were some robots. The smell of robots always reminded Buddy of Ashley and the machines she made, so this probably wasn't so bad.

"Bad robots!" Eddie exclaimed, recognizing their logo from one of his shows.

If Eddie said that the robots were bad, Buddy was willing to believe him. But what would they do about it?

Eddie pointed at a rock near where the robots and

gnomes were talking. The two of them crept behind it and sat to listen.

"That's settled, then," the lead gnome said. "We steal all the sausages and the candy. Then all the children and the dogs will have to do what we say, or they won't get any."

"Affirmative," the lead robot said in its electronic voice.

"Once we have all the sausages and the candy, we will jump up and down on the shops to crush them so that no one else can get sausages or candy."

"Affirmative."

Eddie and Buddy looked at each other. This was a desperate business. It was a good thing they were there to stop it.

Eddie was hungry. He needed a snack before he went to save the world. Fortunately, the corner of a cheese slice was sticking out of the ground behind their rock. He pulled it out, took off the plastic wrapper, and ate it.

Buddy pawed at the spot where Eddie had found his cheese. Something else smelled tasty down there. Together, they started digging, flinging the dirt aside until they revealed a dog bowl full of delicious chunks of meat, and beside it a plate of pasta in cheese sauce. It didn't seem odd to either of them that there was no dirt on the food they had dug up. After all, why would food have soil on it? Eddie extended a fork from his robot finger, and they started to eat.

A long shadow fell across them.

"May I join you?" asked a thin man dressed in black.

The man looked funny, and he smelled funny to Buddy, but there were lots of funny things in this place, like the rabbits with wings that were flying past at that moment. Funny wasn't a reason to reject someone.

"Okay," Eddie said. He stuck a hand into the hole to see what the man might like to eat and came up with a packet of potato chips. "You want?"

"Not to my tastes, thank you. I thought I might simply enjoy your company. Looking at your aura, I believe that I know your mother and brother."

Eddie shrugged. Everybody he met knew his mom. Most of them knew Dylan. It hardly seemed worth pointing out.

"What are you doing here?" the man asked. "I got a sense of great excitement as I approached, but all you're doing is eating."

"Cheese!" Eddie exclaimed, holding up a dripping forkful of pasta.

Buddy barked and licked his bowl clean.

"Ah, I see, the limited but powerful ambitions of the young and the simple. What a pitiful waste."

Eddie wasn't sure what that all meant, but the man said it in a friendly way, so he didn't object. Besides, he was nearly out of pasta, and that meant that it was time to go and stop the robbers.

Eddie and Buddy emerged from behind their rock, followed by the strange man. The gnomes and the bad robots were outside the shops now. They had water pistols, which they were pointing at the shop windows, and they were shouting. The butcher had emerged from behind his counter, and the giant gummy bear had stepped out through its doorway, both with their hands in the air.

"Please don't hurt me," the butcher said.

"I'm for children to eat," the gummy bear said, "not bad gnomes."

"Hahahahaha!" the lead gnome said. "No one can stop us!"

"Affirmative," said the lead robot.

"That's what you think," Eddie called.

He raised his metal hand into the air. Buddy, who had seen this on cartoons, lifted one of his paws and, despite the difference in height between them, reached as high as Eddie.

Eddie looked sternly at the strange man.

"Oh, am I part of this too?" the man asked. "That never normally happens."

He joined his hand with theirs, long, pale fingers outstretched.

"Best friends power!" Eddie said.

There was a flash of light around the three unlikely heroes. When it passed, Buddy wore a special suit of robot armor, with his head pointing from one end and his tail out the other. Eddie was still a robot, but a bigger one than before, taller than any of the villain robots. The strange man hadn't changed.

"I'm almost disappointed," he said. "But I think my role here is rather different from yours."

Eddie and Buddy ran into town. They charged straight at the robots and gnomes, who turned to face them, water pistols at the ready.

Buddy leapt onto the first gnome, knocking him over, then sprang off him and on to the next one. Eddie grabbed two robots, lifted them into the air, and flung them into the distance. The rest of their opponents jumped onto them, and soon the street was a whirl of tumbling bodies—gnomes and robots and a dog all grappling with each other. One minute, Eddie was being lifted into the air by his opponents. The next, he was the one in charge, swinging them around and flinging them away.

"They've got us!" the lead gnome shouted. "Run, boys!"

The gnomes dashed off while Buddy barked after them, wagging his tail from side to side in triumph.

"On no, I am defeated," the lead robot intoned as Eddie lifted him over his head, then dropkicked him out of town.

Quiet descended over the square. The butcher held out a string of sausages. "These are for you."

Buddy accepted the sausages with gratitude and more than a little dribble.

"And I'm for you," the giant gummy bear said to Eddie. "Can you eat this much candy?"

"Yes." Eddie nodded enthusiastically.

The strange man stepped up and stretched out a finger toward Eddie.

"Time for my reward," he said. "I wouldn't normally bother with such a young and undeveloped meal. It seems wasteful. But I think it might help draw your mother out, and that is worth sacrificing many other meals for."

Eddie didn't understand what the man was saying. He tipped his head to one side and stared up, confused, as the finger descended. Buddy, on the other hand, could tell that something was wrong. The man's smell had changed, become bitter and unpleasant, worse than the gnomes.

Buddy pushed Eddie back and stood between him and the strange man, growling.

"What is all of this?" the man said. "The best friend to the rescue? I hardly think that will help here, against me."

Buddy lunged. He caught the man's finger between his teeth and bit down hard.

"Ow!" The man staggered back, staring at his finger. It was bleeding pale, glowing blood. "That should not have happened." With his other hand, he ripped a hole in the air, stepped through it, and vanished.

"Good doggy." Eddie patted Buddy on his armored back.

"Are you ready now?" the gummy bear asked, holding out its jelly hand.

Eddie nodded and took a bite. What a day!

CHAPTER TWENTY-NINE

Lucy made sure to reach Silver Griffins HQ bright and early on Monday morning. The weekend had been fun, but she was intently aware that a serious threat was out there in the dreams of LA and that someone needed to deal with it.

She hopped off the train at the HQ subway station, her backpack over her shoulder and a steaming cup of tea in her hand. She walked up to the station keeper's office and tapped on the window.

"Hi, Normandy." She set down her cup and opened her backpack. "I have something for you."

She held out a paper bag. Slowly, the window lifted, and Normandy the gnome peered out at her.

"Agent Heron," he said flatly. His uniform was crumpled, and the buttons didn't have their usual shine.

"Long weekend?" Lucy asked.

"All weekends are the same length."

"You look like you didn't get much rest out of this one. Pushing yourself too hard at pottery class, maybe?"

"I didn't go. Didn't feel like it."

Lucy frowned. Was this tiredness from the hard-working gnome, or had Mr. No got to him? Even Normandy must need time to chill out occasionally, but…

"I brought you muffins." She handed over the paper bag.

"Oh." Normandy didn't even look inside.

That was it. Lucy didn't think her baking skills were especially extraordinary, but Normandy always showed gratitude and enthusiasm. Not today. Today, he had the dead-eyed stare she was seeing on too many people.

"I'm sorry for what's happened to you, lad." Lucy reached across the counter to squeeze his hand. "Don't worry. I'm going to fix this."

She strode away down the corridor, then up the stairs that led to the secret door into the Observatory. There weren't many people around yet, which made it easier to hurry through the building, past the planetarium, the pendulum, and the exhibits about the universe, to the Griffins' offices.

"ID, please." The receptionist pointed at the box on his desk.

Lucy was so relieved to see that he was his normal self that she didn't object to proving who she was. She tapped her wand to the box, waited until the light turned green, then walked on into the office.

The place was quiet, which Lucy initially put down to it being a Monday morning. By the time she'd finished one cup of tea, made another, and half-finished that, all while doing some research on the magical web, the place still looked only half-occupied. She was hugely relieved when

Jackie strode in, slung her bag under the desk, and flung herself down in her seat.

"Uh, this city," Jackie said. "You think the weekend's going to make up for everything else, then that lets you down too."

"Bad date?"

"Not even. But my favorite takeout place has shut down, out of the blue. There's a sign in the door, just says, 'I can't be bothered.' I admire the honesty, but where am I going to get pizza now?"

"From any of the dozens of other pizza places?"

"Well, sure, but this one was my favorite."

"It's worse than one pizza place. There's something far bigger going on."

Lucy explained what she had learned so far about Mr. No and the effect she had seen from his draining magic.

"Not Dylan!" Jackie's shock quickly turned to anger. "Don't worry, Lucy. We'll get this guy. No one touches your kids."

"Thanks. The problem is, how do we track him down? And how do we fight back?"

"Is there any pattern to who he's been targeting? Specific professions, maybe, or a geographical area?"

"Not that I've found so far, at least not beyond the fact that he's focused on LA. I had Ashley run a computer analysis on the victims I know about, and nothing stood out. Part of the problem is, I don't know who all the victims are. How can we track them down when the only symptom is that they stop caring about things?"

Jackie drummed her fingers against the desk and stared into space, lost in thought.

"We can't just ask around for those symptoms," she said. "Too many potential false positives: people who are depressed, ones with fatigue, struggling with grief, there are dozens of reasons why someone could dramatically lose their motivation."

"I wanted to do some sort of detection spell for the magic, but it's happening in dreams, so that won't work in the waking world, and I can't plan to be aware of this while I'm asleep. It's happened once, but that was luck, as far as I can tell."

The door to the regional manager's office opened, and Kelly appeared. Her makeup was immaculate, but her usually impeccable suit looked a little creased.

"Are you all right, Kelly?" Lucy asked warily.

"Of course I am. Why wouldn't I be?"

"Not feeling demotivated?" Jackie asked.

"No! Why, what have you heard?"

"It's just that you seem a little…"

"Distracted," Lucy said.

"You'd be distracted if you were doing this job," Kelly said. "I've been here practically all weekend, and I'm still not on top of everything that needs doing. How does this place not fall apart when someone like Applegate is trying to lead us?"

At least Kelly still cared. That came as a relief.

"Now there's another problem." Kelly scowled. "Jenkins' assistant just called. He said that there's something wrong with his boss."

"What sort of thing?" Lucy asked.

"I don't know, but I have this report to write, prison transfers to arrange, and I don't have time for—"

"We'll check on Jenkins." Lucy got out of her seat. "It's probably nothing important. You know how many minor accidents they cause in that lab."

"All right but let me know if it's more serious."

"Will do."

Lucy and Jackie strode off along the corridor, then down the stairs to Special Equipment and Weapons.

"It could be unrelated," Jackie said. "Like you said, they're always having accidents down there."

"Do you think Nigel would have called if it was one of those accidents?"

"No."

"Well then."

They passed through the blast doors at the entrance to the lab, stepped over a dozen tiny pig-like creatures caught in the traps, and around the corner to the firing range. Music was playing from the speaker system, but instead of the usual grinding guitars, it was a mix of bubblegum pop and light, edgeless R&B.

Nigel stood, staring in horror at the speakers.

"He couldn't be bothered picking the next album," he said, "so he let it switch over to the radio."

"Makes a nice change," Jackie said. "I don't feel like it's assaulting my ears."

"You don't understand." Nigel pointed an accusing finger at the speakers. "Listen to this. It's barely even music, and he let it play. This never happens!"

Lucy and Jackie walked through a door into SEW's complex of workshops and storage rooms. Toliver Jenkins was sitting in a folding chair in the middle of one of those rooms, a magazine in his lap and a bag of corn chips in one hand. He idly leafed through the magazine, occasionally stopping to pop a chip into his mouth. Around him, half-completed projects sat untouched.

"Hello, Jenkins," Lucy said. "What are you working on?"

Jenkins shrugged. "Not much."

"You must have something you could show us."

He waved a corn chip at the room around him. "Take a look if you want. There's nothing very interesting."

This looked bad, but Lucy had to be sure. She walked to the side of the room and assessed what lay on a workbench, then picked up the most exciting device she could see. It seemed to be a cross between a tablet and a multi-tool, with dozens of different tools and sensors sticking out around the sides of a screen.

"What about this one?" she asked.

Jenkins looked up, shrugged, looked back at his magazine.

"Take it if you want," he said. "I can't be bothered making it work."

Lucy put the device back down. This was like she had seen in others. Not identical since Dylan had given up on reading entirely, but near enough to fit the pattern.

She walked back into the testing range, and Jackie followed.

"I think something attacked his mind," Lucy told Nigel, who stared at her in alarm. "The good news is, it doesn't seem to get any worse than this. The bad news is, we don't know how to make it better."

"But, but, but..." Nigel looked utterly lost. "What will I do? My whole job is working on inventions with him."

"Could you make some inventions of your own?" Jackie asked.

"Is that allowed?"

"You tell us."

Nigel ran his hands over his face and wailed. "I don't know!"

"There, there." Jackie patted him on the shoulder. "How about you do some science for us?"

Nigel nodded eagerly, a lost soul thrown a lifeline in the familiar form of someone telling him what to do. "Yes, what can I do?"

"Observe Jenkins. Record what he does. Let us know if anything changes or if you notice any unexpected patterns."

"Yes, yes, of course." Nigel smiled a watery smile. "Some good, old-fashioned science." He scurried toward the workshop door, then stopped and turned to point at the speakers. "What about this?"

"Today, you pick the music, Nigel, Lucy said. "Your boss won't mind."

"We'll all be glad of the change," Jackie muttered.

The two witches headed for the exit.

"Do you think he was targeted?" Lucy asked.

"Could be," Jackie said. "If anyone was going to invent a weapon against your Mr. No, it's Jenkins."

"So, Mr. No is making moves to protect himself. That'll make him harder to take down."

"True, but it might mean he's nervous. If you're one of the few people to get away from him, maybe you have a way to fight back."

"I hope so. I wish I knew what it was."

Loud guitars blared from behind them, joined a moment later by a growly sort of singing.

"So much for a change," Jackie said. "For a moment there, I thought this thing might have a silver lining. Turns out I was wrong."

CHAPTER THIRTY

Mr. No stalked through the dreamscape of LA. There were fewer points in the darkness now than at night. The place was lit mostly by workers who had been on night shifts, plus a few people who were sick and needed extra sleep. Only the most dedicated of party animals would have been up all through Sunday night, and there weren't many of those, with their feverish dreams of excess and their bodies sunk into a deep slumber.

He had hunted fiercely all through the past two nights, but he still wasn't satisfied. He had eaten enough to sustain him, and more besides, but that couldn't deal with this craving because it wasn't only about sustenance. He needed something more.

Mr. No was self-aware enough to admit that the problem came from the Heron boy and his dog. The way the dog had fought back, its success in hurting him, had caught him by surprise. More than surprise, it was a deep and abiding shock. He hadn't been hurt like this since that dwarf back on Oriceran, the one who had set the trap. At least then, Mr. No had been able to finish the business, to strike a deal, free himself, and get something in return for his pain and loss. He had felt some satisfaction. This time, someone had simply beat him, and that unfamiliar feeling disturbed him. It was an itch he needed to scratch, and he didn't know how.

So he had hunted. He had stalked. He had leapt upon any dream he found that looked like it might have some connection to the Heron woman. Some had undoubtedly been misses, random humans dreaming about witchcraft. Others were closer, like that strange wizard with the laboratory. It all still felt futile, like grasping at thin air. It didn't help.

Then he peered into a dream and saw a familiar face. The Silver Griffin who had escaped him thanks to the Wilderghast. Another one who had gotten away.

Mr. No grinned although no one would see it. This was one way he could make the world right. This would scratch the itch.

He pulled the dream open and stepped in.

Ellis hadn't meant to fall asleep in the middle of the morning, but it had been a long weekend. After catching the Wilderghast, he'd had to deal with the admin around its containment and transfer to Trevilsom. Then another fugitive had been spotted in LA, meaning an unexpected chase through Saturday night. With Sarah working odd shifts, his best chance to see her had been a meal in a diner well past midnight on Sunday, then a walk in a moonlit park before she went back to work. It had all been worth it for that part, but now his body and brain were all worn out. Sleep had caught up with him.

Of course, he wasn't aware of any of that as he walked down the corridors of his old high school, spinning a set of keys that would have suited a jailer in a medieval prison, huge chunky things made of cold old iron. Through the little windows in the doors of classrooms, people he had known stared at him, from classroom bullies to ignorant teachers to neighbors who had hassled his grandma. All of them were firmly locked away, and Ellis had no intention of letting them out.

"Please," his old science teacher cried from his lab. "I didn't mean to hold you in detention unfairly."

"I ain't holding you unfairly now," Ellis said. "This here is justice."

He whistled and walked down the corridor, which changed into something darker, a stone tunnel with doors of solid oak and iron bars. Monsters stared out at him, creatures he had locked away. They tried to grab him but couldn't reach him. One almost managed to capture the keys, but he rapped it over the knuckles with the hefty keyring, and it drew that clawed hand back, hissing and spitting.

"If you didn't want this, you shouldn't have attacked innocent folks," Ellis said.

The corridor changed again. Now it was white-walled with guidance lines on the floor, signs to wards on the walls, and doors large enough to get a wheeled bed through. Doctors, nurses, and porters rushed back and forth.

At the end of the corridor was a door to an operating room. Ellis peered through the glass section of the door and saw Sarah at work with her colleagues around an operating table. Their patient was a giant version of the Operation game, and every time they tried to cut him open, his nose lit red, and a buzzer went off.

Sarah smiled and waved at Ellis.

"Sorry I wasn't there for our date," she said. "I can't leave until we finish this."

"It's okay." Ellis held up his keyring, which had turned into a plastic swipe card like folks used to unlock doors in offices and hotels. "I have the key."

He was about to open the door when a shadow fell across him.

"Is that really how you see her, trapped in her job, waiting to be rescued by you?"

Ellis looked up at the tall, slim man with a pale face and bald head. His teeth were sharp and his eyes bright. Ellis knew that he should have been frightened, that there was something nightmarish about the man, but the feeling didn't come.

"I know that ain't how she sees the job," Ellis said. "She done told me a dozen times how much she loves it, how much it means to her. So no, I don't see her as someone who needs rescuing, and I ain't arrogant enough to think that I'd be the one to set her free." He looked down at the key card, then back up at the menacing figure. "I guess this is about what I want, and what I can't have, and about overcoming that. It's about me." He frowned. "Now what kind of damn fool thing is that to say about a hospital door?"

"It's the sort of thing that shows you're smart and self-aware." A pointed tongue flickered across frost white lips. "Qualities that add piquancy to a meal. Maybe my day isn't entirely wasted."

Ellis frowned. He wanted to get away from this guy, who was ringing all kinds of alarm bells in his brain, but he didn't want to move away from the door and put more distance between himself and Sarah. Two different logics battled for supremacy in his brain.

"I know you, don't I?" he said. "I've seen you before, but where?"

An odd, angular edge of memory was in the corner of his consciousness, something involving a hallway and monsters, and Sarah again. Except that he'd never been in a hallway like that, so how could he have a memory of it? Why had this guy been there? Why was he here now?

A pale finger reached out toward Ellis, who stood frozen. He knew that he shouldn't let this guy touch him, but he couldn't back away. Those cold, menacing eyes held him hypnotized, unable to escape as his breath frosted and the world darkened around him.

"Oh, yes," the man said. "This is much more like it."

From the corner of his eye, Ellis saw Sarah in the operating theater, still working on her patient. She couldn't leave, and he wasn't going anywhere without her, especially not with this guy so close.

Despite everything, the sight of her face made his heart beat a little faster. She tucked a few strands of red hair back from her face, and he smiled. He couldn't wait to be close to her again, to talk, to laugh, to make each other happy.

The cold finger reached out, touched Ellis on the forehead. Ice crept into him, but the warm feeling that came from seeing Sarah held it back for a moment.

Ellis pressed the key card to the lock. The door swung open. He stepped away from the tall man through the door and woke up with a smile.

The dream evaporated around Mr. No, leaving him alone and frustrated in the darkness. How was this happening to him? How had that blasted wizard gotten away again?

It didn't matter. No one could escape him forever. Even that dwarf had paid the price after he had trapped Mr. No.

The dwarf. He had understood how to cross the gap between reality and dreams, how to use magic from the outside to contain Mr. No. If he could do that, then surely he could understand what was happening to Mr. No now. The dwarf would have a way for him to beat these wretched witches and wizards and children and dogs.

Yes, he should find the dwarf again. It was long past time for a meeting between them, not so much a reunion between old friends as a new deal between old acquaintances. If there was anyone Mr. No could find, given time and patience, it was the dwarf. After all, Mr. No already had a part of him.

CHAPTER THIRTY-ONE

Lucy sat at her desk with a cup of tea in one hand and a cookie in the other, deliberately not looking at her computer screen. In her experience, sometimes the best thing you could do for a problem was to set it aside for a while, not do anything, and let the conscious brain spin its wheels while the subconscious got to work.

Was that what happened at night when the brain drifted into dreams? Did that explain why a dream creature like Mr. No could steal people's motivations—because he could touch on the subconscious and disrupt the work happening there? Or were the two unrelated, and he happened to be a dream walker who fed on ambition? That was the sort of thought that wouldn't have occurred to her while she was staring at the digital case file, trying to force the facts into an orderly shape. It might be a useful thought, it might not, but there was no way of knowing until she'd had it. That was why these pauses were so important.

She sipped her tea. Tea was important too.

The door to the regional manager's office—did it still count as Applegate's office, or should she think of it as Kelly's for now?—burst open and Jackie stormed out, slamming the door shut behind her. She flung herself down in her seat, muttering under her breath, and hammered the keys for her password so hard that Lucy was half-afraid she would break the keyboard.

"Is everything all right?" Lucy asked.

"Oh, it's all freaking brilliant," Jackie said. "I really needed some extra paperwork right now. That's going to make me far better at my job."

"Kelly getting to you a bit?"

"A bit?" Jackie pushed her keyboard aside and leaned over to glare across the desks. "A bit? She's a colossal pain in my ass. Apparently, I'm not investigating my cases properly because I haven't filed form who-gives-a-shit, and when I gave her majesty a progress report, she told me I needed to get out in the field more. Make up your mind. Either you want me filling in forms, or you want me out there!"

"Sounds tricky."

"Oh, and you know how I've been showing that tunnel teen around the place?"

"Twylan?"

"Yeah, of course, those kids are friends of yours, right? Well, anyway, Kelly's shown zero interest in helping out, but now she's telling me I have to run all my planned activities for Twylan past her. When I said that I wasn't really planning, just showing Twylan what seemed relevant each time she showed up, Kelly said that wasn't good enough and spouted off about planning an enriching curriculum and showing the best side of the Silver Griffins to the world. Because heaven forbid that we should give the kid a fun time and make her want to come work here." Kelly flung herself back in her seat. "Seriously, whose dumbass idea was it to put the controlling queen of everybody else's business in charge of this place?"

"Would you rather it was you in charge?"

Jackie scowled. "I just want someone who will do it right."

"You mean, do it your way?"

"I get your point, but Applegate didn't do things my way, and he still kept the place running smoothly. There has to be someone sensible who could be in charge instead of her." Jackie's eyes lit up. "How about you? You have the training and experience, and you're a reasonable human being, despite being British."

"Thanks, I think, but I'm not going to launch a coup."

"Not a coup, just a—"

"Lucy?" Sam had appeared beside their desks and was carefully not paying attention to Jackie or what she said. "Kelly would like to see you."

Lucy glanced between the PA and Jackie, who was still boiling over with frustration.

"Can it wait a few minutes?" she asked. "We're in the middle of something here."

"Sorry, but she said right away."

"Of course she did." Lucy sighed and got out of her seat. "Why don't you go for a walk, Jackie? Blow off some steam. We can talk again when you get back."

Lucy walked over to the manager's office and knocked tentatively on the door.

"Come in!" Kelly shouted.

Lucy fixed a smile on her lips, walked in, and closed the door carefully behind her. Then she went to stand in front of Kelly's desk, one hand on the back of a chair, putting on her best show of interest and attention.

"You wanted to see me, Kelly?" she said.

Kelly nodded but didn't offer her a seat.

"How's Jenkins?" the temporary manager asked.

"Okay, last time I checked," Lucy said. "The infirmary said that there was no point holding him since there was nothing life-threatening, so he was only taking up a bed. They've sent him home like they did with Applegate."

"You haven't arranged for reports from his home?"

"That didn't seem necessary. Nothing's likely to change."

"Just because something is unlikely doesn't mean it won't happen. We need to keep a tight watch on this."

"Surely what we need is to catch the culprit and find a solution? That's what I'm working on."

"Keeping a watch on senior Griffins who have been affected will be part of that. Get on it."

Lucy took a deep breath and forced herself to stay calm. It was hard to take this sort of thing from Kelly, with her snappy tone and the lack of basic manners like saying "please" and "thank you," never mind listening to and trusting in Lucy's expertise. But Kelly was in charge now, and she had to respect that.

"I'll arrange for someone to check in regularly on both Jenkins and Applegate. Was there anything else?"

"How is your investigation proceeding?"

"I've been researching Mr. No, talking to informed

sources, and looking for reports in the historical records. So far, I haven't learned much more than what the dwarf told me."

"What about the victims? Any pattern there?"

"Again, I've looked at it, but the only pattern I can see is the recent increase in attacks against Silver Griffins. That tells us that Mr. No has concerns about being caught and is preemptively trying to stop us, but it's not very helpful in catching or countering him."

"So, you've made no progress?"

"I wouldn't say that."

"It sounds like what you're saying, and given what I've seen today, I'm not surprised."

"What you've seen today?"

"You were sitting around drinking tea and doing nothing, then gossiping with Agent Kowal. That's not what the Silver Griffins pay you to do."

"Actually, I was thinking about—"

"I don't want to hear excuses, Heron. I want to see you working."

Oh, so she was "Heron" now? Kelly was getting into this whole position of power a little too much, and Lucy felt a need to knock her down a peg or two.

"Might I remind you, *Kelly*, that we are still the same rank around here, and I'm the lead officer on this investigation? If I spend all day playing cricket or listening to Beatles records, that's my business, as long as I get results."

Kelly's fingers clenched together, knuckles whitening, and she glared up at Lucy. The muscles in the sides of her neck stood out, and there was a scary intensity to her stare. Lucy had never seen her so tense.

"Results are exactly what I'm concerned with," Kelly said. "We might be the same rank, technically, but until Applegate comes back, the buck stops with me. If we mess up an investigation, or mismanage our budget, or fail to file the paperwork, then I'm ultimately responsible for that. It will go on my record. Others will see it as my fault. I'm not going to let any of you sabotage me."

Lucy forced herself to hold back an angry response about what a manager's priorities should be. This was the first time Kelly had been in this position, and she was feeling the pressure. Adding to that wouldn't help. Better to hold back, give her support within reason, and hope that Applegate came back soon.

Kelly drew a deep breath, leaned back, and rubbed her eyes.

"That came out wrong," she said. "Of course, this isn't only about me. But if we mess up, that has serious consequences for LA and the whole magical world. It's my job to make sure those mistakes don't happen. That means it's my job to make sure that you're doing your job right."

It was a relief to hear that Kelly had some perspective on the situation, even if she still saw everything through the filter of how it affected her.

"I'll let you know if I make any significant progress on the case," Lucy said. "Could you maybe leave me to get on with it until then?"

"As long as you report in, I won't need to chase you for reports."

That was a long-winded way of saying no, but Lucy didn't think she would get anything better.

"Is that everything?" she asked.

"For now," Kelly said. "You can get back to work. Remember, more investigating, fewer tea breaks."

"Of course." Lucy would have to take her tea and thinking time away from the office, where Kelly wouldn't notice what was going on.

For now, though, she should find out where Jackie had gotten to and make sure that no junior Griffins were feeling the force of her wrath. Maybe they could go for a run and blow off steam that way. Kelly wouldn't approve of such activities during work hours, but if it made them more productive, wasn't it for the best? What Kelly didn't know couldn't hurt her as long as they did their paperwork.

CHAPTER THIRTY-TWO

To her surprise, Lucy found Jackie in the Griffins' pigeon loft. It wasn't really a loft, but a large, wood-walled room full of nooks in which the pigeons could make their nests, underground like the rest of the base. There were tubes to provide bird food and water and larger passages through which the pigeons could return home after carrying messages. A gnome with a hose and a stiff broom was busy cleaning the floor, which got very messy due to the constant presence of birds and everything they did.

Jackie was in a corner with Twylan, coaxing pigeons into cages with the offer of worms.

"Hi, guys," Lucy said. "What are you up to?"

"Going to take some pigeons out on a field trip," Jackie said. "To teach Twylan how our communication system works."

Lucy had expected to find Jackie still frowning and furious, but instead, she was grinning. It wasn't a relaxing smile, and Lucy couldn't help suspecting that some sort of mischief was going on.

"Did Kelly approve this part of your curriculum?" she asked. There was no point beating around the bush. If mentioning Kelly got Jackie mad, that would only show that she'd been angry underneath already.

"Oh, yes," Jackie said. "She said she wanted me to run my plans past her, so I emailed them before we came here."

"Do you think she'll have had time to see that?"

Jackie shrugged. "If she has everyone so wound up that her inbox is three hundred emails deep, all from people covering their asses, that's hardly my fault. She said to give her a look at my plans, and I've done that. As far as I'm concerned, I'm doing exactly as told."

Lucy wasn't going to argue. She'd come to calm Jackie down, not aggravate her, and if a small act of dissent through being technically correct did the job, she wouldn't get in the way.

"Guess I'll leave you to it then." She headed off.

Twylan watched Lucy go, then turned her attention back to Jackie and the cages.

"Um..." She wasn't sure what to ask or how. Something was wrong.

"Don't worry, kid." Jackie closed the door on the last cage. "It's nothing you need to worry about. Now, do you want to travel by portal?"

"Won't the subway do?"

"Oh, it would do, but a portal is quicker and more fun. Besides, I put it in my lesson plan." Jackie grinned that triumphant grin that had been making Twylan nervous. She picked up her backpack and checked that the cage doors were properly closed.

"Okay..."

They made their way down the corridor to the transport department, each carrying two cages full of cooing pigeons. The wizard on duty looked up from his computer with a raised eyebrow when they came in.

"I got your message," he said. "Are you sure you need a portal to a tunnel under another part of LA?"

"It's part of the plan to show this potential recruit how the Silver Griffins work," Jackie said. "Our manager was very clear that I should both have and stick to a plan."

"Okay then." The wizard rechecked his screen. "We have no planned arrivals or departures for the next half-hour so I might as well send you now."

He scribbled some numbers down on a sticky note, then went to the blank wall at the end of the room, raised his wand, and started the spell.

Jackie turned her attention to Twylan. "A lot of the staff down here are experts in portal magic. They're great at getting a portal open at the exact spot where it's needed and less likely to accidentally open it in front of mundanes than if I did the spell."

"The flattery is appreciated," the wizard said as he completed a circle with his wand, "but it won't make this happen any faster."

It didn't need to go faster. A moment later, there was a golden glow, and the portal appeared, a void interrupting the wall's brickwork.

"Thanks," Jackie said. "We'll make our own way home."

She and Twylan stepped through the portal and appeared in another underground space, outside the schoolroom of the Underfoot Brigade. The portal closed behind them.

In their cages, the pigeons cooed and looked around. They were better able to sense where they were than ordinary pigeons, even common messenger pigeons, thanks to their training by the Griffins. They looked and listened, detected the electromagnetic pull of the poles, and sensed the surrounding flows of magic. Within minutes, they would have worked out their best route home.

Twylan and Jackie stood in the classroom doorway, watching a lesson approach its end. The Underfoot Brigade students had been doing art, and mismatched pieces of chalk and charcoal, pens and pencils, pots and tubes of different sorts of paint littered their desks. As with so much about their way of living and thus their education, they relied on whatever they could get their hands on. There was a sense of excitement as they added the finishing touches to their work.

Their teacher walked down the classroom to meet the new arrivals.

"What's all this, Twylan?" she asked.

"We brought something we thought the class might like to learn about, Ms. Fields," Twylan said. "Agent Kowal can explain."

Heather shifted her attention. "You're Lucy Heron's friend, right?" She held out her hand.

"That's right, Jackie Kowal." Jackie set one of the cages down so she could shake hands. "You're Heather, the Tolderai chief?"

"That's right. So, what do you want to interrupt my lessons with?"

Jackie held up one of the cages. "These are magical messenger pigeons, as used by the Silver Griffins. I'm teaching Twylan about them, and I thought her friends might like to have a go too."

"All right, that sounds good. I can postpone math so they can do this."

While Heather set the kids to tidying away art supplies, Jackie and Twylan took the cages to the front of the class. Excited conversation rippled through the room as the Underfoots realized that something unusual was going on.

"You join the class, Twylan," Jackie said. "Ms. Fields can help me with this."

Once the classroom was in order and quiet restored, Jackie held up a bundle of small slips of paper that had been in her bag.

"Today, you're going to pass each other notes," she said. "And you're going to do it by magical pigeon. First, I'll show you how it works." She put a piece of paper down in front of Kix the gnome. "Write something on that, but keep it clean. It's going to your teacher."

While Kix was writing, Jackie took a pigeon out of one of the cages.

"We magically train creatures," she explained. "They'll go to whoever or wherever you send them, but you have to be careful. They don't only go by what you say to them or how you address the paper. They also get a sense of what you're thinking. That's the only way they can understand the directions."

She took the piece of paper from Kix, wrapped it around the pigeon's leg, and tied it in place with a thread attached to the note. Then she raised the pigeon so that it was near her mouth.

"Take this message to Ms. Fields," she said in a loud stage whisper.

She let go of the pigeon, which immediately took flight. It circled her head uncertainly for a moment, then fluttered over to Twylan's desk and perched in front of her.

"So, who was I thinking about when I said Ms. Fields?"

The class laughed and all called Twylan's name. The pigeon, still looking confused, hopped one desk closer to the teacher. Jackie whistled, and the bird flew back to her.

"Let me try that again." This time, she looked at Heather as she gave her instructions to the pigeon. "Take this message to Ms. Fields."

Released, the pigeon darted across the room and landed on Heather's shoulder.

"Much clearer this time because I was focused. Now, if you could read the message…"

Heather unfastened the paper from the pigeon's leg and silently read it.

"Thank you, Kix." She blushed slightly. "That was kind of you to say."

"You are the best teacher!" Kix declared. "Or was I not supposed to say what was in there?"

The question went unanswered, as at that moment the paper collapsed into a handful of wriggling worms. The pigeon hopped down onto Heather's wrist and started gobbling them up while the Underfoots laughed, pointed, and made grossed-out noises.

"Now it's your turn," Jackie said. "Get into pairs so you can send messages to each other. I'll give each pair a pigeon and some enchanted paper, and you can give it a go."

Soon, the classroom was full of fluttering wings, enthusiastic chatter, and more than a few misdirected messages. The pigeons, who never usually got to take this many notes in an hour, got as excited as the teenagers, thanks to the plentiful supply of worms.

"This is brilliant," Kix said to Twylan. "Do you get to do this all the time in the Silver Griffins?"

"Not this, but I see lots of cool things," Twylan said. "I'm not a Silver Griffin yet."

"You will be one day, right?"

"I hope so." Twylan tied her message onto a pigeon, whispered directions in its ear, and set it to fly with unerring accuracy to Leontine.

At the front of the room, Jackie and Heather leaned against the teacher's desk, watching the teenagers at work.

"Good lesson," Heather said. "You're a natural with the kids."

Jackie made a face. "I can just about manage with older ones like this, but I'm not a kid person. I got lucky this time."

"Twylan doesn't count?"

"She's practically a grownup already."

"You're not the broody type, then?"

Jackie shook her head. "I'd rather not have anyone fight their way out of me. And you?"

"It's part of the cycle of nature, so one day, maybe. For now, dealing with this lot is enough."

There were cries of alarm as two misdirected pigeons tried to get out the door and two magical teens chased after them.

"Make that more than enough," Heather said.

CHAPTER THIRTY-THREE

"I'm home!" Lucy walked in through the front door and got as far as putting her bag down before Charlie dashed out of the kitchen, laptop in hand.

"Great," he said as he kissed her on the cheek. "I have to go into the office. Gail called. There's a server issue."

"But I only just—"

"Eddie's in the living room, Ashley's down in the tunnels, Dylan's out with his friends. I'll see you later."

He was gone.

Lucy sighed. "Nice to see you too, sweetheart."

She knew that she shouldn't complain. There had been days when she was the one rushing in or out, disrupting everyone else's schedule, not to mention the time that a swarm of tiny black bugs had attacked the house because of her. It still would have been nice to get more than such a passing conversation.

She went into the living room. Eddie had cartoons on but was more occupied in carrying out a battle between two plastic dinosaurs.

"My valley!" he cried out as the T-rex descended on the triceratops. "No, my valley!"

There was a clatter of plastic teeth against artificial skin as the monsters battled for supremacy. It was a deadly confrontation, as the combatants took it in turns to roll onto their backs, feet in the air, while their puppet master made horrible gurgling noises to signal their demise.

Buddy wandered in and sniffed Lucy's ankles.

"Hey, lad." She knelt and patted his head. "Are you here for some love and attention, or have you run out of dog biscuits?"

Eddie looked up. "Cookies?"

Lucy laughed. "Well, that certainly got your attention. Yes, we can have cookies if you help me make them."

Eddie got up off the floor and followed her into the kitchen, carrying his dinosaurs with him.

"Cheese cookies?" he asked.

"Sure, I have a recipe for that." Lucy went to the cereal cupboard and got out a box of Rice Krispies. "I know it might seem unlikely, but this is the start of the recipe. First though, hands."

Eddie pushed a step-stool across the kitchen, making a racket as it scraped along the floor. Lucy looked down with concern at the flooring, which like the rest of the kitchen was still very new, but Eddie's furniture removal didn't seem to be damaging anything except her eardrums. He reached the sink, climbed up on the step, and turned the faucet too far, spraying himself with water.

"Let me help with the tap there." Lucy turned the water down and handed Eddie the soap.

Once they'd both washed and dried their hands, she

put an apron on Eddie and donned one of her own. Then she set his step in front of a low folding table that the kids had been cooking on since Dylan was a couple of years old.

"Here." She put a grater, a plate, and a block of cheddar on the table. "Can you do some grating?"

Eddie nodded enthusiastically and set to work. Lucy kept an eye on him in case his fingers got too close to the grater while she fetched ingredients from the cupboards and set the oven to preheat. By then, Eddie had grated most of the cheese they needed.

"Let me finish that." Lucy grated the last little bit into the heap.

The air shimmered around Eddie, and he turned into a mouse, perched on the edge of the table with his whiskers twitching. Lucy laughed.

"You're right. This is a dream biscuit for a mouse. What would Eddie's dream biscuits look like?"

The mouse tipped its head thoughtfully to one side for a moment. Then the air around it shimmered, and the small boy in the apron reappeared.

"Dinosaur," he announced.

"Biscuits shaped like a dinosaur, or biscuits made out of dinosaurs?"

One of those options hadn't occurred to Eddie, and it took him some serious consideration to pick between them.

"Dinosaur shapes," he said at last.

"Interesting." Lucy weighed some flour into a bowl, then put it in front of Eddie and added the cheese. Well-versed in the ways of baking, he immediately started mixing the ingredients. "What would these dinosaur biscuits taste like?"

"Chocolate. And peanut butter and jelly. And marshmallow. And cheese. And pasta."

"Interesting combination." Lucy added ground red pepper to the bowl and chopped a couple of sticks of butter before dropping them in. "All of those tastes mixed, or layers, or maybe different dinosaurs for different flavors?"

Eddie enthusiastically squashed the blobs of butter in with the other ingredients, relishing the slippery feeling on his fingers. Baking was fun in so many ways, from spending time with his mom to tasting what he'd made at the end that he sometimes forgot the sheer joy of squishing butter. It nearly distracted him from the serious question that still needed addressing.

"Different bits of different flavors." He held up a handful of half-made cookie dough and pointed at one end. "Chocolate." He indicated the other end. "Cheese." He gestured at the middle. "Peanut butter and jelly."

"That's quite a biscuit."

"Cookie."

"Sorry, yes, quite a cookie." She added two cups of Rice Krispies to the bowl. "Last thing to mix in."

While Eddie stirred the Krispies into the sticky dough, Lucy cut a piece of baking parchment and laid it out on a baking sheet.

"How about cake? If you could make any cake in the world, what would it be like?"

"Big!" Eddie made an expansive gesture with his little

arms, and in the process spattered Krispie-filled dough across the floor.

Lucy laughed. "Well, that's no surprise. Can you tell me more about it?"

"Chocolate and peanut butter and icing."

"What sort of icing?"

"Toffee." He licked his lips. "Red toffee icing."

"This sounds more realistic than I expected."

"Tall as our house and filled with M&Ms."

"That's more like it." Lucy placed the baking tray next to Eddie's bowl. "Now, we want to make pieces about this big." She formed a one-inch ball of dough in her hands. "Can you do that?"

"Yes." Eddie started making balls, all of them a little irregular, some much bigger and others much smaller, but all more than good enough for a fun baking day. At least they would all fit on the sheet. As Eddie set them down, Lucy flattened them with a wet fork, occasionally moving one to make room for them to spread as they baked. Once they'd portioned out the whole batch of ingredients, she put them in the oven.

"Hands again please, Eddie."

Again, there was some overenthusiastic splashing, this time accompanied by blowing soap bubbles around.

"We know what your dream cake tastes like," Lucy said as she helped Eddie dry his hands, "but what shape would it be?"

Yet again, he tipped his head to one side with a thoughtful look. With his apron half-undone and his hair tousled, he looked particularly adorable. "Bear," he said at last.

The air around him shimmered, and a moment later a bear cub stood in the middle of the kitchen, an apron hanging around its neck. The bear tried to roar, but it didn't quite have the voice to sound scary, especially not with one paw caught in the apron strings.

"Oh my!" Lucy put her hands to her cheeks. "What a ferocious beast!"

"Roar!" The bear cub stumbled forward and wrapped its forelegs around her leg in a furry hug.

"Aw, I love you too." Lucy leaned over to cuddle him. "You know what my ideal cake would be? Layers of chocolate and lemon, with a really rich, gooey filling and sparkling butter icing, shaped like you, to celebrate my amazing baking buddy."

The bear turned back into a little boy.

"Not eat me!" he said, looking shocked.

Lucy laughed. "All right, maybe not shaped like you. It could be your name instead. How does that sound?"

He nodded, then sniffed the air. "Smells like cheese."

"It certainly does." A delicious, savory aroma was drifting from the oven. "In a few minutes, it'll taste like cheese too. Until then, do you want to watch cartoons and come up with more ideas for cakes we'll never make?"

"Yes!" Eddie took her hand and led her to the living room.

CHAPTER THIRTY-FOUR

Gruffbar strode across the factory floor, machines roaring all around him. This was the kind of client he liked, one who made things, who contributed something to the world, and most importantly one who worked with mechanisms and machines. They might not be Gruffbar's all-consuming passion as they had once been, but devices still fascinated him, and being around them made him happy.

He stopped, curious to have a closer look at one of the machines. Huge gear wheels spun, and pistons rocketed back and forth. A dial slowly clicked down while lights flashed on an electronic display above his head.

Intriguing. He puffed on the fine cigar the client had given him and scrutinized the display. When that didn't tell him anything, he looked at the machinery again, trying to work out what any of it did.

Never mind the machine, what did this client do again? The thought was there, on the very edge of consciousness, but he couldn't quite grasp it. He puffed on the cigar some more. It was very good. He drew a deep breath, relishing the sweet smoke and beneath it the tang of engine oil.

Someone was approaching. He couldn't hear their footsteps so much as he could sense their presence, looming across the factory toward him like a shadow in the recesses of his mind. Goose pimples dotted his arms, and the hairs of his beard stood on end.

That uncomfortable sensation finally cut through the haze and made him realize where he was. This wasn't a real factory. There wasn't an actual client. Good as it was, even the cigar wasn't real. He was dreaming.

"Dammit." He turned to see who else his subconscious had added to the mix. When he recognized the tall, black-clad figure, the cigar almost fell from between his fingers.

"You," Gruffbar hissed.

"Me," Mr. No replied.

"Am I dreaming you, or are you really here?"

"Real is a difficult word in this land where I roam. For the purposes of what you mean, yes, you could consider me to be real."

"Great." Gruffbar flung the cigar down and ground it out underfoot. He didn't need distractions now. If he somehow made it through this in one piece, he could always dream up a new cigar, and if not, he wouldn't care. "Have you come to take what's left?"

Mr. No pressed a thin finger to his lips and stared at Gruffbar.

"I suppose I could," he said. "Even your leftovers would be a delicious treat compared with some of my recent meals. A creature of such driving and forceful ambition that you have created a whole second life for yourself after giving up your first love to me. Many creatures would find that admirable. I certainly find it curious."

"I still have tricks. Ways I could fight back. Remember last time."

"I do remember last time, and that's why I know you have nothing now. Then you were prepared, you built a trap for me, you laid your ambush out of sight, beyond the realm of sleep. This time, I am the one who has caught you unprepared. No time to make machines, write runes, steel yourself for battle. I have you exposed."

Gruffbar slumped. He had dreaded this moment from the minute he had seen that Mr. No was back. He wasn't the dwarf he had once been. The drive and passion taken from him meant that he would be hard-pressed to make the devices he had made then, to defend himself or other people. He relied on someone else to sort out this mess, and others could never be relied upon. Without their work, he could only bluff, and while that might work in a court-room, it was no use when your opponent could look inside your head and see the truth.

"I'm a lawyer now, not an engineer," he said. "I suppose after this I'll have to become something else." He folded his arms and stared defiantly at Mr. No. "I won't beg, so you'd better get it over and done with."

Mr. No shook his head.

"You mistake me, Gruffbar. I haven't come to get vengeance on you. That would do nothing to slake my hunger. No, I am here to seek your help."

Gruffbar stared at him, stunned. Around them, the dream machines pounded with greater intensity, pistons flying back and forth, gearwheels racing, motors roaring.

"You want a lawyer?" he asked, dumbfounded. "How can you get into legal trouble when you don't even enter the mortal world?"

Mr. No laughed. It was a hollow, horrible sound.

"Oh no, Gruffbar Steelstrike. I want help from the old you. I want the engineer."

Gruffbar leaned back against the machine, seeking something solid and reassuring in a world spinning around. How often had his dreams been like this in the first days after his confrontation with Mr. No? He hadn't longed for his old passion to return, for the driving desire to make machines to seize hold of him again. Of course not. That was the point of what Mr. No had taken. Still, he'd felt the emptiness somewhere inside, and when he'd considered his life prospects—when he understood how remarkable an engineer he'd been—he had wondered what life would be like if he could follow that path. However, a lack of desire was self-fulfilling. He couldn't want what he didn't want.

Now, a fraction of yearning returned, fed to him by Mr. No. It was the hook on the line of a sinister fisherman, and like a fish, Gruffbar felt it reeling him in.

"Why would you want that?" he asked. It was a lawyer's question, not an engineer's, driving at motive and intention rather than questioning the practicalities of how to do a thing.

"I have encountered some difficulties," Mr. No said. "A handful of witches and wizards who can resist me in their dreams. Somehow, they're breaching that line between the realms of the conscious and the subconscious, the world of clear intention and that of chaos. If I want to defeat them, I need a way to cross that barrier, and you're the only person I know who has intentionally done it, who has created weapons to cross the divide. You made them to use against me before. Now, you will make them to help me."

Gruffbar snorted. "You're wasting your time. I can't do that anymore. You took the will for it from me, remember?"

"I did not take, you offered."

"It doesn't matter. You have that part of me. I can't do what you want."

"That is the beauty of this new deal I am offering you, Gruffbar Steelstrike. You will need your reward to do what I want. It is a bargain of perfect symmetry."

Gruffbar thought he could see where this was going, but he was too good a lawyer to let it stay as implication, to leave a soft space the other party could wriggle through when they decided they didn't like the deal.

"Explain," he said.

"Don't tell me you're so foolish as not to understand."

"Say it." Gruffbar held out a hand, and a lit cigar appeared between his fingers. He puffed and waited.

"Very well. I will restore what I took from you. It was most delicious and having it gives me warmth, but I can do without given what else is at stake. I will make you an engineer again, the most passionate and driven of engineers, one who will master the making of things both magical and mundane. You will be who you were before as if I had never even appeared in Mount Steelstrike. You will be whole. In return, you will use that gift to make what I need so I can fight these witches and wizards and children and pets that plague me."

Mr. No's normally unflinching face curled into a look of hatred. He had been thwarted, not once but three times. He had been humiliated, beaten not by great cosmic powers but by ordinary, pitiful humans, the creatures whose minds he dismantled as easily as picking legs off a fly. He would not let that stand. He would show the world, show himself, how much stronger than them he was. The control would be his again.

Gruffbar puffed on his cigar and considered the offer. To be whole again. To be the person he once was. It was tempting. However, that person, that passion, hadn't been part of him for a long time. He had become someone else, had found a new love in legal work, a new life here on Earth. To embrace the person he had been would mean obliterating the person he was now, and he liked being that person, even if the work was more challenging and the results less glorious. He wasn't ready to see himself wiped away.

Besides, if he completed this deal he would be helping Mr. No, the creature who had ripped away that part of him, left him lost and aimless for a long, painful time. The being that would have done the same for everyone Gruffbar had loved if he hadn't let his will be torn away in return for theirs. The hatred that memory stirred had driven him to return to LA, to contact the Silver Griffins so they could wipe Mr. No off the map. Why would he help any creature he regarded that way?

The answer was simple: self-interest. If he didn't make some sort of deal, what more might Mr. No take from him?

"I don't want the old me back," he said. "You're not getting that deal. I'll offer you another one. Leave me in peace, don't take anything more, and I won't tell the Silver Griffins how I trapped you. I won't give them the weapon they need. They'll have to work it out for themselves, and maybe they won't be quick enough."

"It's unwise to threaten me," Mr. No said. "I could rip out your desire now, leave you with no motive to fight back, to do anything that hurts me."

"You said it yourself. I'm extraordinary. You took away the essence of me before, and I found a new purpose. Who's to say I won't do it again? I was an engineer. Then I was a lawyer. Maybe next I'll be a hunter, tracking you to the ends of the dream realm. Is that what you want?"

It was such a strong bluff, Gruffbar almost had himself convinced. He kept his face blank and puffed on his cigar, waiting to see if Mr. No was as easily persuaded.

The creature reached out a cold, pale finger.

"It doesn't work that way," Mr. No said, but he hesitated before touching Gruffbar. "I think. But…" He withdrew the finger. "Very well. A new deal. Neither of us acts against the other. If you break this deal, I will destroy you, Gruffbar Steelstrike. I will rip your will to shreds."

"No worries," Gruffbar said. "I'm a lawyer, not a hero. I'm not going to risk a good thing."

Then he slapped himself across the face and woke up with a start.

CHAPTER THIRTY-FIVE

Ringo's van pulled up outside a house above Silver Lake. He and Charlie climbed out.

"This is the place," Charlie said after double-checking the address in his phone. "Our first client."

"Apart from ourselves, you mean." Ringo patted his van.

"Hey, I already drive electric, remember? I don't need help cleaning up my act."

Ringo rang the doorbell, and they stood waiting.

"You might want to take off the shades," Charlie said. "Make yourself more open and accessible, like that book on marketing a business said."

"Oh yeah." Ringo took off his shades and put them in the pocket of his camouflage pants.

The door opened, and a man appeared. He was six-foot-five, slimly built, and wearing slacks, a button-down shirt, and sandals. To most people, he would have passed for human, but there was a telltale gleam in his eyes, and he had the sort of floppy haircut some elves used to cover their ear tips in case the illusions concealing them failed.

"Hi, we're here about the car. I'm Charlie, and this is Ringo."

"Enchanted. You can call me Phillipe," the elf said, with a hint of a French accent. "I've used that name long enough that it might as well be true. Please do come in."

He led them through the house. As they went, Charlie noticed that the place had many gadgets, including a voice-activated household assistant, remote-controlled lights, and a robot vacuum cleaner working its way around the living room carpet.

"Max tells me that this technology is still new," Phillipe said. "That I'll be one of the first people in LA to have it installed in my car."

"Absolutely," Charlie said. "If it doesn't work, of course, we'll restore everything how it was for free."

Ringo kicked him in the ankle with a small headshake.

"Of course, Charlie's joking about it not working," Ringo said. "You're going to be on the cutting edge with your cleaned-up car, and when every magical is using this technology, you'll be able to say that you were one of the first."

"I do like to be ahead of the curve," Phillipe said. "I don't know if you noticed on the way through, but I have almost everything here controlled by an app, and I've had solar panels installed, of course."

"Very cool. Do you work in tech?"

"Oh no, I'm a sleep therapist, but I think we all have a duty to embrace the future."

Lights came on automatically as they walked into the garage. In the middle stood a mid-90s Lincoln Town Car.

"This, of course, is the exception." Phillipe patted the

hood. "I've hung onto her out of a mix of sentimentality and environmental concerns, but the balance is tipping on that last point. If you can make her run cleanly, that would be magnificent."

"Of course," Ringo said. "Give us a moment to look her over. Then we'll fetch our tools and get to work."

Fifteen minutes later, Charlie and Ringo had the car raised in the air by magic, levitating in the middle of the garage while they placed the jack stands, then let the vehicle settle atop them to deconstruct its insides. Pieces of exhaust pipe floated out amid a cluster of filter components while Ringo etched a spell along the inside and Charlie assembled electronic components.

"I can't believe we're doing this already," Charlie said with a grin. "A few weeks ago, it wasn't even an idea. Now we're running our own business."

"I've been my own business for years, but this is still pretty awesome," Ringo said. "Don't get me wrong, I enjoy bounty hunting, but the idea of a more regular income is appealing."

"Would you give it up to do this full time?"

"Maybe, man." Ringo shrugged. "On the one hand, I'd be giving up midnight chases and wand fights, which the chicks dig. On the other hand, I could end up with my name on the side of a corporate headquarters somewhere, which, you know, same deal."

"Funnily enough, attracting women isn't a big part of why I'm doing this."

"Yeah, you're pretty well sorted on that front. Not my sort of lady, but I get it." Ringo set aside one piece of pipe and moved on to enchanting the next. "To be honest, I mostly say that stuff as a joke. It's part of the culture among hunters, you know? A lot of old-fashioned guys and girls, turning everything into a pursuit. Again, it's fun, but it's not exactly a stable life."

Charlie set aside his soldering iron and picked up his wand. Even with electronics, magic was sometimes the quickest way to fix something in place.

"My life's been so stable, this could turn into the biggest change since we started having kids," he said. "Not that I want to invite instability in, but the idea of a little uncertainty is weirdly exciting."

"You think we can make this work as a business?"

"I hope so. Imagine how cool it would be to see clean cars all over LA and know that we'd fixed them up."

"Not just LA, man. Dream bigger. All over the country."

"All over the world."

"An international corporation, sneakily fixing up every car a magical owns."

"The first covert corporation."

They both laughed.

"Seriously, though," Charlie said, "it would be great to get beyond individual cars."

"You mean like Max's factory idea?"

"Even just trucks. Do you have any idea of the environmental impact of haulage in this country? If we can improve some big, long-distance engines, we can make a huge difference."

They brought the parts of the car back together, along with their new components, and slotted them into place, some by magic, others by hand. More work with wrenches and wands got everything tightened up before they lowered the car to the floor.

"Let's give it a go," Ringo said.

He climbed inside the car and started the engine while Charlie stood by the exhaust, holding an adapted device for detecting emissions.

"Looking good," he called as all the dials stayed in the green and digital sensors flashed low figures.

A cough made him look up. Ringo staggered out of the car, waving a hand in front of his face, followed by a cloud of fumes. He switched off the engine and stood back, catching his breath.

"We must have put something together wrong," Ringo croaked, "because that is definitely not clean air."

They opened all the doors and ventilated the car, which retained a lingering smell of fumes.

"Should we clean it?" Ringo asked.

"Let's fix it first, then we can worry about that."

They raised the car again and carefully disassembled it.

"I guess this is the problem with saying that we'll fix any car," Ringo said. "We have to adapt our approach every time."

"We should get better with practice."

"As long as we don't choke to death on fumes first."

With a flick of his wand, Charlie opened the exhaust pipe and peered at its grimy interior.

"Is that in the right place?" He pointed at one of the runes that held the spells in place along the inside.

"I had to move it up a little because of how the pipe's different from on my van. I figured it would still be on the right side of the filters."

"Except that I had to move the filters down a little because of differences from the van. I thought it would all still be on the correct side of the spells."

Ringo laughed and shook his head. "We're going to have to get better at communication if we're going to make this work."

"Or we come up with some standard operating procedures. If there's one thing I've learned from IT, it's that procedures can fill gaps that would otherwise take up a lot of thinking and talking."

"I do like not having to think."

Identifying the problem hadn't fixed it, but at least now they knew what they were dealing with. A series of experiments followed, carefully rearranging the positions of spells and filters, subtly adjusting the magic, and altering surrounding components until everything fitted together. At last, they found a solution that seemed to work. They'd put the exhaust back in place and were lowering the car to the ground when Phillipe came in.

"I thought you might want coffee." He held out mugs. "And I will admit, I was curious to see the progress of your work."

"You're just in time," Ringo said. "We were about to test it out. You want to do the honors?"

Charlie cast a cleaning spell over the car's interior with a hasty flick of his wrist, removing the smell of fumes before its owner got in. Then Phillipe took the driver's seat and fired up the engine.

"She sounds quieter than before," he said. "I'm impressed."

"Cleaner, too." Charlie examined the readout on his

measuring instruments. "Not perfect, but a lot better. I suggest that we come back in a couple of weeks to see how it's settled in. We can do some fine-tuning then, get rid of the last toxic fumes."

"Sounds perfect." Phillipe switched off the engine and got out. "I'll make sure to give her a good run around, shake out any kinks, as they say. Now, how much do I owe you?"

Once they'd settled the bill and handed over the new company's first receipt, they stuck around a little longer to finish their coffee and talk technology. Charlie was amazed at how many ways Phillipe had found to apply gadgets to help people sleep.

"Technology is not a fix-all," the therapist said, "any more than magic is, but it is good to make the most of both of them, yes?"

"Our thinking exactly," Charlie said. "If we can use magic and technology to make the world better, isn't that worthwhile?"

Charlie and Ringo walked back out to their van in silence, each lost in their thoughts. Only once they were in their seats did they turn to each other and high-five.

"We did it!" Ringo exclaimed.

"Our first job!"

"Here's to hundreds more."

"To trucks and factories."

"To a big corporate office with our names on it."

"Here's to dreaming big and not worrying if we fall short because we'll do a lot of good on the way."

"Here's to going for a celebratory beer." Ringo grinned as he started the engine. "First one's on me."

CHAPTER THIRTY-SIX

Heather led the Tolderai down through the tunnels, their way illuminated by magical light as they descended deep into the darkness beneath LA. They followed her along abandoned transit shafts, storm drains, and places dug out for mysterious purposes, through concrete and brickwork, into the belly of the urban beast.

"Do we need to do this?" Carol looked around nervously. She wrapped her arms tight around herself, crumpling her loose blouse. "It's so dark and not in the natural way of night or winter. It's unnatural, oppressive."

"She's right," Mackam said. "It's like descending into the pit of some foul demon, no light, no air, no plants. Only humans would make somewhere as awful as this."

"Humans or dwarves," Carol said. "I went down one of their mines once, trying to be friendly and learn from other magicals, but the whole place made me feel sick."

"Trust me, this is going to be worth it," Heather said.

"That's what we said about working with the Silver

Griffins and joining that replanting project," Mackam said. "Look how those turned out."

"At least those started pleasantly before they became awful," Carol added. "This isn't even starting well. It's just cold and gloom and awfulness."

There were murmurs of assent from the other Tolderai. No one was enjoying themselves, and it wasn't their way to keep that bottled up inside.

"Enough." Heather turned to glare at them. "Since when did this tribe become so moaning and self-defeating? Cold and darkness, these are things we face every winter, every night, and we endure because that's what nature does. As for being surrounded by what's unnatural, I came to this city to do what was necessary for our future. I've spent months here. If I can endure that, you can cope with a few hours in these tunnels."

"That sacrifice was necessary," Mackam argued, "to defeat the Choking Dread. That's finished now. You can leave this place behind and stop dragging us all into its horrors."

"No. We can't leave the city behind because this is where we'll save nature, where we'll do the hard work. Most people live in cities now, and that means that city thinking is shaping the world. Cities pump out pollution. They flood the areas around them with roads, and they expand across the landscape like spilled blood spreading through water. I'd love nothing more than to cut ourselves off from all this, but we can't, not if we're serious about keeping the forests safe. So, we have to find a way to work with cities."

"There's working with cities, and there's this." Mackam waved a hand, taking in the concrete all around them. "If we have to be here, we should be in the parks and gardens, where there's some glimmer of life, or at least up in the air, and feeding weeds to undermine the buildings."

"Life can thrive anywhere, given the right support. Look at it this way, Mackam: the man can't see you while you're down here. Whatever you get up to, it will go unseen, which is part of my plan. Don't you want to be out of sight?"

Mackam looked up at the ceiling, where tons of concrete and dozens of feet of earth separated him from the nearest surveillance camera. "All right. I'll give this business a chance. But I'm watching, chief, and if you've lost what makes us Tolderai, don't think I won't challenge for your title."

Heather turned to Carol. "I know the other plans started nicer than this, but I wouldn't be dragging you down here if I didn't think it was worth it. Will you trust me a little while longer?"

"I suppose I should." Carol gave a lopsided smile. "Come on then, chief, show us what you've got."

Heather led them on, down ladders and long-forgotten shafts, into the depths. At last, they arrived at the end of a downward-sloping tunnel, where decades-old digging machinery lay rusting and abandoned.

"What is this mess?" Mackam prodded at one of the machines with his knife. "What forgotten beasts and misdirected schemes?"

"I don't know," Heather said. "No one else seems to

know either. That's why this place is perfect for us. It's as deep as the tunnels go, and no one even remembers it's here. That means we can do what we want, and the first step is to carve out a cave. Mackam, can you get rid of the machines while the rest of us dig?"

"Oh yes, I'll slay the monsters."

Mackam grinned and placed his hands on a rusting digger. The air around it shifted, and a storm cloud spread like a second skin across the machine's surface. As Mackam chanted, the storm grew in intensity but not in area. Only ever an inch from the digger's surface, his magic bombarded the machine with wind and lashing rain. Lightning flickered from his fingertips. Weather happened in fast-forward, turning metal to rust in a matter of minutes.

Meanwhile, the other Tolderai set to work. They took seeds from their pockets and scattered them at the end of the tunnel, then cast life-giving energy into them. Roots burst from the seeds and drilled into the ground, shattering packed dirt and shoveling it out in ripples. Behind them, Heather planted a single acorn, then channeled her power into it, growing it into a squat oak. The tree's bark peeled open at the front, becoming a portal to an isolated patch of forest that the acorn had come from. Instead of piling up in the cave, the churned earth was flung through that portal and away to be used for planting later.

Slowly but surely, directed by the guiding magic of the Tolderai, the shifting roots carved out a wide cavern. As the last of the digging machinery crumbled into dust, Heather called a halt.

"That's a good start," she said. "We'll need more caverns

later, connected so we can tend them all, but this is enough to show what I have in mind."

She walked to the middle of the cavern, pulled a paper bag from her backpack, and tore it open. Seeds scattered at her feet then spread across the floor on a magical wind. Some were large, others small, a mix from different plants in different places.

Heather closed her eyes, took out her wand, and spread her arms wide. She chanted, and the life force flowed through her. The seeds started to spout, more roots questing into the dirt while tiny shoots rose toward the magical light at the cave's roof.

"Mackam," Heather directed, "make it rain."

Mackam spread his arms wide and drew on the same power he had used against the machines. This time it was gentler, less focused, and less intense, a soft layer of cloud that rose to the ceiling and spread there then darkened into rainclouds. Drops began to fall, slowly at first, then faster, pattering on the bare earth, on the first unfurling leaves, on Heather's head and shoulders and outstretched arms. She almost smiled as the water soaked her through, nature touching her directly.

With the fall of magical rain, the plants grew faster. Seeds sprouted into saplings, then into trees. Flowers unfurled in bright colors around their roots. Grass and clover filled the space between them until the whole floor of the cave was lush and green while living wooden pillars reached up to its roof.

None of the Tolderai spoke, but they reached out to touch the plants, or to touch each other, a hand on a shoulder here, two heads pressed together there, smiling and laughing as a darkened, lifeless pit became a perfect place of life.

Heather turned to the assembled Tolderai and opened her eyes.

"This is our new mission," she said. "A series of caves here beneath LA, and afterward, who knows where else. We will provide fresh lungs for the city, forests that humans can't destroy because they don't know about them. They will breathe fresh air into the world, safe and secure down here."

"Can they survive like this, away from natural light and water?" Carol looked up from a rainbow spread of tulips.

"If we tend them with our magic, provide light and water, then yes. This isn't like the forests above, where we can plant them, nurture them, and move on when they are strong. As long as these forests are needed, we will have to tend them. They will need us here in LA, providing constant care as we expand the caves.

"I know it's not a flawless plan, but it's one we can do on our own. We're too used to working alone to work well with others, our vision of the world sitting at an angle to theirs. This way, we don't need to worry about what others think and feel. We will make the world better without them."

"The Silver Griffins won't like it," Mackam said. "Secret forests in their city. Powerful spells under the feet of the mundanes."

"That's why we won't tell them. You know as well as anyone, Mackam, that secrecy is the surest sort of safety. We will tell no one. This will be our secret, our mission, unacknowledged and unrewarded by an ungrateful world. Will you accept that mission with me?"

The cave resounded with the cheers of every witch and wizard there.

"Then let's get to work. I want three more caves connected to this one before we stop for the day."

CHAPTER THIRTY-SEVEN

Mr. No crept through the space between dreams, a sinister black figure moving spider-like across the minds of the unwary, looking for tasty morsels he could consume. He was more than his hunger, but it was the hunger that drove him.

No, he realized as he stepped from the flamboyant dreams of a cheerleader to the bright surrealism of an advertising executive's imagination, it wasn't only hunger. He had gone beyond that.

In one way, what propelled him had become more basic, the need to defend himself against a threat. When he was the only one with any control of the dream world, he hadn't even realized that he felt safe. He could simply take for granted that he was untouchable, that nothing would harm him. Yes, Gruffbar had done that once, but it had been a freak event and easily overcome. Now, he had been thwarted three times in a matter of days. Absolute control over his encounters with the world had slipped away. If these creatures, these dreamers, could escape his grasp then perhaps they could hurt him, and that could never be allowed. He had to hunt down the most powerful, the most dangerous, and remove them from his world.

There was something more sophisticated too, a higher desire than he'd felt before. He didn't need to eat the dreams of the witch Lucy Heron, but he longed to. Her combination of power and desire to do good was so much richer and more nuanced than what he usually ate. The longer he went without it, the more he thought about it. The more he came to appreciate what her mind represented, the more desperately he wanted it.

He should have been able to find her easily, but something was standing in the way, hiding her presence from him. Thus, he walked from dream to dream, looking for any sign of her, sniffing the air for the distinctive scent of Silver Griffins and the Heron family.

He had gotten lucky several times, finding minds with a hint of Lucy about them. People who knew her or whose lives had been touched by her. People she worked with, people she was friends with, criminals she had captured and victims she had saved. Those kept him going.

The colleagues were particularly tasty. He had relished Jenkins' dreams. The wizard researcher was a strange little man, but his mind was like almost no one else, fizzing with wild ideas and the uncontrollable urge to act on them. Even in his dreams, Mr. No had found him inventing, and it had been immensely satisfying to watch his imaginary laboratory, with its crackling generators and miles of tools, fade away as Mr. No feasted on him.

Still, he hadn't found Heron, and the urge for her became stronger with every night.

For Mr. No, navigating the dream world was about finding the connections, the similarities between dreams that joined them together, that showed minds that were close to each other even if their sleeping owners were miles apart. He had followed trails of dreams about spells and the Silver Griffins, and they had led to dead ends. Tonight, he was trying something more mundane. Tonight, he stalked dreams about Lucy's neighborhood. Mr. No strolled through the imaginary version of Echo Park.

The first place he found himself was on Sunset Boulevard, not the real one, but the Boulevard of tourists, the location of Hollywood hopes and broken expectations. It was a gleaming place of bright sunshine, in which the dreamer mangled the mundane reality of shops, cafes, and bars in with the wild expectations from before he had seen the truth. That dreamer strolled along the sidewalk, a cocktail in one hand and a film script in the other, stopping every few yards to talk with a celebrity. One moment he was chattering away with Humphrey Bogart—black and white, just like in his films—the next with Ruth Bader Ginsburg and the members of Mötley Crüe. Mr. No knew a lot about human culture from his time in dreams, and if he'd had anyone to gamble with, he would have placed a bet that this man was far older than his dream self looked.

"Do I know you?" the guy said as he reached Mr. No. He looked puzzled, and understandably so. This was the first person he'd met all dream who hadn't appeared on the front of a newspaper or the first screen of a news site.

"Not personally, no," Mr. No said. "Perhaps by reputation."

"Oh, are you a writer?"

"More of a reader."

"So, you do reviews? Only I've got this script, and I know it would make the perfect movie if I could convince someone to make it."

"Of course you do."

Mr. No accepted the proffered manuscript and flicked through it. The story and dialogue were every bit as derivative as the dream they were in. Not surprising, barely disappointing.

"I think it's safe to say that this is the finest work you will ever create."

"Really?" The man's smile said he had mistaken the comment for a compliment.

"Oh yes. One small thing…" Mr. No reached out, touched his cold finger to the man's forehead, and sapped his dreams of celebrity. Around them, Sunset Boulevard lost its luster, and the sky went dim.

Visible across the jumbled dream geography, Mr. No spotted Dodger Stadium. As the dream unraveled, he stepped through the pieces and reached the complex before it could vanish. From there, he could sense a dozen more visions of the stadium all around. He picked one by instinct and stepped into it.

A century of experience had taught Mr. No to expect something specific from sports dreams. The dreamer was almost always playing, usually on a famous team, and unless it was a nightmare of shame and embarrassment, they would be the star player. It therefore came as a refreshing surprise to find himself in the audience, one row back from the dreamer, watching the teams at play.

The teams were a pleasant surprise too—no MVPs

here, no lost sporting greats, no family members filling out the roster. Instead, animals were playing, with an alligator stepping up to bat and a group of mice collectively covering first base.

"Who's winning?" Mr. No leaned forward to speak with the dreamer.

"I don't know," she said. "Does it really matter?"

"Most sports fans would say so."

"Oh, I'm not a fan. It's just that I've lived near this place my whole life and I finally gave in to curiosity. It's not what I expected, but the atmosphere is great, isn't it?"

To her left, an old lady was knitting while she watched, while to the right, a family had spread a picnic blanket across the tops of the chairs and were enjoying sandwiches and lemonade.

"Very relaxing," Mr. No said.

There was no point feeding on this woman. She wasn't caught up in ambition or deeply held desire. Perhaps another day, with another dream, she would be worth his time. For now though, she might serve another purpose.

"You said that you're local. Where around here do local people like to go?"

"Try Echo Park Lake. It's nice for a walk at this time of year."

"Which way is that?"

"Over there." The woman pointed, and the seats parted, revealing a straight path to a body of water with a patch of parkland at the end and houses built up around it.

"Thank you." Mr. No rose from his seat and walked off down the path. Arriving a few seconds later at the lake, he stopped to sense others like it in adjacent dreams. Then he followed his instincts again and stepped into the next one over.

This time, the lake was frozen, and cartoon hippos were ice skating on it, in time to an orchestral soundtrack. There was snow in the air and the distant sound of bells. Another dream that had become a surreal mashing together of elements, not desperately felt desire. It happened, of course, but Mr. No's methods of navigation usually steered him away from such pointless wastes of imaginative energy.

The dreamer was in the middle of the lake, a woman in her sixties dancing with the hippos. Mr. No skated out to meet her.

"How do you do?" He sketched a bow. It seemed like the right tone for the dream. Judging by the woman's smile, such old-fashioned gestures suited her.

"I'm very well, thank you," she said. "How are you?"

"I'm fine. I was wondering, do you live around here?"

"Yes."

"Do you know someone called Lucy Heron? I believe she lives in the neighborhood."

He had tried to be subtle about these things, but what was the point? It wasn't as though most of these people would remember their dreams, and none would give his presence any significance. He could ask whatever he wanted without worrying that it might come back to him.

"It's a big neighborhood, honey," the woman said, laughter in her voice. "I'm afraid I don't know her."

"Such a shame."

"I tell you what, though, there's an older guy I used to

work with, Al. His next-door neighbor is a Lucy. It's a long shot, but maybe that's her?"

"It will be worth a try. This Al, can you see him here?"

Mr. No gestured toward the people walking around the lake. This was the easiest way to reshape a dream, a small suggestion that would easily fit what the dreamer already saw. Human minds were so open to influence. Most of them, at least.

"There he is!" The woman pointed.

"Thank you." Mr. No bowed again and skated off.

The dream Al stood on the bank. He had a wrinkled face, wild gray hair, and a baseball cap in his hand. He didn't move or speak, an inanimate figure forgotten by the dreamer. That was fine. Mr. No didn't want this Al. He wanted the real one.

As with the stadium and the lake, Mr. No sensed another version of Al lying in another dream. That version burned brighter: the man himself. Mr. No cut a hole through the imitation Al and stepped through into the real Al's dreams.

This Al was in his garden, cutting the dead heads off roses. Every time he nearly finished, more appeared, but he didn't seem to mind. He hummed to himself and kept on pruning, moving around his garden in a never-ending loop.

"Are you Al?" Mr. No asked.

"That's right." Al smiled. "Pleased to meet you."

"Do you have a neighbor named Lucy Heron?"

"Sure do." Al pointed over the fence. "That's her kids you can hear."

Licking his lips in anticipation, Mr. No peered over the

fence. Sure enough, three children and a dog were at play. He knew that blasted hound and both of the boys, though the older one was far livelier than Mr. No had left him. Mr. No grinned. This was it.

"Cute kids, aren't they?" Al stood next to him, a rake in his hand. "Look, there's Mom."

The back door opened and a woman emerged. An older man's dream version of Lucy Heron, a little more glamorous than the real thing, but unmistakably her.

"Thank you so much." Mr. No didn't even think about whether he should drain Al. What was the point when he was so close to a grand feast, something more satisfying than anything else?

He climbed over the fence, strode across the yard, and approached the smiling simulacrum of Lucy.

"Hi." She held out a plate. "Want cookies?"

"Oh no, I have something far tastier in mind."

Mr. No slashed the air with his hand. The dream Lucy split open, and he stepped through the gap, into the real Lucy's mind.

CHAPTER THIRTY-EIGHT

Lucy stood on a footbridge in a garden. The bridge was made of wood, painted a bright and friendly green. Underneath was a pond full of water lilies, some of which looked real and others to be made of oil paint. They were all beautiful, and every time she looked at them, they were different, subtly rearranged to create a new effect.

So, this was Giverny, home and inspiration to the artist Claude Monet. She had always wanted to visit, but it had never been possible. Now, at last, life was quiet, and she had the time.

She looked up from the waters to take in the garden around her, a medley of the photographs, paintings, and videos she had seen of this place. Willows trailed their slender branches in the water. Tulips and daffodils stood tall in bright beds. Other flowers filled any available space between the paths, creating a beautiful assortment of colors and shapes. Birds hopped and fluttered between them, singing about the joys of nature, while bees hurried from flower to flower, busy with the business of pollination. Sunshine warmed Lucy's face, and a gentle breeze soothed her skin. The place couldn't have been more beautiful if it had tried.

"Is this really what you want from life?" The voice was like a trowel scraping across the edge of a paving stone. It sent a shiver of unease through Lucy. She turned to see a pale man in a black suit standing next to her. He seemed familiar, but why? What was he doing here, this figure of coldness and gloom, in a place of warmth and light?

"I've always wanted to visit," she replied, not wanting to be rude.

"Not to live like this, the rural ideal, the artist in their inspiring element?"

"I guess when I was younger, it was something I dreamed of, but I didn't have the right sort of talent to get into art school. I'm happy to be a fan, not a creator."

"What do you dream of?"

"Making a better world, of course. A safer one." Lucy frowned. Memories were breaking through the treacle-like texture of the dream, angular points of reality intruding through the soft curves and gentle feelings. "You know that, don't you? You know who I am and what I want."

"I do. I hoped that you might consider it for a moment before I snatch it all way."

The sky darkened as clouds swept in on a storm wind. The willow branches rattled. The birds took flight in a great flock, then turned into crows, wheeling and cawing, waiting for a chance to feed on the aftermath of destruction.

Lucy backed away from Mr. No and raised her fists.

"You're not going to take my will from me that easily. I'm not some poor kid or a sap like Applegate."

"That's more like it." Mr. No grinned. "The hero facing down the terrible monster. A battle of good versus evil. These are the moments you live for, aren't they?"

The petals fell from the flowers. Then the stalks shriveled away. The trees withered, dropped their leaves, and died. Lucy stood alone on a battleground, the earth torn to craters by shelling. There were barbed wire and bodies, broken tanks and fallen planes, the glowing aftermath of battle spells fading into darkness. She was a lone warrior facing a threat that would destroy the world.

All of this was a dream. On some level, she had already known, but now the thought became conscious. She had created this place. It reflected her mind. Did that mean she could control it?

She tried to picture a tank rolling forward and crushing Mr. No, but nothing came. Something simpler then. Let the mud swallow him. Let it become thick and oozing until he sank into the depths and disappeared.

"The look on your face." Mr. No smiled a sinister smile. "Trying so hard to bend this space to your will, and yet..." He held his hands wide. "Here I am, perfectly safe."

"I wouldn't get so cocky, sunshine. If I can turn Monet's garden into a battlefield, I can turn you into a greasy smear across the landscape."

"That's where you're wrong. What you made here, the bright version and the dark was your subconscious, and that is the part that makes dreams. Now your conscious mind is in charge, and it has no power here. As long as you didn't understand, you had power but no control, no ability to direct it. The minute you realized what was happening, you gained control but lost power. You can choose to do what you want, but this world…" He waved at their grim surroundings. "It is what it is, the creation of your subconscious, and no amount of careful calculation will give you control of that."

He walked slowly forward, the pointed tip of his tongue running like a worm across his lips. Lucy backed away, stumbled at the edge of a crater, and fell into a puddle of mud.

"This is going to be so delicious," Mr. No said.

She scrambled back through the mud until her back pressed against the unyielding armor of a ruined tank. Mr. No followed her, finger outstretched.

"That's it," he said. "Keep willing yourself to live. Keep dreaming of beating me. Let me feel how much you want it all. Tenderize this delicious piece of psychic meat."

"I'm not afraid of you," Lucy said as the finger reached for her forehead.

"That's fine. It's not fear that I want."

He pressed his finger against her skin. It was icy cold. Lucy felt it drawing something out of her.

She mustn't let this happen. She thought of her family and friends, all the people Mr. No would prey on if she wasn't there to bring him down. She couldn't let him have the people she loved.

"This again," Mr. No said. "Like the other wizard, using the thought of others to protect you. He caught me by surprise. You haven't, and you're trapped here with me. Sooner or later, I will break through."

Lucy shoved him hard, sent him stumbling back through the muddy water that filled the crater.

"No!" she screamed.

"Oh, yes."

He raised both hands and reached for her.

Lucy shoved past him and ran. She ran through mud and water over tangles of barbed wire and tumbled bodies. She ran past ruined tanks and wrecked planes. She ran like her life depended upon it. Not only her life but those of everybody she loved.

Mr. No came with her. He never seemed to run, and yet he was always there, any time she paused or looked back over her shoulder. However hard and fast she ran, he was never more than a few feet away.

She had driven him off before. There must be a way to do it now, to at least survive this and fight another day. But how?

The last time she had been holding her wand when she fell asleep, and it had come into the dream with her. She should have done that again, should have done it every night just in case. That wand had some power over dreams. She had seen it touch on them before. Now she didn't have it.

Except that, as she thought about the wand, as she wished for it, she felt a tingling in her hand. It was almost like touching its wood, feeling its metal bands on her skin, its familiar and uneven shape.

She stopped running. There was no point to it anyway. Instead, she focused on thinking about the wand.

"How sad, you couldn't run forever." Mr. No appeared

in front of her and raised his finger, reaching for her. "Now it's time for me to eat."

That feeling of the wand in her hand hardened, solidified, became real. She was clutching it, as sure and certain as if she was awake, an object more real than anything else around her.

The wand gave her power.

She took a step back, out of Mr. No's reach.

"Again?" he rasped between jagged teeth. "Run, by all means. It only builds up my anticipation."

Lucy didn't point the wand. This wasn't like magic in the real world. It was something different. It created a bridge between the part of her that had made the dream and the part of her stuck inside it. As conscious and unconscious minds connected, she willed the world to be different.

The ground around Mr. No's feet bubbled and squelched. He sank, first up to his ankles, then up to his knees.

"That is unexpected," he said as the mud oozed up his thighs. "However, I'm not this easily beaten."

He reached out a hand, and somehow, he was holding the barrel of a broken cannon fifty feet away. He heaved and dragged himself out of the mud. When he stood upright, there wasn't even a stain on his suit.

"Let's try this again." He reached out, and just like that he was right in front of Lucy, touching her face.

"No, you don't," she snapped. A pulse of energy burst from the wand and flung Mr. No back. He crashed into the cannon and slid to the ground.

"She has claws now," he snarled. "So do I."

He twisted his hand through the air. The cannon turned, became whole, and fired. Lucy raised a wall of mud in time to absorb the shot, but then the weapon itself crashed through and pinned her to the ground.

"You think you're the only one who can reshape dreams?" Mr. No lurched toward her, hunched and strained. "I will burn up whatever part of my strength it takes to defeat you and make sure that I remain the master of this realm."

Barbed wire tangled itself around Lucy's legs. Broken vehicles dragged themselves through the mud to form a circle around her, with only one way in, and that way occupied by Mr. No. Lucy could see a dozen ways to fight back, but none that he couldn't counter. Nothing she did here was stronger than him. Sooner or later, he would wear her down.

Perhaps, if she couldn't win the battle yet, she could live to fight another day.

"Wake me up," she whispered to the wand. "Please."

There was a flash of light and a jolt like electricity running through her body. For a moment, she heard Mr. No cry out in frustration. Then she woke up in her bed, clutching the wand tight.

She drew deep breaths, trying to calm her frantically beating heart. She had faced Mr. No twice now, and both times she had gotten away. However, getting away wasn't enough. She needed a way to beat him once and for all.

CHAPTER THIRTY-NINE

Ashley sat in front of her screens, watching feeds from the Mini Griffins. Her agents were out around their neighborhoods, looking for people with similar symptoms to Dylan. She didn't know if that could help in curing him—the way people's bodies and brains worked wasn't as easy to understand as robots or quantum physics—but gathering and analyzing data was something she understood. If that were all she could do to help Dylan, she would give it her best shot.

She had brought Dylan down into the lair with her. He never seemed to care where he was at the moment, but having him there would help to motivate her, a reminder of what was at stake. It also meant that she could show him to the other Mini Griffins, so they knew what to look for. With both of them down here, Eddie and Buddy had come along too.

Sadly, all her work seemed to be turning into a dead end. After two hours of searching, none of the Mini

Griffins had found anyone in the slumped, demotivated state that Dylan was stuck in.

"The problem is, people like that aren't going to come out," said Mia, who as a twelve-year-old was one of the older and wiser Mini Griffins. "I mean, if I lost all motivation, I'd be sitting inside watching TV or maybe lying in bed."

"I'd be playing computer games." Tommy's voice emerged from another feed, originating in the West Hollywood neighborhood where he lived.

"I thought you loved computer games."

"I do, but my mom says they're as bad as doing nothing, so that's what I'd do. I'd win, see."

"That's not how this works. If you love computer games, you'd stop wanting to play them."

"Then I'd go out on patrol."

"Same thing. You wouldn't want to."

"That doesn't make sense."

"Ashley, can you explain it to him?"

Ashley wished that she could, but what had happened to Dylan was so alien, she struggled to wrap her head around it. She'd always been so passionate about the things she did, from building robots to digging the underground headquarters to running her YouTube channel, she couldn't imagine what it would feel like not to be motivated like that. The horrible unfamiliarity of it was part of what made Dylan's state so tough to deal with.

Noise made her look around. Eddie and Buddy were leaping around excitedly near one of the computer stacks, and she worried about what they might do.

"I think we should end patrols for today," she said.

"We're getting nowhere, and I have something else to deal with."

"You've not lost all your enthusiasm, have you?" Tommy asked, alarmed.

"Not like that. I'll see you guys tomorrow. Griffin Central out." Ashley shut off the feed, got out of her chair, and went over to where Eddie and Buddy were bouncing around. "Can you move away from the computers, please?"

"Okay." Eddie picked something up off the floor, threw it into the open space in the middle of the room, and ran over to it with Buddy. The two of them leapt up and down and made excited noises, Buddy yapping, Eddie imitating him.

"What are you so excited about?" Ashley asked.

"Buddy dog's toy." Eddie pointed at the thing on the ground, a stuffed toy made of tough enough material to withstand some time between a dog's teeth.

"Okay, Buddy's excited about his toy, but why are you excited?"

"Buddy's excited."

"Why are you excited?"

"Buddy's excited!"

"Wait, you're excited because he is?"

"Yes!" Eddie leapt up and down with Buddy, who grabbed the toy and flung it against the wall.

Ashley looked from them to Dylan, slumped in a beanbag in a corner. An idea had occurred to her. She went over to her workstation, did a quick search of YouTube, and put a video up.

"Look, Dylan," she said, pointing at the screen. "He's talking about Vikings."

Dylan, usually so passionate about history, barely looked up.

"Seriously." Ashley grabbed a tablet, put the same video on it, and dropped it in Dylan's lap, where he couldn't help seeing the screen. "He's so enthusiastic! Doesn't that get you excited for history?"

Dylan gave an indifferent shrug, but his eyes stayed on the screen, and Ashley thought she saw a hint of a smile at the corner of his mouth.

If she was wrong, then this would be a complete waste of time and electricity, but if she was right, then maybe she could fix her brother. She needed someone better at people than her, someone who could tell if anything made a difference.

In the corner of the room was a cellphone her mother had provided, a phone with only one purpose: to let her call a trusted adult in an emergency. This wasn't exactly an emergency, but it was important, and she thought that would do. She scrolled through the short collection of numbers in the address book and found the one labeled Sarah Smith.

"Hello, Doctor Sarah?" she said when the woman answered the call. "This is Ashley Heron. I hoped you could help me with something..."

Twenty minutes later, Sarah arrived in the lair carrying a bag of medical instruments, some magical and some mundane. She hooked a few of them up to Dylan, who didn't protest or even ask what she was doing. Then she stepped back and held up a large crystal with spells engraved into its edges.

The video had finished a while back, but the tablet still

sat in Dylan's lap. Ashley hit play, and another history video began. This time, the historian was talking about Italian princes. She spoke with great enthusiasm.

"Well?" Ashley asked.

"Give it a minute," Sarah said. "You have a great idea here, Ashley. Other people can have a huge effect on our moods, including spreading their enthusiasm. Still, even if this can counter the effect of the magic, it might take a long time."

For once, Ashley was having trouble staying patient. This wasn't a new machine she had made. It was her brother and his health. Over the past few days, it had felt like he wasn't there although his body was in the room. That had been upsetting her more than she liked to admit. She desperately needed it to end.

"There is a change," Sarah announced while looking from her electronic monitors to the crystal and then back at the screens. "It's fairly low level. I'm not sure it's enough stimulation to make a lasting impact."

"Fine." Ashley grabbed her brother by the arm. He was four years older than her and a lot taller, but that wasn't going to stop her. She dragged him to her computer chair, Sarah following with the measuring equipment, and sat him down in front of the bank of monitors. Then she switched all those monitors on and pulled up a different video on each one. A dozen different historians and history YouTubers started talking at once, all of them raving about the things they were passionate about, a wall of enthusiastic noise. Seeing so many people getting carried away, Buddy started jumping up and down, and Eddie next to him.

"Yay history!" Eddie exclaimed while understanding almost nothing he saw.

Ashley ignored the screens and focused on Dylan, willing her blank-eyed brother to revive. Surely this had to work?

"It's a cool idea." Sarah laid a hand gently on Ashley's shoulder. "I'm not sure that extra noise is going to help, especially if it gets so that he can't follow any of it."

Surely it had to work? Except that Dylan's expression still hadn't changed. Ashley sucked on her fingertip as she struggled to think of a solution. What if the videos weren't enough? How else could she get through to him?

"Dylan?" She took hold of his hand and summoned one of the few bits of the past she knew about. "You know who's my favorite person in history? Ada Lovelace. She came up with algorithms before there were working computers to run them on. She was so brilliant, so ahead of her time, she invented a thing that no one could use for a hundred more years. She thought that computers could be more than calculating machines and look what we ended up with!"

She waved her arms, taking in the technology that filled half the room. Dylan turned his head to look at her.

"You're unusually excited," he said with a small smile.

"I am! That's because history's brilliant, remember?"

Dylan frowned, then nodded. "It is."

"Why don't you pick something that looks brilliant to you?"

She put his hand on the mouse and pointed at the monitors. Dylan scrolled over to one showing an image of an ancient Aztec city, and his smile grew a little. Quickly,

Ashley muted the rest of the feeds so that he could listen to that one.

"It's working." Sarah looked up from her crystal. "Something in his brain is shifting. Ashley, you did it. He's getting his enthusiasm back!"

Ashley hugged her brother, so relieved she could almost cry. If they could draw him out of his lethargy, they could help anyone who Mr. No had fed off. People would get better.

The problem would be stopping him from hurting any more.

CHAPTER FORTY

"How do you always end up dragging us to vegan places?" Ringo asked, looking down the menu of the Mohawk Bar. "I mean, it's not like I mostly came for the eating, but still…"

"There are meat options if you want them," Max said. "Mostly, I thought you'd appreciate a place with good beer."

Ringo sipped his and nodded. "That is good." He looked at Charlie. "How's yours?"

"Can't tell," Charlie said. "I'm still high on the novelty of a guys' night out."

Max laughed. "That makes it sound like we're going to get wasted, watch sports, and stay out until the small hours dissolving our brains."

"Hey, I'm up for it if you are," Ringo said. "But I guess that's not how the night will go with two dads on the team."

"Definitely not." Charlie raised his beer. "That needn't stop the celebration. Here's to our first successful job."

They clinked glasses, and all took a drink.

"Seeing as this job went well, do you want two more?" Max asked.

"Are you serious?" Charlie said.

"Absolutely. Phillipe told some of our mutual friends about the work you did, and they asked if I could get bookings to fix up their cars."

"It's not even been a week. We've not checked how effective the work was. Don't they want to wait until after that?"

Max laughed. "You don't know the minds of people with money to spare. If there's a chance to get something cool and exclusive, some of them will always want in, and they'll want it before anyone else can get it. Besides, the planet can't wait for us to prove what we already know— that your modifications will work. We need to get cars cleaned up as fast as we can."

Charlie looked at Ringo, who grinned.

"This is what we wanted, right?" Ringo said. "I say grab all the work we can."

"Now we've done a test job, don't we need to get the rest of business set up? Like having a website so people can find us."

"I'd save that part," Max said. "Right now, the fact that people can only find out about you by word of mouth makes you seem more exclusive, so it adds to the buzz."

"We don't want to be exclusive. We want everybody using us."

"Eventually, yes. By building excitement now, you can increase your business further down the line. Trust me.

I've done enough corporate work to see the dark arts of marketing."

Charlie shook his head. It was weird to think that people were talking about them and their business. It still barely seemed like a real thing, despite the legal paperwork and the bank account, even despite the job they'd done for Phillipe. Still, it was a thing, an important thing, and one he was proud of.

His train of thought was interrupted by someone talking loudly behind him.

"Holy cow!" a man in a suit exclaimed. "You won't believe this, but that was some recruitment guy, offering me my dream job."

"Really?" said the guy he was talking to, a short man in a Hawaiian shirt. "Congratulations."

"Listen, it was nice meeting you, but I have to get home and tell my wife."

"Of course. Enjoy."

Something about the Hawaiian shirt guy's tone seemed off to Charlie. Sure, he was smiling, but the tone was smug and superior, not friendly. Out of the corner of his eye, Charlie watched the suit guy leave while the Hawaiian shirt guy finished off his beer. Then he too headed for the door, brushing past a woman in a blue dress as he passed. When he opened the door, her eyes widened, and she stared at a man walking in.

"Oh my God," she said to her friend, loudly enough for Charlie to overhear. "My dream guy just walked in. How do I look?"

Charlie turned to his companions.

"Is it me," he whispered, "or is something up with the guy who just walked in?"

Ringo covertly pulled out his wand and cast a spell under the table.

"You're right," he said. "The guy's an illusion."

Charlie glanced out the door. Hawaiian shirt guy stood in the street, pretending to play with his phone while slyly watching the woman panic as she tried to work out how to start a conversation with the non-existent man.

"That guy outside in the loud shirt, I think he's an illusionist," Charlie said quietly. "He's somehow working out what people want and tricking them into thinking they've found it."

"Why would anyone do that?" Max asked.

"For fun," Ringo said. "It's a pretty shitty way to entertain yourself and one that might get his magic noticed."

"We should call in the Griffins." Charlie reached for his phone.

"I don't suppose there's another way to tackle it?" Max asked. "I know it's their job, but since Kelly's been running things, she's super stressed about how much work the Griffins have. If there's anything we can do to reduce it, that would be great."

"I've chased down suspects plenty of times," Ringo said. "Charlie must have picked up a trick or two from Agent 485. Why don't we do this ourselves?"

"Why not?" Charlie downed the last of his beer. "We're already on a mission to clean up the world, right?"

They headed out the door. The guy with the Hawaiian shirt was heading east down Sunset Boulevard, and they followed him.

"He's probably looking for somewhere else to pull his tricks," Ringo said. "The longer he sticks around, the more likely he'll get caught out, so this is how he stays safe as well as getting plenty of variety."

"So, what do we do?" Charlie asked. "We can't simply walk into a bar and confront the guy in front of whoever he's tricking."

"I have an idea, but it's a little unpleasant."

"You mean like injuring him unpleasant?"

"No! Only some discomfort."

"Do it," Max said. "Before he causes more trouble that the Griffins have to clear up."

Ringo muttered something under his breath. His wand, which he held pressed against his forearm to hide it from passersby, glowed for a moment.

The guy in the Hawaiian shirt stopped and clutched his guts. His head swiveled from side to side, briefly evaluating what was around him, then he rushed into the nearest bar.

"You gave him indigestion?" Charlie asked.

"Let's just say that I've used this trick before, and it always gets my target into the bathroom." Ringo put his wand away and led them into the bar their target had run into. "Max, grab some drinks and a table, make us look like regular customers. We'll be back in a few minutes."

Ringo and Charlie walked through the bustling bar to the men's room. It was empty except for one stall, from which groans and gurgling noises emanated.

"Make sure no one else comes in," Ringo said quietly.

Charlie drew his wand and cast a simple charm. The men's room's door frame expanded and stuck.

Ringo walked up to the occupied stall and tapped on its door with his wand.

"You okay in there?" he asked.

"I must have eaten something awful," the guy said. "My guts have gone nuts."

"I saw what you were doing at the last bar. The imaginary phone call, the pretend boyfriend."

There was a moment of strained silence, then a shuffling sound.

"I don't know what you mean," the man said. "If you're with the Griffins you have to tell me, right?"

Charlie almost laughed out loud. If the guy had wanted to pretend that he wasn't magical, he shouldn't have mentioned the Silver Griffins. That was one excuse they didn't need to worry about.

"That's the police, not Griffins," Ringo said. "We're not either. We're concerned citizens who gave you a little belly ache so we could have a quiet chat."

"You did this to me? You asshole! When I get out of here, I'm gonna make things come true for you in the worst way possible. In fact, I don't think I'll wait until—"

"Dearmo." Ringo pointed his wand over the top of the cubicle. A wand clattered to the floor, and he snatched it up before the guy could retrieve it. "Well, look at that, a wizard. You have two choices now, Mister Magic. Either I remove my spell, you come out, and we have a chat with the Griffins, or I don't remove the spell first, and they get to see you in your current state. What's it gonna be?"

There was a mumble from behind the door.

"What's that?" Ringo asked.

"I said take the spell off," the guy said.

"Okay."

Ringo's wand flashed. There was some rustling, then the door opened, and the guy stepped out, loud shirt and all. He scowled at them.

"Who are you guys anyway?" he asked.

"Just some small businessmen making the world a better place." Ringo looked at Charlie. "You any good with portals?"

Charlie shook his head. "Not great."

"Guess I'll give it a go then."

Ringo drew a deep breath and started chanting. As he did so, the Hawaiian shirt guy rushed at Charlie.

"Stupefacio!" Charlie exclaimed.

Magic leapt from his wand and hit the guy in the face. He stood stunned, eyes wide, body wobbling.

Across the bathroom, Ringo had finished opening a portal. He poked his head through, then pulled it back out.

"Looks like I landed in the Griffins' break room, not their transit room, but it'll do." He grabbed the prisoner and dragged him through the opening. Two minutes later, he reappeared and closed the portal behind him. "All done. Shall we get back to celebrating?"

Charlie unjammed the door, and they emerged into the bar. As promised, Max had a table and three beers waiting.

"Gentlemen," he toasted, raising his glass. "Here's to yet another success."

CHAPTER FORTY-ONE

Jackie and Lucy stood by the coffee pot in the Silver Griffins' break room, steaming mugs in their hands. The room was still a disjointed mix of styles and features, the physical embodiment of too many cooks spoiling the broth, but at least they were getting used to it. The room might not be as relaxing as it had been before redecoration, but familiarity bred a certain sort of comfort.

The break room had become the most productive place to discuss their cases since Kelly couldn't see them there and wouldn't complain that they weren't working. It wasn't the ideal way to work, but it would do until their regular manager returned.

"I got a call from Applegate's wife this morning," Jackie said. "Ashley's enthusiasm therapy is having some effect. I don't know what gets Applegate excited, and I'm not sure I want to know, but he's on the way back to normal."

"That's great," Lucy said. "I'm so proud of Ashley. We still need to find a way to bring down Mr. No, though, or he could return and steal those people's dreams again.

There's no point fixing a broken leg if you're going to let an elephant trample on it."

"Stopping Mr. No is going to come down to you. You're the one who can fight him in dreams, remember?"

"Only enough to get away. That's not a solution."

Twylan appeared in the doorway, clutching her long brown coat around her. Even with all her recent visits and all of Jackie's encouraging words, she didn't seem confident in the fact that she belonged there.

"Hi kid," Jackie said. "Sorry, I forgot you were coming in today."

"That's okay. I can go read for a bit if you want."

"No, join us." Jackie poured another cup of coffee and handed it to Twylan. "This stuff's not great, but it'll get you through the day."

"Or I have some tea bags if you'd prefer something that tastes good," Lucy offered.

"This is great." Twylan smiled. "What are we doing today?"

"Nothing as exciting as playing with pigeons and portals," Jackie said. "Today, I need to do some work so you can help Lucy and me on a real case."

"Really?" Twylan's eyes went wide, and magic danced like electricity across her cheeks. "That's so cool."

"You'd think. What if I told you that we're going to watch people sleep?"

"I'd say that sounded creepy, and not in a cool haunted house way, more a bad ex-boyfriend sort of way."

"That's one slogan we don't want to wind up with: Silver Griffins, the world's worst ex-boyfriend." Jackie laughed. "These are volunteers, so I think we're okay. Come on. You can bring the coffee with you."

They walked down the corridor to a large meeting room, which they'd refurnished with beds instead of tables and chairs. The lighting was soft, the atmosphere still. Nearly all the beds were occupied, mostly with gnomes although some held witches and wizards. All the sleepers were hooked up to magical and technological monitoring devices. A few of the gnomes had dream catchers hanging on the wall above their heads.

"What happened to them?" Twylan whispered.

"Nothing sinister," Lucy replied in an equally hushed voice. "We wanted to watch people sleeping so we could look for signs of what happens when Mr. No enters their dreams and drains their spirits. We asked our agents and support staff for volunteers, and here they are."

In one of the beds, a gnome twitched, muttered something in her sleep, and rolled over. The readout on her monitors shifted a little, lines dancing and numbers rising, then it settled back down.

"There's a monster attacking people in their dreams?" Twylan asked.

"Uhuh." Jackie nodded. "Pretty cool, right, in an awful way."

"We're trying to find a way to fight back," Lucy explained. "But it's hard to affect what goes on in people's dreams."

"The pillow!" Twylan said.

Jackie frowned as she fished around for a half-forgotten memory. "Why is that ringing a bell?"

"I'll be back." Twylan raced off, leaving the two agents to look at each other in confusion.

"You're her mentor," Lucy said. "You should know what that's about."

"Hey, it's not on me. I have no idea how teenagers think, and I'm glad of that. Let's look at the patients. Twylan can explain herself once she's back."

They walked down the room. At the foot of each bed was a tablet with the gathered data for that patient's sleep. They peered at each one in turn, looking for signs of anything unusual. Even if they found anything, they wouldn't know if it was related to Mr. No until the sleeper woke, but that data was what they had, so they kept looking at it, like a fortune teller trying to read a palm in the dark.

They were almost around the room when Twylan rushed back in, carrying a pillow covered in dizzyingly patterned cloth.

"Isn't that one of Jenkins' toys?" Jackie asked.

"For putting objects into people's dreams." Twylan held the pillow out for the other witches to examine. "I thought it could help."

Jackie slapped a hand against her forehead. "Of course! I didn't know about Mr. No when Jenkins showed us this, and I'd dismissed it with all the hundreds of wacky ideas he throws around, but maybe we can use it to give someone their wand or a weapon to fight Mr. No with."

"That's a great idea." Lucy took the pillow and headed for one of the beds. "Let's give it a try."

Jim, one of the junior Griffin agents, was soundly asleep. His wand lay with his wallet, phone, and keys on the bedside table. After a few minutes' discussion of how the pillow worked, Lucy put the wand inside the magical version, then carefully lifted Jim's head and switched the mundane for the magical one. Jim slept through it all. After years of dealing with tired and grumpy children, Lucy was an expert at moving people without waking them up.

"Now what?" Jackie whispered.

"Now we wait."

They sat in chairs at the end of the room, quietly waiting to see what happened next. Lucy read some recent reports, and Jackie checked her emails on her phone while Twylan read through the Mr. No case file, catching up on what had been happening in people's dreams. As she read, she realized that she had heard Griffins talking about parts of it when she was visiting, but that with the distraction of everything Jackie was showing her, she had never put the pieces together. There was probably a lesson in that, though she wasn't sure what.

Jackie nudged the others.

"Look," she whispered.

Jim was twitching in his sleep. He murmured in a strained voice, rolled over, then rolled back again. A line raced wildly up on his heart rate monitor.

"Did we do that?" Twylan asked in alarm.

"More likely we have great timing." Jackie got out of her seat and went to stand beside Jim. "This could be a Mr. No attack."

"Should we wake him?" Lucy asked as she and Twylan joined Jackie. "If this is an attack by Mr. No, getting Jim out of the dream might save him."

"No," Jackie said. "We need to know if this works, for the good of everyone who sleeps in this city."

Jim moaned once more and twisted around, the sheets tangling around his legs. His eyes flicked open, and he sat bolt upright.

"You okay there, Jim?" Jackie asked. "You're into surfing, right? How do you feel about that today?"

"What are you talking about?" Jim rubbed his eyes. "I mean yes, I get it, this is a test, and I still love surfing."

"Did you see him?" Lucy asked. "Tall lad, wears a black suit, trying to touch your forehead with his finger."

Jim shook his head. "I had a nightmare. Dinosaurs were chasing me, and clowns were riding the dinosaurs, but I was running through molten jelly, and they were catching up, and…" He shuddered. "It did not end well."

"Didn't you have anything you could fight back with?"

"Um, not really. I guess I could have thrown the jelly at them? I'm not sure that's a great weapon."

"No wand?"

"Oh, um, yeah." Jim yawned. "I think my wand was around there somewhere, but it didn't seem important. You know how it is in dreams, you see all sorts of things, but they don't always mean what they do in real life." He rubbed his eyes again. "Have I got time to sleep some more before work? I feel more tired than when I went to bed."

They left him to his rest and returned to the break room for fresh coffee, or in Lucy's case tea.

"I thought that would work," Twylan said. "Mr. Jenkins said that he put a sandwich in his pillow and had a midnight snack."

"It was a great idea, kid," Jackie said. "I guess we've

fallen foul of dream logic. If we put something into a dream, and it's not what the dreamer is already thinking about, then it's only going to be one more bit of weirdness. Jenkins probably knew that he got hungry in the night. Jim had no idea that he could fight back, and neither do most of the people who run into Mr. No."

"I do," Lucy said. "I've recognized him in my dreams. I've fought back. I've even brought my wand in to help me. So, if I sleep with something in the pillow, maybe I'll know what it is and why it's important. I can go in armed."

"That's great, but what kind of weapon would be any use against Mr. No?"

"I don't know, but one way or another, I'm going to work it out."

CHAPTER FORTY-TWO

"Kelly wants to see you," Sam called as Lucy walked back to her desk.

Lucy groaned, but what could she do? Kelly was in charge, and she had to cooperate with her. She walked over to the manager's office and let herself in.

"You called for me, Kelly?" she asked.

Kelly looked up from the heaps of papers spread across her desk. She was wearing her usual sharp suit and precise makeup, but her hair looked like a wind machine had blown it around. She tugged at it with one hand while the other tapped a pen against the tabletop.

"I still don't have your report," she said. "Where is your report?"

"What report?"

"The summary of cases you've dealt with this quarter, to feed into the management report. I emailed you about it. I emailed everyone about it. Everyone needs to send a report."

"Oh, yes, of course. I'll do it soon. I'm busy with a case."

"You need to do it now. I need to complete my executive summary so I can get an overview and consider the distribution of cases going forward. Do you understand?"

"I think so, but is it really that urgent?"

"Yes! I have to do it now because I won't have time tomorrow or next week, and after that we're nearly onto the next quarter's reporting, and I have meetings all afternoon, and... Look, just send me the report!"

Lucy drew a deep breath and forced a smile. There was no point arguing about priorities when her boss was in a mood like this.

"Of course, Kelly. I'll do it as soon as I can."

"Good." Kelly looked down at her paperwork, then up at Lucy again. "Wait, you said something about a case. Have you made progress on the Mr. No investigation?"

"Yes, I think we might have found a way to fight back against him."

"And you didn't tell me?"

"I mean, we only just—"

"The biggest case we're dealing with right now, and you didn't inform me? This is completely unacceptable. I should write you up for this. I will. There's going to be a disciplinary, and, and..."

"Enough!" Lucy snapped, slamming her hands down on Kelly's desk. "I am done putting up with this crap from you, Kelly. I'm doing the work. I'm solving the case. I don't need you riding me every bloody minute of the day."

"Yes, you do, or you'd never get it done! I see you sitting around gossiping and drinking tea."

"We were talking about the case. Now we have to hide to have those conversations because everyone's afraid they'll get grief from you if they slow down for even a second."

"They should be. Do you have any idea how much work there is to do? How many cases need solving, how many incidents to follow up on, how many tiny details get forgotten because people get sloppy and stop paying attention? This place is a mountain of work, and it's my responsibility to make sure it gets done because none of you can get it right, everything gets forgotten, and if I don't follow it up, who knows what we might miss?"

"If you do try to follow up every detail of everybody else's job, who's left to do your job?"

"Exactly!"

They stared at each other, both quivering with frustration.

"There is so much to do," Kelly said, her voice so strained it sounded as if she might break at any moment. "I need the rest of you to do your jobs right before I sink beneath this mess."

"You can't manage every last little detail." Lucy tried to let go of her anger and show some empathy. Kelly was struggling. "Sooner or later, you have to trust people to do the work well enough."

"What if they don't do it well enough?"

"Then the Silver Griffins hired the wrong people, but I don't think that's happened." Lucy eased herself into a chair. "Kelly, are you okay?"

For a moment, Kelly's expression stiffened. Then her lip wobbled, and she sank back in her chair, hands pressed to her face. "There's so much to do. The harder I try to get through it all, the more things come up. It's like fixing one problem only for it to make ten more."

"Can I help?"

"This is my job. I should be able to do it."

"This is Applegate's job, and if you'd got it in normal circumstances, you would have had support and advice and training on how to take over. You were thrown in at the deep end. It's okay to admit that you're drowning."

"Not drowning." Kelly managed a half-hearted smile. "Just sinking a little."

"Then let me and Jackie help."

"If I do that, I've failed."

"No, you've delegated. That's part of the job."

Kelly let out a deep breath and tapped the pen against the table again.

"Fine," she said at last. "I'll use you and Jackie."

She got on the intercom to Sam, and a minute later, Jackie walked in. She raised an eyebrow as she looked from the stressed-out Kelly to where Lucy sat, carefully calm.

"You and Lucy are going to help me manage this place," Kelly said.

"Not like that, we're not." Jackie folded her arms.

"Excuse me?" Kelly's eyes narrowed as she glared at Jackie.

"If you want our help, you can ask nicely."

Kelly turned her glare on Lucy. "You said—"

"I said you need help. I didn't say that you could demand it from people. That's not how being a leader works, at least not a good leader."

Lucy could almost see the conflicting parts of Kelly's mind warring across her face, the control freak battling the woman in desperate need of help. Was she ready to let other people have their way, now she had the power to tell them what to do?

Kelly leaned back again, eyes closed, and sighed.

"I'm sorry," she said. "What I meant to say was, can you please help me with some of the work of running this place while Applegate's away?"

Jackie pouted. "I think you should at least look at me while—"

"Jackie," Lucy hissed. "Now's not the time. She asked. I think we can answer."

"Fine." Jackie rolled her eyes. "We'll help you, *boss*. What needs doing?"

Kelly opened her eyes and surveyed the jumble of forms and reports that littered her workspace.

"First, there's this quarterly report," she said. "According to the management procedures, I need to get a report in from everyone about the cases they've completed and the ones that are ongoing."

"Get Sam to do that," Jackie said.

"But it's my job."

"Sam's your PA. Everyone knows Sam. Sam knows everyone. That's how Applegate got it done."

"What if the reports aren't all in on time? Then the figure will be wrong. Sam doesn't have the authority to make people do the work."

"Applegate never got all those reports in. He pulled the figures from the database, then used a few quotes from different people's reports for color."

"But the procedure says…"

Jackie laughed. "You think Applegate did every bit of

work the procedure told him to? That man liked his lunch breaks far too much for that."

"But…" Kelly stared at the reports in front of her. "I've been trying to do everything perfectly, to fill his shoes, and you're telling me…"

"I'm telling you that our boss wore extra-large shoes so no one could see the shape of what was inside. Like clown shoes but polished up to look more professional. You two did the management training course. Surely you learned about things like this?"

"The management training people thought that we should follow procedures," Lucy said.

"Then they were a bunch of suckers. What's next?"

They worked their way through the mountain of tasks facing Kelly. Some were set aside for later, and some delegated to other Griffins. Slowly, cautiously, Lucy and Jackie pried Kelly's iron grip off the tiny details of running the office.

"What about the cases?" Kelly asked as they neared the end. "Shouldn't I know what's going on with all the cases? Applegate always seemed to know."

"I don't know if you're over or underestimating Applegate, but you're definitely wrong," Jackie said. "No one can know about everything that goes on here. The human brain isn't big enough. Applegate's just really good at sounding confident and repeating details back to you."

"I thought he was so smart."

"He is, in a specific sort of way."

"It's like peering behind the curtain." Lucy shook her head. "Instead of the *Wizard of Oz*, there's a bloke in a clown suit with shoes ten sizes too big."

"Hey, if it works, it works." Jackie grinned. "So, are we done here?"

"I think so," Kelly said. At last, she seemed to relax.

"Actually, there's one case I'd like to talk about," Lucy said. "Mine."

When Kelly had been demanding information from her, she'd wanted to resist. Now that her temper had passed and no one was bossing her around, she realized there was a lot to gain by talking it through. There was a reason Kelly had risen through the Silver Griffins. For all her faults, she was good at field agent work, the business of hunting down and capturing magical menaces.

Quickly, Lucy talked through the outline of what had happened: the attacks in dreams, people drained of aspirations, her confrontations with Mr. No while she was asleep. Then she explained Jenkins' pillow and the potential it held.

"The problem is, what do I put in it?" she asked. "I can already take my wand into dreams, but that isn't enough. I need something that will help me fight back, something I can catch Mr. No in."

"Could you ask your dwarf contact?" Jackie asked.

"I don't know how to contact him, and if he wanted to talk, I think he would have found me."

"Is there a night wizard we can talk to or some sort of dream elf? Maybe a sleep therapist? I know that's a long shot, but they might have ideas."

Kelly laughed. "Now you two are acting like me. You're making it too complicated. If you want to catch something in a dream, there's one obvious tool to take with you, and it's barely even magic."

CHAPTER FORTY-THREE

Lucy stood on a heap of paperwork, like a statue on top of a plinth. Around her, chocolate chip cookie fish swam through a sea of ice cream and jello.

"I think it's safe to say that I'm not awake." It felt weird to state her thoughts out loud, but she'd promised the other Griffins that she would, right before they cast the spell that sent her off to sleep. They were going to try to find a way to watch what she was doing, and if that worked, she wanted them to get the full show. If not, well, then she was merely a crazy lady talking to herself, but that was what parenting would drive a person to.

"First things first." She held her hand out and thought about her wand. She felt it before she saw it, the wooden handle with the metal bands, lumpy yet somehow perfectly comfortable, fitting exactly to her grip. That solidity increased, and there was a tingle of magic, then the wand was visible. It seemed more real than anything else around her.

She looked across the expanse of sugary sea. Cords ran

through it, thick threads that crisscrossed each other below the surface.

"I guess I'm as ready as I'll ever be," she said, to reassure herself as much as to inform any observers. "Let's do this."

She drew a deep breath, then raised her wand. She hadn't tried this before, but she thought she knew what she was doing, and the wand seemed to agree. It felt more like it was steering her than she was guiding it so her hand moved without her willing it to. As she slashed down, a tear opened in the air in front of her. The gap widened, a gash in the wall of her reality, and she stepped through.

It was dark in the dream realm, a space as black as night, littered with the gleaming points of light that were other people's dreams. Every so often, one would wink out as the sleeper awoke, or a new one would appear as someone sank into unconsciousness. Lucy could sense where her dream was, the wand providing a connection back to it, linking the parts of her mind together. Now, she needed to find something else.

She held the wand out. "Come on, show me what you've got."

The wand twitched to one side, then up, pointing to a spot of light. With her other hand, Lucy reached out. One moment, that dream seemed far away. The next, it was between her fingers.

"This is crazy," she whispered. "And amazing."

She touched her wand to the dream, and it expanded until its light surrounded her.

She found herself standing in the White House. A guy she vaguely recognized from the local news, some councilor or community campaigner, stood behind the desk, a stern look on his face. He had the sense of solidity about him that told Lucy he was the dreamer.

Standing with her back against the wall and a grandfather clock by her side, Lucy hid in shadows, watching as two men approached the desk. One was a secretary, a bundle of papers in his hands and a cluster of pens sticking out where his hair should be. The other one, emerging through the French windows, was Mr. No.

"Mr. President," the secretary said, "the Chinese have invaded from the west and the Mexicans from the south. Canada is threatening to come in on their side, and the British have said they're sending in King George. Your country has never needed a leader like you more."

"I know, Brian." The dreamer puffed out his chest. "Don't worry, America is in safe hands."

"My, my." Mr. No approached the dreamer. "This is grand. Are you going to save the country?"

"Not only the country," the dreamer said boldly. "I'm going to save the world."

"Of course you are." Mr. No reached out a long, pale finger. "One thing first..."

Lucy's wand pulsed with magical power in her hand. She stepped out of the shadows and raised it. "Not so fast."

The dreamer looked at her in confusion.

"Who are you?" he asked. "Did the Chinese send you?"

"Security detail, Mr. President," Lucy said. She didn't want to have to fight the dreamer as well as Mr. No. "There's an enemy agent here."

"You!" Suddenly, there was a gun in the dreamer's hands. He pointed it at Mr. No. "Treacherous commie scum."

"Oh, you don't have to worry about me." Mr. No waved the man away dismissively and stepped around the desk, his gaze fixed on Lucy. "I've found something far more appealing. Though why she's here, I have no idea."

"Because this time I'm the hunter in dreams," Lucy said. "That makes you my prey."

She pointed her wand straight at Mr. No and let the magic fly. It hit him like a fist to the face, knocking him off his feet. He slammed back through the White House windows, which shattered around him, and through the very fabric of the dream, leaving a dark tear in the air. Lucy ran through the gap after him, leaving the dreamer behind.

Mr. No crouched in the darkness between dreams, clutching a hand to his smooth face.

"You think you can beat me that easily?" he said. "I'm no petty dwarf lord or elf princeling to be battered into submission." He rose to his full height and held out his hands, pale magic flowing between them. "I am the master of this place."

"Not a master, a parasite, a desperate, needy creature sucking the life from others." Lucy held her wand out, power pulsing through it. "Your time is up."

Another bolt of magic flew from her wand. This time, Mr. No caught it in the air, tangling it in his magic. He laughed, a sound like a saw blade running over stone.

"You call this fighting?" He flicked his hands, and the spell flew back at Lucy, who flung herself aside, dodging the attack. "I will show you a fight."

Bolts of power hurtled around Lucy, who fled from

them, rushing through the darkness back toward her dream.

"I am full of potential," Mr. No screeched. "Full of power. Full of strength. Nothing can stand against me here because I am all the strength in this place, and I am going to crush you."

A blast of magic shot past Lucy's head a moment before she dived into her dream, away from the darkness and the figure stalking through it. She landed face-first in the sea of ice cream and jello. Cookie fish flashed past as she swam to her paperwork podium, careful not to get tangled in the threads that ran beneath the waves, and climbed up the paperwork, dripping with melted desert.

When she looked back, Mr. No had appeared. He stood ankle-deep in the ocean, indifferent to the cream waves lapping at his pants. There was a red mark down one of his cheeks where Lucy's magic had hit him and a fierce gleam in his eyes.

"You think you can escape me here?" he sneered. "You're no more the master of your dreams than you are of the realm around them."

He waved a hand, and the fish flew out of the ocean. They crashed together in an explosion of crumbs, becoming a single mass of cookie that transformed into an angry chocolate-chip-covered bear, waving its claws and roaring at the top of its voice. It charged toward Lucy, running along the top of the waves. Within seconds, it was almost on her. She waved her hand, and a giant child's fist appeared out of the sky, grabbed the cookie bear, and carried it away.

"Two can play that game."

"True, but I have been playing for centuries, while you have only dabbled in the moments since you found that wand. Do you think you can stand against this?"

He raised his hands again, and lightning crashed from the sky. Patches of jello and ice cream exploded as the lightning hit, and with each new bolt, it came a little closer to Lucy.

"I will strike you down," Mr. No said, "and I will finally suck all that delicious power and ambition from your head. What a feast!"

"You hurt my kid." Anger lent her voice the strength to be heard above the howling storm. "You hurt my friends. You tried to hurt me. For all of that, I'm going to make sure you never walk free again."

"Do you think you can defeat me with the stuff of dreams?" Mr. No laughed. "I am the master of them. Everything here bends to my will."

"Not with the stuff of dreams, but with something from beyond. Something designed to deal with cursed creatures like you."

Lucy raised her hand. The threads that ran beneath the waves rose, and as they did, it revealed the hoop between whose sides they ran. A ring that seemed massive only because Lucy had dreamed everything else so small. Aside from her and the wand, it was the one piece of the real world in this place, but her relationship to it had become unreal. An object she could have held in the palm of her hand was now big enough to surround them and for Mr. No to become tangled in its rising strings.

"Before they were called dream catchers, people used these things to ward off evil," Lucy said. "Like anything in the world of dreams, our imaginations give them power. Now this one's going to catch more than a dream, going to do more than ward off evil. It's going to trap the evil that stalks between dreams and tangle it up for good."

"No." Mr. No pushed at the threads, trying to drag them off his legs, but he only got his arm caught in them. "No, this shouldn't work. This can't work."

"But it does. An enchanted dream catcher, and you a creature of dreams. It was meant to be."

The threads had risen well above the ocean now, almost to the top of Lucy's paperwork pillar. She crouched and touched her wand to the strings. Power flowed through her, and a little of her ambition, the dream of making the world a safer place. The strength that Mr. No had sought to devour instead wrapped the magic around him and tied him in place.

"No!" he screeched. "No, you can't do this to me! It's not possible!"

"It's a dream," Lucy said. "Anything is possible. Now that I have what I came after, it's time for me to wake up."

———

Lucy woke in one of the beds in the Silver Griffins' improvised sleep lab. Kelly, Jackie, and Twylan stood around, watching her.

"Are you okay?" Jackie asked.

"I don't know," Lucy said. "It's hard to care."

A look of horror crossed her friends' faces. Lucy burst out laughing.

"I'm sorry," she said. "I'm kidding. I'm fine and still set

on making the world a better place." She pulled the dream catcher out of her pillow. It was cold and heavy with contained power, writhing in her hands as Mr. No struggled desperately, futilely to break free. "Here, Kelly, find somewhere safe to lock that up. It's time for everyone to dream safely again."

CHAPTER FORTY-FOUR

Back home, far from LA, a little girl named Ines dreamed of roller coasters, of cartoon characters, of stuffing herself full of candy. It was the first time she had dreamed so well in weeks—since getting back from the once-in-a-lifetime holiday she hadn't been able to enjoy.

When she woke up, she asked her parents if she could go to Disneyland again. They were so relieved to have their girl back, they went straight out and booked the trip.

Farhad woke and looked at his rideshare app. He hadn't taken a job in weeks, which was crazy. How was he going to save up this way? He pulled on his pants and shirt, grabbed his keys, and dashed out the door, phone in hand, ready to make his fortune.

Selma woke up in front of the TV. How long had she been sitting on this couch, eating chips and watching garbage? She felt as though her butt had become one with the furniture.

She grabbed her notebook. A new design for a microchip had come to her in her sleep. The idea wasn't complete, of course, because dreams weren't reality, but with some hard work and some research, maybe this would be the breakthrough to make her name.

Ed woke up in the care home and ran a hand through his gray hair. There was a phone by the side of his bed. He didn't need to look up the number he was after, the one with the Australian dialing code, as it had been somewhere in his mind the whole time like it was every day.

Unlike all those other days, for years and not merely weeks, today he made the call.

"Hello?" his daughter's voice said from the other end of the line.

"Hi," he said. "It's Pa. I miss you. Could we maybe talk?"

A city councilor woke from dreams of presidential glory. The White House hadn't been quite like in his daydreams, a little too full of wizards and war, as if someone's fantasy drama had spilled over into an episode of *The West Wing*. That was dreams for you though. They weren't supposed to work like the real world.

Maybe there was a lesson in it all. Perhaps he shouldn't spend so much time worrying about national ambitions or raising his status. If he thought about making a difference, instead of only where the political path went, he could make a real difference right here in LA. He'd start by finding extra funding for some tree planting projects.

"Did you see the local news today?" Charlie asked as the Heron family sat for dinner.

"No, I was busy helping Kelly out," Lucy said. "Applegate's making the most of his medical recovery time. Why, what's in the news?"

"Park!" Eddie banged his fork on the table.

"That's right," Charlie said. "The city council is talking about creating some new parks, planting more trees, and making space for kids to play. There's a new homelessness program on the way too, and an urban regeneration scheme. It's like they all suddenly learned to dream a bit bigger." He smiled at Lucy. "I wonder how that happened."

"It does feel like something's changed, doesn't it?" she said. "Not only the people who lost a part of themselves. It's like all of us are coming out from hiding under the blankets on a stormy night, looking around and seeing how much potential the world has. You should see the gadgets Jenkins is coming out with. They make his dream inserters, and monster generators feel small and ordinary."

"This whole mood is good for business. People are getting more ambitious about living green. We have five clients booked in for car conversions now and more approaching Max. I think this business could take off."

"That's fantastic." Lucy looked around the table. "What about you, kids? Have you been thinking about doing great things?"

Everybody's attention turned to Dylan, who nodded vigorously.

"If I'm going to be a great magical archaeologist, I need to focus on my magic," he said. "I'm going to ask Twylan to give me more training, so I can learn how to shape spells more precisely, not simply control and hold back the power I have."

"Twylan might be a bit busy, sweetheart," Lucy said. "She's working on proving that the Silver Griffins should let her in early to make use of her magical talents."

"If she's too busy, I'll find someone else. I'm not going to let anything hold me back. And I'm going to study extra hard at school, so I can go to a good college and learn about archeology and get out there and find all the past we've forgotten. I'm gonna find civilizations no one's ever even heard about."

"Wow, that does sound impressive. What about you, Ashley?"

Ashley looked up from where she had been carefully arranging spaghetti on her plate. Despite their thick layer of sauce, the pasta lines managed to look like equations or a complex diagram for some incredible construction.

"Huh?" she said. "Sorry, I was thinking about an idea."

"What was it?"

"Well, if I made machines that were essentially robots in

the shape of string, they could rearrange themselves into different shapes depending on what we need them for. They could carry your shopping or hold cars up for Dad to get underneath and fix them or tie up criminals when they try to escape. I'm not sure how the distributed intelligence would work yet, or the command interface, but once I've made a few, scaling up and down should be easy. You just add more strings."

"It's a different sort of string theory." Charlie grinned. "Sorry, science joke."

"No, actually…" Ashley pulled a sheet of paper from her pocket and a pencil from behind her ear. "There are some principles from string theory that could apply if I can work out how to…"

Her voice trailed off, but the scribbling continued.

"Jar!" Eddie said.

"It's only a design, not a machine at the table," Lucy said. "I don't think that's against the rules."

Eddie frowned for a moment, then nodded, assimilating this small refinement on the rules he knew. "Okay."

"What about you, sweetheart?" Lucy asked. "Have you got anything big you want to do?"

"Elephant!" Eddie exclaimed. A larger than usual patch of air started to shimmer around him.

"No!" Lucy and Charlie cried out in unison.

"Okay then, whale."

"No!" they shouted again, frantically waving their hands. There were some animals that their house wouldn't be able to hold, at least not while keeping its walls intact. "No magic at the table!"

The shimmering subsided, and Eddie sat back in his seat.

"Can I design?" he asked.

Lucy laughed, got up out of her seat, and fetched him a pencil and paper. "Sure, sweetheart, you design all the elephants and whales you want."

A moment of quiet descended across the table as the kids ate their dinners and contemplated their grand dreams.

"What about you, honey?" Charlie asked. "Have you got anything you want to do that you didn't before? Going to push harder for promotion at work, become the world leader of the Silver Griffins?"

Lucy looked around the table. What she had here was a big enough dream for her. There was love and comfort, laughter and pride. Sitting in her home, with her family around her, knowing that they were happy, healthy, and safe, she felt no burning desire for more, and she was fine with that. Not everybody in the world got to be happy, so why wish herself out of it?

"Not really. I quite like things as they are."

"You must have something else you want to do, even if it's a little thing."

Lucy contemplated the options, all the grand schemes and activities she might enjoy doing with life.

"I think I'll take up art again," she said at last. "I'm never going to be the next Frida Kahlo, but it's something I enjoy and isn't that enough?"

Charlie smiled. "That's all a dream ever needs to be."

Medieval European items with magical powers are going on display at the Los Angeles County Museum of Art. Some of these items are potential targets for theft. Can Lucy Heron and the Silver Griffins keep the items where they belong and out of the hands of those who shouldn't have them? Find out in <u>MOM'S THE WORD.</u>

Rice Krispie Cheese Cookies

INGREDIENTS
- 2 sticks butter, softened
- 2 cups all-purpose flour
- 2 cups grated sharp cheddar cheese
- 2 cups puffed rice cereal (like Rice Krispies)
- 1/2 teaspoon ground red pepper

INSTRUCTIONS

1. Preheat oven to 325-degrees F. Line baking sheets with baking parchment or silicone lined baking mat.
2. Combine all ingredients.* Form into small balls, approximately 1-inch in diameter. Placed on lined baking sheets about 1-inch apart. Flatten each ball slightly with a fork that has been dipped in water.

3. Bake at 325-degrees F for 12-14 minutes, or until lightly browned.

It's grown up decadence with Rice Krispies and a red pepper kick. My mother used to make these for her bridge parties. I think of them as suburban chic and still love them. Like a Rice Krispie treat grew up and still wanted some of the fun. Enjoy till next time...

Get sneak peeks, exclusive giveaways, behind the scenes content, and more. PLUS you'll be notified of special **one day only fan pricing** on new releases.

Sign up today to get free stories.

Visit: https://marthacarr.com/read-free-stories/

AUTHOR NOTES - MARTHA CARR

Here's a question I've been noodling for a while. Is it possible to grow roots in a community during a global pandemic? I've been wondering because I moved into this dream house in this new city eighteen months before the first lockdown. Timing.

Add in that I live alone with the good dog, Lois Lane and the sweet pittie, Leela. This was going to take some out-of-the-box thinking.

First, I needed to be more proactive and reach out to neighbors nearby. Nicole up the street started a Zoom game night once a week in the beginning and I made a point to show up and participate. Another Martha a few blocks over shared mask patterns and I dragged out my sewing machine to relearn how to use the thing. There were a few weeks that every spare moment I wasn't writing, I was sewing. Martha even kept busy doing a craft a day, or more and would share her new creations with me over Zoom.

Soon a small group of us were sitting in Nicole's front

yard around two large inflatable pools (some of us were in them, drink in hand). When the weather got colder, I invested in a fire pit and the party moved to my backyard.

My future daughter in law, Jackie Venson played her blues guitar from my garage for Mother's Day last year and people spread out along the sidewalk to listen. That led to another concert with more people spread out along the empty field across the street.

There were Zoom lunches and brunches, and home-made cookies left on doorsteps and endless chats and even Zoom yoga. Curbside pickups from a long list of local restaurants and food trucks and I even took a printing class of four people, double-masked.

I read a few books, chapter by chapter, live on Face-book back at the beginning and started Fan Pizza Friday over Zoom, first weekly, and now monthly and still going strong.

On my birthday last September, the Offspring rented out a movie theater and fifteen of us watched Tenet, sitting far apart in the theater. I even made goodie bags and handed out cupcakes with the Wonder Woman emblem on top. It was a taste of the old reality – suddenly mixed with the new when we noticed that all the posters on the walls were from February 2020.

Then, for all of us in Texas there was a monster snow-storm that took out the power and the water – and neigh-bors came out to share food and spare bedrooms.

After all of that, here we are in the hopefully waning days. And here's the biggest lesson I learned from it all when it comes to connections. They actually grew stronger because we were all actively trying to be there for each other and ourselves.

Over time we grew more vulnerable, shared stories, celebrated milestones and leaned on each other more readily when hard times came, and several friends and neighbors lost a parent to Covid. We were there for and with each other through all of it, despite keeping a safe distance and despite wearing masks.

It taught me something about the resilience of human beings and the general kindness we are willing to share and that's what I'm going to take with me and do my best to keep practicing. More adventures to follow.

Thank you for reading both this story, and these author notes here in the back!

So, for those following my 'Misadventures Cooking Chili,' I have a small update for you.

Using whole peeled tomatoes (canned) absolutely worked way better than diced tomatoes and tasted more like my mother's chili. I still used almost an 8 oz can of tomato sauce for additional flavor, but the 'something' that I loved from my mother's chili was absolutely there.

Unfortunately, I found what was left on the stove in the morning, having stayed out overnight and wasn't safe to eat...DAMN!

I took a moment of silence.

This brings me to my next comment, which can be filed under 'growing older.' I'm getting tired of eating smaller and smaller portions, feeling too full to eat again, and still gaining weight.

I mean, seriously. If I'm going to gain weight, how come I don't have the option to at least eat a lot?

Age slowed my metabolism. Which, in effect, was a slap in the face to eating more of what I like at that time of my life when I can afford to eat anything I want to eat.

Except, I can't.

For medical reasons, I need to keep to a minimum 1 pound a month weight loss. I completely understand why the drug combination Phen-Fen was a massive cultural diet event. If you could get around the whole 'damage your heart valves horribly' side-effect (one of the drugs was yanked off the market for this problem, thankfully.)

C'mon science! It's time to build the super cool stuff we sci-fi and urban fantasy writers dream up that would allow a bit of cheating.

How about just on the weekends?

Maybe just Saturday?

I'm told this thing caused exercise might be a solution. I'll have to check into that.

Maybe I'll do that on Saturday, too.

You have a fantastic week!

Ad Aeternitatem,

Michael Anderle

Solve a murder, save her mother, and stop the apocalypse?

What would you do when elves ask you to investigate a prince's murder and you didn't even know elves, or magic, was real?

Meet Leira Berens, Austin homicide detective who's good at what she does – track down the bad guys and lock them away.

Which is why the elves want her to solve this murder – fast. It's not just about tracking down the killer and bringing them to justice. It's about saving the world!

If you're looking for a heroine who prefers fighting to flirting, check out The Leira Chronicles today!

AVAILABLE ON AMAZON AND IN KINDLE UNLIMITED!

OTHER SERIES IN THE ORICERAN UNIVERSE

THE LEIRA CHRONICLES

SOUL STONE MAGE

THE KACY CHRONICLES

MIDWEST MAGIC CHRONICLES

THE FAIRHAVEN CHRONICLES

I FEAR NO EVIL

THE DANIEL CODEX SERIES

SCHOOL OF NECESSARY MAGIC

SCHOOL OF NECESSARY MAGIC: RAINE CAMPBELL

ALISON BROWNSTONE

FEDERAL AGENTS OF MAGIC

SCIONS OF MAGIC

THE UNBELIEVABLE MR. BROWNSTONE

DWARF BOUNTY HUNTER

MAGIC CITY CHRONICLES

ACADEMY OF NECESSARY MAGIC

OTHER BOOKS BY JUDITH BERENS

OTHER BOOKS BY MARTHA CARR

JOIN THE ORICERAN UNIVERSE FAN GROUP ON FACEBOOK!